The BRIGHT SIDE of BROODING

A MILITARY ROMANCE

CLAIRE CAIN

Cover design by Jess Mastorakos - Jess@jessmastorakos.com

E-Book ISBN: 978-1-954005-14-3

Print book ISBN: 978-1-954005-16-7

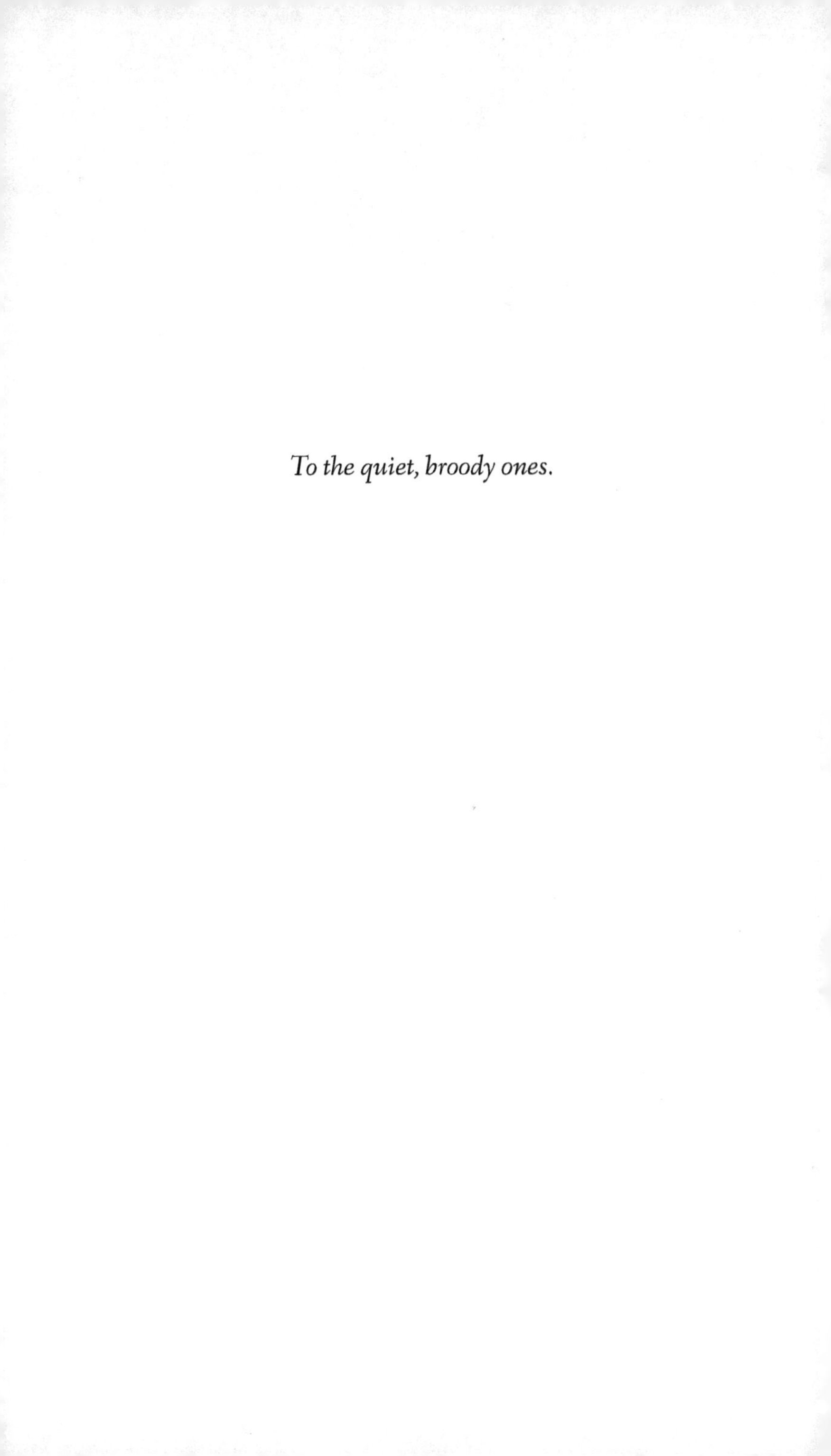

To the quiet, broody ones.

CONTENT WARNING

Dear reader,

The Bright Side of Brooding is a military romance about two very different people falling in love while living in Germany. While it's generally lighthearted, it may contain content not suitable for some readers.

The heroine's background includes an abusive upbringing to include hunger. The hero also grieves due to death of a dear grandparent.

I hope readers who find this content to be particularly sensitive can make the best decision for their health and happiness. I want you to walk away with only happy, lovely feelings, and I hope you'll feel safe proceeding with this information in mind. If you have questions or need more information, contact me at claire@clairecainwriter.com.

My very best to you,
Claire

A NOTE FROM THE AUTHOR

This series focuses on soldiers stationed overseas. OCONUS is the military acronym that stands for Outside the Continental United States. So really, it's what military personnel say when they're stationed somewhere other than the 48 continental states.

Any posting in Germany is an OCONUS duty station.

This series was formerly titled the OCONUS Bonus Series, but since that's not very clear for civilian readership, we've got a fresh series title. I couldn't skip this little intro, though, because the OCONUS setting is such a big part of the series. Being a service member outside the US is unique!

I hope you'll enjoy a peek at my fictionalized version of being stationed in Germany, which is based on my time living in Bavaria as a military spouse—truly some of my favorite years so far.

CHAPTER ONE

Summer

I perused the bread neatly sorted into identical baskets hanging from the wall behind the bakery's counter. Buttermilk. Multigrain. Rye. Baguette.

Rye, I think.

I requested the last loaf of rye, and a multigrain for myself. While the woman retrieved them, I fished out several euro coins and placed the amount onto the dish on the glass counter. The woman stretched her neck and counted the money without touching it, then nodded and handed over the fresh bread wrapped in waxy bakery paper. I slipped them into my waiting canvas bag, then with a *"Danke, Tschuss!"* and a wave of my free hand, I departed.

Excitement bubbled in me like water at a rolling boil—time to deliver the food! I wouldn't see Specialist Jacobs, most likely. He was a nice guy but tended not to answer the door, like most of them, when I dropped off his meal. I'd been delivering dinner to him and several other soldiers who'd been injured in a crash during a training rotation two weeks ago. Of the six men involved, only one had refused my efforts.

My stomach dropped at the thought of Sergeant Masters, but I pushed it away, forced a smile, and let my full, teeth-and-cheeks grin blare out at the general population of the parking lot while I scuttled along to where I'd parked. Even if you don't feel happy, you can trick yourself into feeling better by smiling—simple as that! So I did.

A German man passing glanced at me, completely stoic, and I remembered myself and tucked away the teeth. Nothing said "I'm an American" like emotional expression in public. *Whoops.*

Then I did smile, quite genuinely, to the tune of my car's unlock beep when it chirped just as I reached the driver's side door. My BMW Sedan was something of a middle finger to my family back home. Even though I'd owned it for well over two years, I still got a little kick of pleasure out of hopping into the luxury vehicle and smelling that leather-seats-and-new-car scent. Eat your heart out, Mama.

Excess in one's hand speaks to excess in one's heart. Oh, I remembered that one well. It always sounded particularly accurate and even godly. Too bad nothing about my parents' existence involved striving for righteousness. Their platitudes focused solely on creating shame with an eye toward unflinching obedience. *Neat.*

I brightened that smile, kicking away memories of my toxic past trying to creep in. I had better things to think about.

Tonight, the car's interior didn't exactly smell like new —not with the dinner I'd put together for the Jacobs family currently scenting the air. Tomato bisque, roasted chicken, salad with double greens and burrata, and an apple torte. Heavenly, comforting, restorative, I hoped. And a break for Jenny Jacobs because the woman had her hands full with three-year-old twins and a husband still not quite on his feet after two weeks in a wheelchair with a broken femur. Poor guy. He'd had one of the most severe injuries.

A few minutes later, I pulled into the Jacobses' drive, dropped the bags of food on the doorstep, and rang the bell before jogging back to my car. End of January in Bavaria meant *cold*, and I had no desire to wait around.

"Thanks, Miss Applegate!" Jacobses' little girls yelled in unison from the doorway where their mom held it open and waved.

They knew me from the clinic. It just so happened I looked after the whole Jacobs family, so I was privy to all of the details on his recovery and his family's health.

I held up a hand, then backed out and headed home, a warm glow clinging to me on the way.

I loved feeding people. *Loved* it. Honestly, sometimes it felt more satisfying than helping folks at the clinic. More satisfying than a perfectly poached egg on homemade crusty *pain de campagne*. Actually no, that was a lie. It *almost* always felt better than things at the clinic, because when I fed someone, that came completely from me. And basically nothing was better than a perfect egg on home-made bread. So.

At the clinic on Kugelfels Army post, I worked as a registered nurse on a medical care team—the standard for military clinics. Having spent my first three years after college on active duty as a nurse in the Army, I knew the dynamics of both military and civilian workers in a clinic like this one. I'd been out of the Army longer than I'd been in, but I still carried the experience with me and credited the knowledge gained with my success thus far, as well as my ability to adapt to life on an Army post and working with soldiers and their families.

Our teams were composed of two doctors, an RN, two LPNs, and two medics. Patients dealt with their doctor for diagnoses, prescriptions, care plans—all normal in the scheme of things. I assisted and wore all manner of hats: filled in for the medics and LPNs where needed, did intake interviews, took blood pressures, and gave immunizations. I assisted with in-patient procedures and answered dozens of questions a day about symptoms and what over-the-counter medicine to take. I got to do a lot for my patients, and I loved that, but I shared that with the other team members.

It might sound odd, but I could be a little selfish in my altruism. I liked knowing I'd been the one to help someone, and having grown up intimately acquainted with the feeling of hunger, feeding people felt like the best, most satisfying version of help I could offer.

I pulled into my place and parked in the garage. Very few homes in our area had electronic garage doors, but I'd lucked out with one. I pressed the button to close the door and shuffled up the walk. The garage stood separate from the house, but I'd take the electronic door and not complain.

I worked my way inside past the sturdy locked door, kicked off my shoes, and slipped on my cozy slippers before shuffling into the kitchen to serve myself dinner. After washing my hands, I dipped out a bowl of soup from the crock I'd left simmering on low while I ran my errands. I sliced bread, then sat down at the table in the same spot I always used.

The crust of the multigrain was perfect. Rye would've been even better for this soup with that earthy, dense quality to it, but there'd only been one loaf so that had to go to my friends. I closed my eyes as the warm, unctuous flavor coated my insides. I used parmesan rind and a little Neufchatel right at the end to really punch up the creamy factor while not making it too terribly fattening.

I growled at the whole concept. I hated the idea of certain foods being *bad* for you. *All things in moderation* had been a beloved adage for decades or centuries or *whatever* for a reason. But clearly, some people couldn't handle eating variety.

You need to calm down.

My inner angel didn't like the train of thought. But I couldn't help it. I reached behind me to the buffet where I'd left his letter, and like I'd done every few days—okay, every single day—reread the letter from Sergeant Nicholas Masters.

Dear Miss Applegate,

I have been made aware it is you who is leaving the exceptionally rich and abundant food on my doorstep each week. I thank you for your kindness. I am not sure what I've done to merit the receipt of your generous meals, but whatever it is, I would very much like to know.

I have savored every bite, and I thank you.

That said, I hope you won't find it rude of me to request you cease the meal delivery and direct it elsewhere. I'm sure there are many families who would relish the delights you offer. I, however, cannot continue to be one.

Very Respectfully,
Sergeant Nicholas Masters

I blinked against the ire rising in me. What kind of fool had written this?

"I mean, come on!" I said to the non-existent crowd gathered around my large table.

Who said things like that? Who *wrote* things like that? Honestly, who? I'd never had a conversation with the man, but I knew him by reputation.

Well... reputation and sight.

"And what a fine, fine sight it is."

Okay, let's face it. I talked aloud to myself a lot. It might've been cute if I had a dog to lovingly waggle his tongue at me, but in reality, it was just me. Get a sauté pan crackling and it sounded like a supportive enough chorus, though.

Anyway, Masters. Truly. The man was... how to describe him? You know that feeling when you go somewhere and you see, like, mountains in the distance with a gorgeous rainbow sunset behind it and little stars twinkling above it and you think to yourself *this is the most beautiful thing I've ever seen?*

Looking at Masters was like that.

No, really. He was *that* good-looking. He looked fake— that's how pretty he was. But the thing is, not *just* pretty. The man was built to the hilt. He had this aura that read *power*. He was also notoriously introverted, quiet, and antisocial.

Six months ago, I'd sat a few seats away from him at a fest. He'd arrived with Thatcher Wild, all around excellent human and delightful guy, and my interest had been piqued. I'd thought, *Hey, self, here's this gorgeous guy right next to you. Maybe you'll say hi to him!*

But almost before I'd fully settled in, he'd gotten up and left without so much as a fare-thee-well for anyone but Thatcher and one other person! I'd wanted to scoff, and loudly, but it wouldn't have done me any good because the band had been blasting.

Plus, I didn't know him. Even if some part of me wanted to know him, in the same way I wanted to know Henry Cavill or Chris Hemsworth—which meant not *really*. But, like, if they were sitting a few seats down from me at a table? Yeah, I'd do my best to have a quick chat and stare that beauty in the face at close range.

Whatever. He likely had no clue who I was aside from the basics of my name and house number, so this wasn't personal. I had no idea why he didn't want my food, but I wasn't quite ready to give up. I'd gotten the tip from my friend Rob Waverly that Masters was a bit of a health nut.

I chuckled at the memory. Rob had been so earnest, like I wouldn't know someone who looked like Masters had to be pretty tuned in to what went into his body. Still, the seared skirt steak, crispy potato stacks, and brussels sprouts salad with warm bacon dressing wasn't *too* bad. I'd been excited to take that to him because, funnily enough, it turned out he lived three doors down from me. I could make things for him that needed to stay crisp, and steak that might overcook if I had to drive it twenty minutes to someone's house. Plus, I'd grabbed the skirt steak on sale—it was destiny. That meal had undoubtedly been an improvement on the first week's beef short rib ragu over pasta and giant, fresh-baked ciabatta loaf. And cheesecake.

It may seem ridiculous that I didn't know the man considering our proximity for nearly a year and a half, but I never saw him. I mean, *never*. I could count on less than ten fingers the times I'd seen him out of his house in the last few months. Half the time, his place looked vacant except that his garden was always perfectly manicured and his porch tidy and swept. Lately, I'd seen someone duck in for a half hour twice a day, which I'd noticed happening during rotations on weekends. I couldn't say whether it happened weekdays, but I figured it might. Girlfriend? Seemed odd for those quick, regular visits, and only certain times... couldn't be a cleaning lady with that frequency.

Since I didn't know the man, the person visiting his house and the reason for it didn't concern me.

I wasn't about to give up on the food. I would try again, but this time, I had a menu that would be grain-free and generally very healthy. I could do healthy. Didn't love to if I didn't have to, because all of the fun cooking used butter, butter, and more butter, but I could do it. Butter just made life better in every possible way. But if that was what Masters needed in order to eat my food and be relieved of cooking one meal a week for himself, then he'd get it.

Two nights later, I signed the letter I'd just written. It said:

Dear Sergeant Masters,

I am very glad to hear you enjoyed the food. I do hope this meal will meet with your approval. A mutual friend informed me that you prefer healthier eating, and so I have done my level best to meet a more stringent nutritional requirement. Included in the bag, please find paprika-seasoned grilled chicken breasts, kale winter salad with toasted walnuts (on the side in case of allergy or aversion), baked sweet potatoes sans filling and bereft of anything delicious other than themselves and a pinch of sea salt and dried thyme, and fresh-cut winter strawberries smuggled in from Spain. Because I find the absence of dessert to be a depressing reality no one should face in these dark winter months, I have included oatmeal chocolate chip cookies. And if oatmeal isn't on the menu, you can find the chia seed cookies. I look forward to your feedback.

Sincerely,

Summer Applegate

There. Put that on your plate and eat it.

I bundled up in a long, wind-proof coat that ended at my knees and donned snow boots. The snow had started just as I'd finished grilling outside, thankfully. I hated cleaning grill pans, so whenever possible, I used the outdoor set-up. I looped a scarf around my neck, pulled a bright blue knit hat with a white snowball pompom on top over my hair, and grabbed the bags. I could be to his house and back within five minutes, I estimated, and then would sit down to my own meal.

I walked as fast as I could with the bags of food and my puffy coat and boots slowing me down. The sidewalks were slicked with a fine layer of snow. His house looked closed for business. The rolladen—heavy metallic shutters that could be raised or lowered over windows—were all lowered. This meant I couldn't see whether any lights were on. No matter, though, as I knew he wouldn't answer the door when I knocked.

I set the paper bags with the food on the porch next to the door, then knocked twice and turned to scuttle back down the path as quickly as possible without biffing it. Done! Hopefully, he'd find it soon and eat it while it was hot. I hated the idea of him discovering it hours later.

Hmm. With a moment of indecision, I turned around and moved to ring the bell. And just as I reached it and pushed, the door swung open to reveal the man himself.

CHAPTER TWO

Summer

Angry wouldn't quite describe his face. But suspicious? Yes.

He cut an imposing figure, I had to admit. He embodied that large, intimidating, mean-mugging type man I typically didn't go for. But every time I encountered Nicholas Masters, whether in life or legend, some element revealed itself that caught me off guard and forced me to notice him.

For example? That letter. Who writes a letter like that? Or when Rob mentioned he lives just a few doors down from my house. This came in the context of him sharing Masters' address when I explained wanting to make food for the people who'd been in the accident. After Rob gave it, he told me not to share it, not to tell anyone I was feeding Masters in the first place, and that the only reason he knew where Masters lived was because he sometimes trained at his house.

What?

I knew Rob was training for something, and it occupied most of his time outside the workday. But to find it was Nicholas Masters training him? It... intrigued me.

Even the time at the fest, when he'd just left. More than a small handful of women had approached him in the hour he'd sat at the table. I'd missed his dismissal of them, but it'd happened, and quickly. This, too, served to intrigue me.

But nothing could've prepared me for the sight in front of me. Because it was—and please don't think less of me for saying so—something right out of a pinup calendar. Whatever the case, I would just be thankful for the moment, even if it came with the storm cloud of his facial expression.

The man stood in his doorway, warm light behind him lending him an unearthly, angelic glow. His feet were bare on the hardwood floor just inside the threshold, and his long, muscular legs were covered in sweatpants pushed up at his calves. And up top?

Nothing. Not. A. Thing. Just miles of stunning golden skin interrupted by designs inking over every part of his arms. Well, skin and ink that covered muscles carved out of will and sacrifice. Muscles defined by refusing bread and cheese and butter, no doubt.

And yes—yes, that would be a sight in and of itself. But in one arm, cradled like a baby, rested a little white ball of fur with cerulean blue eyes blinking back at me and a long tail flicking with impatience.

He was topless. With a kitten. In a snowstorm.

Seriously.

And sure, *he* wasn't the one in the snowstorm, I was. And everything felt more... magical and heightened in a snowstorm, didn't it? That was just fact. Hallmark and Gilmore Girls and my own Appalachian mountain upbringing had taught me that.

"Sorry to interrupt your evening," I said, my voice weird and high, but whatever. He'd come to the door without a shirt, so I couldn't be blamed.

Yes, I'd been a nurse for eight-plus years. I'd seen bodies and more bodies. So a shirtless fit man didn't exactly fall into the novel category, nor did it necessarily set me all a-twitter or anything. But these were after-work hours, and I'd been caught unawares, and with an empty stomach, too.

"Can I help you?" Barely any inflection. Just the tiniest, barest little hint of a turnup at the end of the sentence.

"Well, uh, I guess? I brought you dinner. I'm Summer Applegate." I raised a hand and twiddled my fingers, only to realize I wore mittens and he couldn't see my fingers. *Genius.* "I know you said to stop, but your friend Rob mentioned that you eat really healthy food, and I thought maybe you didn't like my food because I don't tend to cook super healthy things. So I wanted to give it another shot, because I hate that you got hurt, and the way I take care of people is to feed them. Or, well, I mean I'm a nurse, so I do actually take care of them too, but in the off hours I feed them. It makes me happy. And I hope it makes them happy. And, so, well, I hope this will work out better for you."

Oh good Lord, stop talking!

I swallowed, mildly horrified at my babbling, though not at all surprised. I wouldn't say I was nervous, exactly, but he made me feel... well, let's just say it. He made me feel like I'd trotted up to his porch in the nude.

Masters squinted, and his firm-looking, sculpted lips flattened.

My stomach dropped. *Ugh.* Would he really refuse the food?

I held out a hand to stay him. "Listen, I know you asked me to stop. I'm not trying to harass you, or anything. I... try this food. If you don't like it, I swear I won't bother you again. You can just let me know one way or another."

I grabbed the handles of the bags and thrust them at him. He still held his cat, who seemed entirely disinclined to leave his embrace, so Masters reached with the other hand and took both in one. I blurred out the view of his sculpted pecs, the neat double stacks of abdominal muscles, the general splendor of his physical person.

"Okay then," I said, a nervous chuckle escaping. "Bye."

I turned and waved again without looking.

"Ms. Applegate."

I stopped and my feet nearly slid out from under me. I moved slowly, returning my gaze to his doorway. *Good night, what a sight.*

"Thank you." A slight nod, furrowed brow still, no smile.

So I flashed him one, and said, "You're welcome."

Then I walked ever so carefully home, full to the brim with... thoughts.

The insane pace at work the next day boiled down to one maddening little fact about the Kugelfels community: it was tiny. If a normal military base was a trusty six-quart casserole dish, Kugelfels was a tablespoon. This might not immediately make sense for those not in health care, so let me explain. If an illness hit the community, it swept through at lightning speed. I'm talking a kid shows up at the elementary school with a stomach bug, and next thing we know, we've seen two hundred cases in a week. And soon enough, half the population is down for the count. Talk about community spread.

This time, the flu had settled on Kugelfels like a shroud. The snow hadn't stopped last night, but even with a late call for soldiers, people tripped through the doors bundled in coats, shivering through fevers, skin sallow from illness.

"My goodness, I do love a good viral sweep," Carla, a fellow RN, chirped as she plunked away at her computer.

"Is it the vomitus or the pre-pneumonia symptoms you like best?" Dr. Crane asked, pure sarcasm.

I chuckled under my breath, though I didn't need to hide it.

"I just love knowing we're helping. We're solving problems. It's not all aches and pains with no real diagnoses. Flu, bam. Strep, bam. Whatever." She turned, winked with an exaggerated smile, and then continued her typing.

Dr. Crane shook his head and left. He was about the grumpiest person I'd ever met, but it was hard to say because I suspected Nicholas Masters could give him a run for the honor. I mentally swatted away an image of the man, glorious torso and fluffy white snowball cat, glaring at me. No time for such things, despite their persistent efforts to gain my attention.

"Green Team, you guys have one waiting, one checking in," Cindy, the acting nurse supervisor hollered into the room as she passed by, alerting us.

The edge in her voice said enough—she wasn't happy with how things were moving. We were behind, as it always happened thanks to late arrivals or things that popped up in appointments, so we needed to move it.

I hopped up, ready to take the person waiting since our

medic was out with, you guessed it, the flu. One more element keeping this day moving. I grabbed my laptop and rushed out into the hallway, only to be caught by Major Hall, the active-duty manager of the clinic.

"Nurse Applegate. I'd love to talk to you when you have a minute. Can you swing by my office when you start lunch?"

Her pale face had the most pleasing freckle pattern dappled across her nose and onto her cheeks. They looked slightly bronze against her whipped-cream skin and gave her this sun-kissed look I envied a little. Her chestnut hair was pulled back into a neat bun at the base of her skull, and her uniform looked tidy as always. Pleasing appearances aside, the woman exuded professional skill and calm.

"Absolutely. I should break in an hour, if that works?"

She nodded with a closed-mouth smile, and I zipped off to room three.

An hour and ten minutes later, I knocked on Major Hall's door.

"Come on in. Have a seat." She gestured to a chair and clicked rapidly at her mouse before focusing fully on me.

"Everything okay?" I asked, betraying my total lack of calm.

"Oh, yes. I'm sorry if I worried you. I have some news, and I wanted to give you a heads-up."

I perked up and leaned forward in the chair.

"The nurse supervisor position will be opening up in a few months."

"Really." *Yes. I knew it. Yesss. Finally!* I made a point not to squirm in my seat or let my feet bust out a little tap dance right there. Not professional, so I'd keep it together.

"You recently earned your Master's in Nursing Science, right?"

"Yes. Last August." After eighteen grueling months of online courses. And I would never go back to school. Ever. Never. Cue T. Swift because the declaration deserved its own song. My friend Emily had taken me out for drinks and dancing, and I'd made every one of my favorite meals for two weeks straight in celebration.

"It's new, and you don't have the kind of managerial experience we typically look for. But you're here. We know you. We know you do good work, and you're a part of the community. I know you're involved with the Red Cross and some other efforts too, and you head up a lot of activities in that community."

"Yes," I said dumbly.

"I think you should apply."

I swallowed, excitement zipping my posture even straighter. "I will."

"You'll want to do whatever you can to bulk up the managerial aspects—really highlight where you've managed projects within the clinic, obviously, but even outside work too, whenever relevant. I know it's not always possible to acquire the experience until you have the job, so I get it. But I do think you can be competitive." She smiled kindly.

"Thank you. I'll do my best."

We talked for another moment about timelines, and I left her office, nearly climbing out of my skin with excitement.

I practically skipped down the hall, but the excitement plummeted when I ran into someone at full speed—*ouch*.

"Oh, I'm so sorry."

Hands grasped my arms to steady me. "No problem, Nurse Applegate."

My stomach soured. Of all people, it had to be him. Kent Dennin.

"Thanks," I said, forcing a chuckle and taking a big step away—out of his reach.

"Like I said, no problem." He held my gaze, then his eyes dipped to my lips and down my front before he held up a hand in a wave.

Cold disgust slithered through me, dousing all sense of excitement over the news from Major Hall. Kent Dennin made my skin crawl. I couldn't explain it except for the way he looked at me. I'd decided that was enough. I avoided him. He worked in another part of the clinic. He was a sergeant, seemed nice enough to everyone, but I didn't want his attention. *Of course*, it'd be him I ran into.

I inhaled, steeling myself, then shoved all that away with a teeth-baring smile. I didn't need to worry about a leering Kent. I could bask in the excitement of a door opening right in front of me. A door I'd been watching since the moment I arrived and noticed there was only one upwardly mobile employment option for me at this clinic. I loved my job, but if I wanted to stick with my plans and grow my earning potential, I needed to move up. This was it.

I beamed to myself. *This is it!*

CHAPTER THREE

Nick

I've been collecting memories, cramming them into my head like a starving man. I don't know if I'll lose them, so I ink them into my skin to keep them safe from myself.

Command Sergeant Major Allen eyed me, his expression typically unsmiling. "You're recovering well?"

I nodded.

Allen, Lieutenant Colonel Wolfe, and Major Nate Reynolds all stood there. Did they expect me to speak? What would I say?

"And you're doing all right—feeling okay after the last few months and such?" LTC Wolfe asked, his voice carefully even. No pity, thankfully.

"Yes, sir. Doing just fine." If fine was feeling the recession of grief for a few minutes a day rather than not at all, then yeah. Dandy.

"Good. That's good," Wolfe said.

"All right, Masters, we'll let you get on with it. See you soon," Reynolds said, releasing me.

I bid them all farewell with another nod and left, heading for the commissary. I needed to grab some fresh lettuce and more bananas—I'd forgotten them on my Saturday grocery run. Routines helped keep me moving, but sometimes, I came out the other side and could barely remember what I'd just done. Such was the case with the last commissary trip.

Soon enough, I'd worked my way through the produce section, dodging a glance or two from fellow shoppers, and made it to self-checkout. I'd made a habit to stick with this method since the last few times I'd checked out, I'd ended up with a woman ogling my tattoos.

"I like your tattoos," she said, then bit her lip in that way women did to bring attention to their lips. I didn't bother looking—she wore a wedding ring. Some women did since they were less likely to get hit on, but I happened to know this woman was married to a contractor.

"That one there—what's that one for?" She pointed to my left bicep. The ink there was a map of the last hike my dad and I had taken, though without place names, it looked more like it traced the veins instead of outlined rivers and mountain ranges.

Since the credit card machine always took a minute, I had no escape. "It's a map," I said, not interested in telling her anything. Not interested in the way she leaned down, offering up a peek down her shirt.

"Ooo, like a treasure map?"

Thick, seedy disgust coated my throat, and I cleared it. "No."

The same woman had hit on me at least two other times. Something about me read like a blinking sign to women like her—I must have an invisible-to-me notifier indicating I was *here for a good time.* Problem was, I definitely was not. Not anymore, certainly, and even in my younger days, I'd never thought of those experiences as exploits or sowing oats or whatever other bull people called it. I'd tried to connect, tried to grow depth.

Biggest issue for me had always been my general demeanor and introversion. At this age, I didn't apologize for it or wish it away. The last decade or so had taught me to truly embrace it, see the interior qualities of my nature as assets instead of weaknesses. Not that I didn't have those too, but I didn't need to apologize for being a quiet, thoughtful person. Gran had taught me that long ago, and I'd finally internalized it.

Piercing, hot pain sliced through my chest. *Gran.* It was coming up on two months since she'd passed. I wondered if I'd ever count days or years by anything other than the deaths of the people I loved.

"Did you need any help, sir?" A man approached, friendly face ready to assist.

"I'm all set." I held up the bagged goods, grabbed the receipt that spurted out of the machine, and gave him a nod goodbye.

Back in the car, the tension in my shoulders eased, even as the too-familiar grief still weighed heavy in my gut.

Sometimes, it was just the attention that got to me—I was a big man and drew eyes. Plus, I'd gained a reputation for being a hard-ass thanks to my reluctance to babble on like some, and my new PT programming that had everyone whining about how difficult it was even though I wasn't doing anything even remotely revolutionary. Soldiers eyed me because of that, and the women around the small community...

I shook that off. Not all women got that particular look in their eye, of course—many were happily married and seemed to have some level of respect for their spouses. But plenty let their eyes wander over me, especially when I wore exercise clothes instead of a uniform. And it always made me feel like I'd left my shoes at home.

At one point in my life, I'd enjoyed the attention to a degree. Eager for the physical interactions, sure, but then hopeful for something more. And the more never once came —not enough to truly know me. I'd tolerated shallow relationships at times, assuaging the worst of my loneliness, until I'd wake up and sense I felt even more lonely being with someone who didn't like my *moods* or couldn't stand how quiet I was, who made no effort to dig deeper than a good time physically, or to hold on when I pushed them away.

The lessons I'd learned repeatedly were that I had nothing to offer a woman but my face and body—at least not anything most women were supposedly interested in. Gran had raged when I'd even hinted at that years ago, but there was the rub. Gran was gone. My parents were gone and had been for more than two decades.

Everyone who'd loved and known me was gone. And some of this ragged, clinging grief was rooted in that—in that loss, but also in the utter isolation that came with the fear that no one else would ever know me again.

I pulled into my driveway, surprised to find how quickly the commute had flown when I was lost in my thoughts.

I pushed inside the house and waited, wondering if I'd

get the cold shoulder or an ambush ankle attack. Depended on the phase of the moon or something. I padded carefully in, especially since I'd had the horrifying experience of stepping on the cat's tail in the first days of having him here, before I realized how he'd lace around my legs and position himself exactly where he would be most likely flattened when I wore my combat boots.

He'd warmed up to me so quickly. From what I'd read, cats often took longer, especially if you didn't get them as kittens. Butter was small, and he was fully grown when Rob dropped him at my house weeks ago. He'd been a shelter kitty, though one severely lonely hour spent searching cat breeds online made me think he was mostly, if not all, Ragdoll.

A distant *thunk* told me he'd jumped down from one of his many perches and would be expecting food and affection, in that order, immediately.

We went through these familiar motions, a welcomed distraction from the waves of cresting emotion that so often crept up on me and threatened to pull me under after days like this. Full, good days. And then something would trip the wire, and I'd be consumed with repeating thoughts about Gran.

Loss.

The knowledge that I had no one left, not a single person who knew me or cared. Not in anything beyond the superficial. Not for years, in truth, but now...

Death was so final. I'd ruminated on that for no small amount of time, obvious as it was.

I gave Butter a small pat on his back, which earned me a flick of his tail I'd learned meant to back off. I chuckled to myself, surprised to find that lightness in me so soon after thoughts of Gran and all that came with them.

On the counter, my eye caught on the baggy of remaining oatmeal chocolate chip cookies from Summer.

Summer Applegate.

The woman just wouldn't quit. She'd delivered meals to many, but she didn't need to feed me. I had few expenses beyond food and Danielle, the pet sitter, and I had no one else to worry about. I could feed myself.

The look on her face when she came to the door had been less attracted and more stunned. She definitely didn't eye me in that way that made me feel bad, so points there. And again, not that I was some irresistible paragon or something, but it got old being looked at like a tool and not a person.

She clearly hadn't expected me to answer the door so quickly. Probably planned to drop the food and sneak off. I never would've answered the door without a shirt, especially if I'd known it was her, but Butter had curled up in the crook of my arm, and I couldn't convince myself anything was worth disturbing him or the low hum of comfort he gave me.

Irritation and a little... something else, not sure what, ticked away in the back of my mind. I'd very politely written to thank her and tell her I appreciated the food but that I didn't need more. She'd ignored me, showed up with a meal that was, without a doubt, one of the finest I'd ever eaten. And I'd eaten every bite, almost to the point of being overfull.

Then I'd written another letter. She couldn't mistake my meaning in this one, for sure. That should take care of it, and I'd be relieved when the next week passed without another meal.

Yeah, keep telling yourself that.

I snickered and moved through putting together a snack

before an evening training session with one of my strongest clients, Art. I didn't like her stubborn ignoring of my *thanks but no thanks* letter, but this time, she'd get it. She had to. And if I regretted that I wouldn't eat her food again? I wouldn't think about that either. Even if it had been practically the only flavors I'd managed to taste since before Christmas.

She'd go her way, finally, and I'd go mine. That sounded just right.

CHAPTER FOUR

Summer

I dragged through my door, thankful I'd dropped off a meal to Bec Jones on the way home and that I didn't have to go back out. I'd made a quiche I'd kept in the fridge—she could heat it up whenever she and Thatcher wanted to eat it. She didn't live all that far from me, but once the flu started circulating late last week, I'd known I needed to make at least a few meal deliveries easier this week.

I dumped my bag full of empty lunch, snack, and coffee containers on the ground in the kitchen, then stripped, showered, and emerged with wet hair, warm sweats, and an appetite. Somehow, I only felt tired until I got home and cleaned up. Eating in my scrubs after seeing sick people all day grossed me out. I wasn't a germaphobe, but I also understood the basics of how diseases spread and had no desire to get the flu or any other fun illnesses, so I took any precautions I could, especially when particularly aggressive strains were at work.

Moving to the kitchen, I grabbed my own piece of quiche and nuked it for a few in the microwave. I filled a wineglass with my favorite red, taking extra pleasure in the fact that I'd found such a perfect Bordeaux for less than four euros at the local grocery. No, really... and it was fantastic.

I took my seat at the table and set my phone down, then took a few bites. Not bad. Not my favorite combination—a roasted red pepper, asparagus, and goat cheese tart, actually, but I'd called it a quiche. I pulled up the notes section on my phone and jotted down the changes I'd make next time I cooked the recipe. A few more bites, and finally, *finally*, I let myself inspect the envelope I'd found on the front porch when I came in earlier.

On the front, in a now-familiar script, *Ms. Applegate*.

Why did my stomach flutter? Just touching this envelope did things to me. Made me kind of... nervous.

I slipped my pinky under the edge, fleetingly wondering if he'd licked the strip of adhesive.

"Okay, really?" I rolled my eyes at myself because *really*.

Inside, on the same cream, textured paper as the last, it said:

Ms. Applegate,

Thank you for the thoughtful meal. I apologize if my first letter caused offense. I didn't mean to. Rob Waverly is correct—much like he does, I also adhere to careful eating guidelines, particularly before competitions. I very much appreciate your efforts to accommodate my peculiarities, and

I can confirm that everything you provided was excellent. Having had the pleasure of three meals from your kitchen at this point, I suspect anything you touch would be delicious. That said, I beg you to consider spending your valuable time, energy, and resources on someone else.

Please accept my sincere thanks, again, for the delectable meal.

Very Respectfully,
Nicholas Masters

Heat burned in my cheeks. The mixed-up feeling the man caused in me grew to a little flame of embarrassment and frustration. How does someone say some of the nicest things I've ever read in a letter and then ultimately still insult me by not wanting to eat my food?

And no, I did not cook for my profession. So I could recognize I might be reacting a bit harshly to his request that I not continue feeding him but—but—!

I pushed out of my seat and stomped into the kitchen, then dumped my plate, appetite gone. "That is a man with an ego too big for his giant, muscular, Hercules-looking body."

I tapped the phone before thinking twice about it.

"Hey, friend. How are you doing?" Ariel Wolfe answered, the sounds of her niece and nephew chattering in the background.

"Hey. Do you have a sec?" I sounded huffy and on the verge of whiny, even to my own ears.

"Sure. What's wrong?"

"So, I'm taking meals to the guys hurt in the accident, right?" I took a sip of wine and put the glass down a little too hard.

"Right. I heard everyone is obsessed with your cooking and talking about how you need to quit the clinic and do a meal-order business. I would totally buy your food, and Livie told me she would too."

In the background, I could hear Livie holler, "I totally would!"

I chuckled reluctantly, resisting the good humor that comment tempted me toward. I didn't much feel like getting happy just now—unusual for me, but I wanted to ride this sense of injustice.

"That's nice. But listen. I got a letter from one of the guys saying I didn't need to bring him a meal again after the second week. Then I found out he's really health conscious. *Fine*, so I made him something super healthy. He left another letter on my doorstep today saying thanks, the food was amazing, and no need to give him another meal."

Silence met me for a moment, before Ariel said, "Wait, he wrote you letters?"

"Yeah. On really nice stationary."

"Huh. That's thoughtful."

"Well—well yeah, it is." My ire deflated a bit. *Ire* didn't accurately reflect the feeling either. But *bothered* sure did. "I just don't get why he won't let me feed him."

Another pause before a light laugh. "Oh, Summer, I like you."

I smiled despite myself. "What? Why?"

"You're hell-bent on helping this guy, even when he's refusing. I'm guessing exactly no one in the history of your feeding people has ever refused your food, so I'm sure that's driving you insane. But maybe he's just being polite? Doesn't want to feel like a burden or something. I get that."

I sobered, connecting with the sentiment more than she'd realize.

"I do too," I said quietly.

Like she knew I needed a moment to think, to simmer over her statements. Eventually, she asked gently, "So... are you going to write back?"

"Write back?"

"Yeah. He's written you letters. Are you going to respond? Or just not feed him?"

I let loose a weird laugh-snort. "That's a primary difference between us, my friend. You'd write him back or just do what he wants, whereas me? I've been over here thinking about what meal I'll make for him next."

Ariel's full, lovely laugh filled my ear, and I smiled again. Our friendship had started fairly recently—only about six months ago—but I liked her so much. She was a bit on the introverted side, kind of private, and even though I was nothing close to an introvert, I got the private thing. I put it all out there for anyone who wanted it... to a point. What I kept to myself was locked up tight.

"Well, maybe include a note and let me know what happens."

We chatted another minute and then said good night, confirming our plans to get together the next weekend. She was preparing to move out of her brother and sister-in-law's place because her mom would be moving back to Germany in a month or so. It was convoluted, but we had a lot to catch up on.

And just now? I had a menu to plan.

CHAPTER FIVE

Nick

I thought of you today and wondered what you'd think of me now, this wandering wraith. But you don't think of me, not anymore. You have gone and left me, empty and untethered to anyone else on earth.

I walked around Rob, watching his form.

"Good. Push." He'd come a long way since we started training together.

The only sounds in my garage were his breathing and the mix he put on when he arrived—AC/DC, Metallica, and such.

"Two more," I said, but he already knew it. I didn't have to prompt him much—he had the drive. Alicia did too, of course. Arturo, the same. They'd all show well at regionals.

"Well done," I said, always conscious of the need to

praise. I could be harsh as a coach, so whenever I could, I gave words of affirmation. Never false praise, mind, but acknowledging successes, however small, could matter. Especially on an off day.

"Crap, man. That was brutal," Rob said, staring sightlessly ahead as he wiped his face with a small towel.

"You're welcome."

He chuckled. "Yeah, yeah. Thanks."

"Hand okay?" His hand seemed fully operational to me, but I'd noticed him flexing and stretching it more than usual last weekend.

He eyed his left hand, turning it front to back. "Yeah. Makes me feel old because in this colder weather, it stiffens up a ton. But grip strength is good."

I nodded. *Good.* We had six weeks until the regional competition. He probably wouldn't be competitive for a podium slot, but he wanted the experience and exposure, and since I'd already planned to go for Art and Alicia, it made sense he should go too. He'd qualified by the skin of his teeth, and now we had six weeks to get him closer to ready.

"You need to watch lengthening on the left side. You're not quite fully extended when you're overhead. Is that from the injury?" I asked, moving around the space, a twinge of anticipation hitting as the realization that my day's obligations were nearly done, and soon, I could relax.

Rob let out a dramatic sigh. "Probably. It feels fully extended, but I can see it too. Yell at me next time."

I nodded.

He moved to an open area in the corner of the space where yoga mats and bands waited. He'd need a good stretching session today and, no doubt, rolling. He'd need to ice later, too. I joined him, feeling tight from the workout I'd done earlier.

The housing office had given me two options to choose from when I first moved here after PCSing from Fort Bragg. The other was an apartment, which wouldn't have worked. Thankfully, I finagled this one somehow, and it was pretty perfect. The garage was a spacious two-car setup, and though it didn't have a door into the house directly, it did have insulation, which helped immensely, especially in these frigid winter months. I used space heaters to make up the difference, but with bodies moving around, it warmed up okay.

I'd collected the equipment for my gym over the last ten years, slowly building what I'd need. I'd planned to begin training people after retirement, but once Lieutenant Colonel Wolfe put me on PT scheduling and planning, I got the bug. I couldn't push the whole battalion like I would people I trained directly, and once a few people approached me about one-on-ones, I fell into it.

I'd never imagined getting to be involved with athletes like Arturo or Alicia. They were excellent before they started with me. Both had experience but had let their training drop off due to the rotational schedule. That they'd both managed to clinch a spot in the regional competition didn't surprise me, though they seemed absolutely floored.

After extensive stretching and rolling out muscles with foam rollers, Rob gathered his things, and I walked him out the side door and into the driveway.

"So, Summer bringing you food tonight? Thursday's your day, right?" he asked from where he dumped his stuff in his car.

My chest kicked—irritation, of course. *Summer.* What a perfect name for the woman. Her face *looked* like summer.

Warm, sunny, beautiful. And damn stubborn, from what I'd witnessed thus far.

Pretty she may have been, but that dogged insistence on feeding me didn't make sense. Why did she even care? Unless it was some sort of weird performative nice girl ritual or something. No one was *actually* that generous and thoughtful, but I couldn't figure out her angle.

I didn't let myself look toward her house.

"Not sure. I told her not to worry about it."

He shook his head. "Why would you do that?"

I raised a shoulder in a shrug. "She doesn't need to do that for me. I've got nothing else to worry about. I can cook."

He looked around like I was crazy, but his attention caught on something. He started, and that response from him pushed me to follow his gaze.

Summer Applegate stood pressed up against her door, her hands in front of her. A man, back to us, hand above her, blocked her from view partially with his head ducked like he was speaking to her.

Alarm shot through me right as Rob started jogging.

"Summer, hey!" he shouted as we both jogged. "Summer!"

At first, neither the woman in question nor the man harassing her seemed to hear him, so he shouted again.

We were at the path leading to her door when her eyes jumped to Rob, then me. Finally, Rob reached the doorstep and pulled the guy away from her with a hand on his shoulder.

"What the hell?" the man said, immediately irate.

Summer's eyes welled with tears, but they didn't spill over. She blinked rapidly, her chest rising and falling. She wore no coat and slippers on her feet. She had sweatpants and a T-shirt on—she obviously hadn't planned on being outside long. This revelation made the man's choice to block the door even more suspect.

"You okay?" I said low, stepping onto the porch but careful not to get to close. Though we'd met and interacted, I didn't want to assume she'd be comfortable with me in her space. At six foot three and two-fifteen, I was something of an imposing figure.

She nodded, lips pressed hard together.

"Get gone, man. Don't come back. Don't let me hear about you coming back." Rob shoved the idiot down the path, and he scrambled off to his car without another word. Rob turned and stomped back up to Summer. "Come here," he said and pulled her into a hug.

Something slipped through me—ugly, and not worth my time. I shoved it away without another thought, inspecting the woman as she closed her eyes tight in Rob's arms.

"What are you doing here?" she asked as she pulled back and looked at him, then flickered to me before settling back with Rob.

"Just finished up with Masters—I told you he trains me, didn't I? The more pressing question is, who was that idiot?" He dropped his dark head, bringing his face close to hers.

Up to this point, I'd assumed they were just friends. Seeing him with her now, I wondered. How else would he know where she lived, after all?

"He works at the clinic. I'm shocked he came here and even more that he felt like he could box me in and talk to me like that. He was about to get my knee to his crotch, so I guess thanks for saving me from smashing whatever poor excuse for family jewels he had."

I wanted to laugh at her stark delivery but clenched my jaw to stave it off. Very unexpected, but this was not the time. Still, that fire lit something in me—or maybe it burned away the irritation her obstinate disregard for my first letter had caused. In the ashes stood a woman, scared, but not cowed. She didn't need me or Rob.

And the oddest thought hit. *I wish she needed me.*

I mentally reared back. Where had that come from?

Later, when I reviewed all of this, I'd roll my eyes at the ridiculous train of thought. Where had the desire for someone to need me come from in my lonely, broken heart? *Gee, I wonder.* Apparently, all I needed was a pretty nice-ish girl in distress, and I got ideas. Pathetic.

"You should report this to your manager or whatever the process is with the clinic. And we should call the MPs."

Her hand shot out and she grabbed his wrist. "No. Definitely not. I'm not dealing with that, and this won't happen again, I'm sure. I have to..." Her eyes jumped to me, then back to Rob. "I have something in the oven. I'd ask you guys to come in, but—"

"No, no. Masters has to get back to his poetry and brooding, and I've got to get home. But report this, and call me if you need anything," he said, already walking back toward his car just down the street.

"Thanks," she said, opening the door.

Our eyes connected before she slipped back inside, leaving my chest tight with concern. Should we be leaving her like this? It didn't feel right, but I didn't know her enough to insist on staying. And then again, she didn't need either one of us.

Back at his car, Rob looked at me with wide eyes. "Idiots are exhausting."

I nodded.

"Well, let me know what she made you," he said, then winked.

I rolled my eyes but couldn't ignore the spark of anticipation. She might not've made me dinner. I'd very clearly told her not to worry about it. But I had to admit I wouldn't mind if she knocked on my door tonight—just to see how she was. It was only right I wanted to make sure she was okay.

CHAPTER SIX

Summer

Rob's crappy beater car buzzed down the street. Whenever I heard it, I wondered how it passed inspection since Germany had such strict noise laws.

I'd stepped inside, more than eager to get away from my unexpected audience and hunched into a ball right on the mat where I usually wiped my feet. I wrapped my arms around my knees and held myself close, wishing the shuddering, cold sensation would flee.

The pounding in my chest halted my progress. Why had Dennin come to my house? How had he even known where I lived? And why did he think I wanted him up in my face?

I counted to ten, breathing in and out through my nose. Finally, I shifted to my knees, then slowly stood. My vision grayed out a little, but I blinked it away and moved to the kitchen. I poured some water into a glass and shuffled to the table where I slumped down on a chair and guzzled the drink.

My mind stayed blank a few minutes, just static lines, until the thought of Rob and Nicholas Masters returned. They must've seen Dennin blocking me against the door. But I could've handled him. I really had been seconds from kneeing him in the groin. I didn't think of myself as violent, and I wouldn't resort to that unless I had no other choice.

Did Rob and his friend think I couldn't take care of myself? I didn't need their help, and while I could admit now I was thankful for it, that itch between my shoulder blades hit home. That nasty feeling I knew would come arrived just on time, even if logically, I could accept they'd helped me and I was glad I hadn't incapacitated the creep at close range.

Debt. I owed Rob and Masters now. The thought sat bitter on my tongue.

The first time I understood that nothing comes free, I was nine. The librarian, Mrs. Mason, had fed me dinner—somehow, she'd found out we didn't eat much in the evenings. School kept us fed during the day, thankfully. My father worked nights most of my childhood, my mom worked all day, and there was this dead zone where the five of us just floated around, hungry, searching the fridge's contents for what we could do with it—until the bigger kids were out of the house and scrounged wherever they went, I guessed. By twelve, I'd learned to cook decently well, even with ingredients like bargain hotdogs and canned beans.

But at nine, after a full month of decent meals, my father found out. And I learned that the kindness of the librarian was something bad—something to feel ashamed of and ugly for. I'd argued that she wanted to help me, so why couldn't she? That had just made him more angry, and he'd raged about how he wouldn't raise his kids to take. That the problem was less in the giving, though he had plenty of criticisms for Mrs. Mason, but in the weakness and stupidity of taking. He'd taken a belt to me, and I'd had to hold my breath when I sat down for two full weeks.

But hunger drives a kid to do crazy things, and maybe Mrs. Mason was crazy too. She still fed me—she'd leave a little cooler packed with whatever food she could keep hidden thirty paces into the woods behind the library. That lasted a while longer than the first time.

My older siblings didn't glance back at me once they left home, each of them already saddled with babies instead of college, bills instead of dreams. My younger sister had taken whatever I brought her and never asked where it came from. I used to think she knew, but in retrospect, I think she sensed she'd be better off not knowing in case our parents found out. Somehow, they always did, and I was the one that took the brunt of the punishment.

Those lessons literally beat into me the shame that owing a debt created. Years of therapy had led me toward accepting that it was my father's shame that'd driven him to make that mindset so clear to us kids, but it didn't mean I'd shed the visceral response whenever I sensed I owed someone. After a time, it was probably for the best my older siblings didn't attempt to help, because I doubted I could've stomached accepting it then.

I'd gotten over the worst of that in college, recognizing my ability to succeed in the world might be hampered by some of the messed up mindsets I grew up with. But of course, meeting with the counselor every few weeks didn't exactly cure me of all wrong thinking.

I didn't know how I'd pay Rob back, but at least we

were friends. He was a good man; I genuinely believed that. But that didn't make his help free. And even if it was free in his mind, it wasn't in mine. Luckily enough, the dinner in the oven tonight was for Masters, whether he liked it or not.

Resolve renewed, I stood, ready to get on with it and put the mess behind me. First, I'd get the food packaged up. Then, I'd deliver it. Hopefully, he'd answer the door in something more than he had on last time, and I would be able to thank him for the intervention and clarify I owed him nothing.

Yes. That would do it. That'd make things even again, and we could all move on.

The door swung open quickly after I rang the bell. Towering, massive Nicholas Masters stood holding the little furball in one hand and looked at me.

Just looked.

Seriously, the guy was not much for talking. *Fine.*

"Dinner?"

He blinked. His lips pressed together and he squinted a little, then nodded. "Thank you."

"Well..." I shuffled around on the porch step, words crawling up my throat without permission. "Now we're even."

His head cocked to one side. "Even?"

Pshhh. Like he didn't know. Like anyone didn't keep track. "For helping me. Now we're even. So... don't mention it. And... thank *you*. Have a good night."

I whirled around, ready to retreat, but his voice stayed me.

"Ms. Applegate."

I whipped back toward him. "Yeah?"

The man had serious, broody male *down*, and being subject to his stern, studious gaze unnerved me. I'd been thoroughly unnerved already today and didn't much want to hang around with this bare naked feeling that came when he looked at me. Irritation pinched my neck and curled my toes in my boots as he just stood there another few seconds before speaking.

"Are you okay?"

A measure of my frustration drained instantly at the question. "Oh. Uh, yes. I'm fine."

Those skewering eyes probed me again, but he nodded. So I nodded back because I didn't have anything else to say.

"I'm here. If anything like that happens again. Don't hesitate."

"Thanks," I said, my voice edging around a bubble of discomfort and confusion. Then I fled because I didn't know how to stand there and act like his offering help didn't unsettle me.

I trudged home, an odd mix of angry and pleased. The latter came thanks to the man's offer, and I interrogated the thought to figure out why. Because it was nice? Maybe. I liked nice. But something in my chest niggled at me, telling me it was more than that. Because he was so drop-dead good-looking? *Maybe.*

I snorted at the idiocy of that thought as I stomped on the welcome mat, knocking as much snow and ice from my boots as possible, then quickly moved inside. *The pretty man was nice to me, Pa!* Not that I'd ever once confided in my father.

The other feeling there, twisted right up with the pleasure, was the anger. I knew exactly where that came from. I'd worked on and off over the years to tamp down the nonsensical response at being offered help, but it still rose up, snarling, especially in the heat of the moment.

The combination of growing up poor, and in a family where accepting help came in a close second to the mark of the beast, left me with a problem. Like now, when I reasoned things out and could see what was true, but still *felt*. The damn feelings kicked me in the shins.

Logically, I understood that accepting help made me human. In fact, I'd created a life out of doing that for others —I loved being a nurse and helping others. I loved feeding people in my spare time. I loved volunteering.

But when I fell into a position where I needed help, it felt almost intolerable. It *was* intolerable.

Of course that depended on what, exactly, someone was helping me with. But honestly, even small things like accepting a ride with a friend to an event or leaning on a girlfriend for emotional support—these things chafed. I wished I could say that time, distance, and therapy had allowed me to surmount the deeply entrenched thoughts about being helped, but I still fought it. As evidenced today, when Rob and Masters had stepped in, like they should've. It's a *See Something, Say Something* world, and I wouldn't want someone to fail to intervene for fear of the person not wanting help. What nonsense.

And yet, here I sat at my kitchen table, bothered down to my toes that not only had Nicholas Masters seen me in that awful situation thanks to Dennin, but now he'd offered his help for future use. Like I was a woman who frequently required it.

"There's nothing wrong with needing help, as long as you know it makes you weak and useless." With mantras like that, it was no wonder I had issues.

To be clear, I did recognize that needing help, and

taking it, was acceptable. Good, even. I supported people doing that... I just found it completely awful for myself.

I'd developed a system over time. If I did accept help, I'd pay the person back. A lot of times, there wasn't a direct way to do that—like with Rob and Masters. But I'd do *something* for them, and that'd loosen the stranglehold of guilt and shame enough to eventually let it go.

Never mind all that. Now I could relax with the garlic roasted chicken and kale salad and flip through the new cookbook I'd ordered as an incentive to get through the flu madness. I'd focus on the perfect photography and the airy white marble countertops the dishes were placed on in the photos. I'd dream up my own presentation, and compose the menu for the next feast night.

I'd forget all about Dennin, and Rob, and Nicholas Masters.

Not more than an hour later, my doorbell rang. A spike of alarm shot through me—could it be Dennin?

I moved quietly to the front of the house, phone in hand, and peeked out the window to see a retreating form, much larger than Dennin's. I waited a moment, then cracked the door to find a familiar-looking envelope.

Grabbing the letter, I looked for him, but Masters must've already ducked back into his house. I did the same, greedily ripping into the little rectangle.

Ms. Applegate,

Thank you for yet another delicious meal. I'm not sure why you insist on spoiling me with these riches, but they enhance my days, whenever they come, and I cannot do anything but say thank you. That, and I can insist that should you ever need my help, you ask. I'm sorry for what happened earlier today, and I hope you're not too rattled— not that you seem like a woman easily shaken, but rather that having someone forcefully at one's doorstep is an altogether loathsome concept. I can hardly stomach anyone at my door, let alone a person I haven't invited.

I hope you'll be able to rest well and relax, and please, tell me if ever I can help you.

Sincerely,

Nicholas Masters

P.S. *To be very clear, I hope you'll consider yourself invited to my door as often as you choose.*

Pure, unadulterated pleasure shimmered through me.

Well, then.

CHAPTER SEVEN

Nick

You are not here. Here, I keep wondering if I am. I am a bulb, flickering brighter, then dim. Dimming, almost burnt out. Almost to the rattle, the tinny absence of a glow. I am almost gone.

Frustration bit at my heels as I stalked down the clinic hallway. I'd finished physical therapy for this week, number four of six required sessions since the accident last month. Also the reason I felt particularly caged lately. I couldn't work out at the intensity I liked, and these sessions hardly seemed to help.

That's not fair, Nicholas. Are you sure that's an accurate statement?

Gran's voice played inside my head as clearly as if she'd

spoken the words to my face. Pain, sharp and hot as always, sliced through my chest. It'd been years—coming up on three years—since she'd really known me. So long since I'd had a conversation as *me*, and not a visiting, vague friend.

Her dementia came on hard and fast, and in half a year, we'd gone from her forgetting my mom's name to forgetting me, standing right in front of her. The helplessness that comes from watching your loved one lose her tether to this world, to things and people she'd known all her life, was ruthless. The grieving that'd started then wasn't all that different from what it was now that she was gone physically, too.

And the memory loss haunted me. Would my parents have faced that? Would I? Suddenly, I felt a pressing need to *live*. And returning to my regular life, working day to day and training when I could... it didn't feel like I was doing that just yet.

"Masters! Hold up."

Alicia Cartwell waved her patrol cap at me when I turned back toward her voice.

A little leap chased that previously vicious grief. Summer Applegate stood next to her, her cheeks tinted just slightly. I approached the women, brow raised. Alicia knew me well enough to know I wouldn't be speaking unless necessary. Wasn't my way.

"Needed to ask you a few things. But first, do you know Summer Applegate? Summer, this is Sergeant Nick Masters. He's my trainer here. He's in the OPFOR battalion as well." Alicia, her blond hair tucked into a neat bun at the back of her head, gestured between us.

"We've met. Nice to see you again."

Nice to see you in something other than a full-body puff coat. Not that I'd say that aloud, but I didn't mind taking in the look of her. I wouldn't let my eyes slide along her scrubs, but I could appreciate the lack of bulky layers just the same. The panicked moment last week with the idiot on her doorstep didn't count.

"Yes. Likewise. Did you need assistance?"

She cocked her head and had a look of efficiency about her. This was a woman who got things done. No meandering small talk about the weather or *how funny* it was that we both knew Alicia. Why did people always think coincidences were *funny*? Anyway, none of that from Applegate, and it immediately made me respect her a bit more.

"No, ma'am. I just wrapped up a PT session."

Understanding lit her eyes. Of course she knew about the incident and had probably received detailed reports of everyone and their injuries—she'd been feeding all of the people involved. But I suspected everyone in the clinic knew all the details of each soldier's injuries and recovery. Mine wasn't all that exciting, so they were welcome to it. I was one of only three who were being seen on post—everyone else had to see specialists on the German economy. And Summer would know that thanks to being privy to medical information. That, or Rob had gossiped about my busted hip. Come to think of it, I should ask him if he talked with her about me. Not that I cared. Just didn't want anything to do with the rumor mill—didn't need Rob feeding the machine.

"Good. I hope it went well."

I nodded.

"Are you on the way out, then?" Alicia asked.

I nodded again.

"Perfect. I'll follow you out." She turned to Summer. "Thanks again. I'll see you soon?"

Summer Applegate smiled at Alicia, full-out, and it hit me between the ribs.

"Absolutely. And Sergeant Masters, I'm sure I'll see you sometime soon, too." Then she directed that spotlight smile at me for a moment before she turned and left.

She certainly didn't linger, nor did she try to throw food at me, so I could appreciate, again, the lack of shiny veneer today. The impression I'd gotten on our last encounter had stripped that away, too. Maybe I needed to get rid of that judgement altogether. But really, I hadn't seen enough to prove otherwise.

Alicia and I walked side by side down the hall and out the clinic front doors. Once we reached the parking lot, she tilted her head to the side and eyed me.

"You know Summer?"

"We're neighbors."

She rolled her eyes. "*I* know that. But I didn't realize *you* did."

I shrugged.

She rolled them again, far more exaggerated this time. "Well, I need to talk to you about the travel timeline for the competition. Also, you should ask Summer to step in for Melanie."

Irritation flared at that. We had a regional competition for FitCross coming up in a few weeks. The fitness organization ran these events internationally, and they gave amateurs and pros alike a chance to compete. The FitCross style paired well with military training since it focused on multifunctional fitness—the idea that an athlete should be able to go run a half marathon or carry a heavy load of hundreds of pounds, or anything else in between.

When you traveled to a larger competition with a team like we were, the organization required you to have a medical person on your team. I had basic medical training like all soldiers and a bit more with being an Eagle First Responder, but not quite enough to satisfy the organizers or myself. Our usual medic had a family emergency back in the States and was on emergency leave for a few weeks—no way she'd be able to take leave for the comp.

"You should. Summer's awesome. She's an RN, knows her stuff. She even has training with athletic injuries and did some kind of orthopedic rotation in her training or something—or maybe she dated an orthopedist? I can't remember. But anyway, she's awesome. I love her. Rob loves her. Arty will get on board if he doesn't know her yet, and you don't love anyone so it doesn't matter."

I bristled. I made decisions for the team. I'd make this one without her input, especially since I didn't think I wanted Do-Gooder Barbie offering help all weekend.

Nicholas!

Gran's censure rang clear. Or maybe that was my own conscience. I didn't need to put Summer down in my mind just because she... bothered me.

Her lips flattened. "Okay. I'll take your silence as a hearty agreement and expect the good news about Summer's joining the team by the weekend. Thanks, Coach!"

She slapped my back and jogged to her car.

I sank into my own vehicle and slammed the door a little too hard, unsure why I felt so completely annoyed with Alicia's suggestion. Summer would be over-qualified for what we needed, which amounted to someone to deal with nose bleeds and assess for signs of larger issues that'd necessitate a hospital visit. We didn't need a person to actually treat muscle, bone, or joint issues.

And why would it matter if she'd dated an orthopedist?

People didn't absorb information by osmosis when they spent time with someone, when they—

I interrupted that idiotic thinking by cranking the key and turning the car on, glad I had a car that still *had* a key. The last few times I'd rented a car to visit Gran, I'd ended up with new ones that started by push-button. Awful.

And there it came again. Thick laces of grief weaved between my lungs and cinched tight. I sucked in air and rested my head on the steering wheel, breathing slow. In, out. In, out. A few minutes of focused breathing, and I pushed through.

The drive home passed in a blur of lush green trees sparkling with frosty snow in the dusk. I'd left work early to get to my end-of-day appointment, so it was the first time I'd driven home before dark in a while. The orderly farm fields stretched out on either side of the road, broken up by lines of towering pines. The pale yellow or brown fields left in neat lines looked like if someone could pick up the scene and stretch it on a canvas, it'd be something out of a Van Gogh painting, swirling and yet orderly on the page.

I parked in the driveway, locked the car, and did not glance to my left to see if Summer's car sat in her driveway. I'd just left the clinic—she wouldn't have beaten me back. I made it all the way to the door, even unlocked it, before my head compelled me to look. Not home yet. Probably out delivering meals or kissing babies or some other altruistic BS she did to keep up appearances.

No one was that beautiful and that nice *and* that good. No one.

A murderous rumble came from the depths of the living room as I entered the house. No greeting today, evidently. He held a grudge better than me.

I unloaded my lunchbox in the sink, rinsed my coffee

mug, filled a tall glass of water, and drank it down. I peered in the fridge and retrieved the container for tonight's meal—I prepped everything ahead each weekend. Summer's insistence on feeding me had thrown my meal planning and prep for a loop. After the first letter and her blatant disregard for my request, I never *really* knew if she'd show with a meal. Well, I did know, if four straight weeks counted as proof—and it probably did—but I didn't like the idea of failing to plan and ending up without a meal.

I scooped the food out on a plate, eager to put something warm inside me and fill up. The hollowed out, aching sensation wouldn't leave. Based on the low pulse in my heart and head, nothing would get this nagging feeling gone today. But food, some writing, a little extra sleep... these would help.

While my meal heated, I opened a small can of cat food. Just the sound of the tin lid summoned the little grump.

"Finally deigning to acknowledge me, huh?" I said as the furry snowball on legs trotted into the kitchen, tail high behind him.

I smiled, a small swell of gratitude rising in my chest. This tiny beast and his moods had grown on me. When Rob shoved him at me two months ago, I'd sworn to myself I'd take him back to the store or wherever Rob had found him. But Rob evidently knew me well enough to put a stop to that by microchipping him and never telling me at which shelter specifically, he'd found the small pile of fur, skin, and bones.

Waverly had shown up on my doorstep four days after I'd gotten back from the funeral. He'd seen me for one workout, given me a once-over, and told me how sorry he was. He couldn't have been that sorry, because he didn't know what losing Gran meant. He knew I'd lost my grandmother who lived in a nursing home in Massachusetts. At some point, I'd explained she had dementia, and even though she never knew me when I visited this last year, it was where I traveled whenever I took leave.

He couldn't know she was the only person left on earth I loved. No one knew that. And he wouldn't understand that I'd been grieving her for years as her cognizance slipped away, while at the same time the loss of her now felt utterly crushing. I could barely admit that she was the last person who shared my blood, and now she was gone.

What did that make me? An orphan, sure, but I'd been that for decades now. There was no other word for when everyone was gone, nothing but alone.

Despite his ignorance of those things, Rob had found me this crusty bastard of a cat, shoved it in my arms along with a small litter box and a bag of food, and said, "You need a companion. Since I'm pretty sure you're not the dating type, a girl or boyfriend won't work, and so my wingman services are useless. So here. Take him."

My little companion licked around his lips, already having destroyed the serving of wet food. Now he'd mow down some dry stuff, and then he'd decide acknowledging me wasn't a bow puncture to the ship of his feline integrity.

I sat at the table, not tasting the meal, listening to Butter chomp his kibble. I tasted food more lately, but it didn't surprise me that tonight, I dined on cardboard. It was one thing that made me feel like a glutton when Summer fed me —it all tasted so good. So damn good, and I couldn't stop myself until I ate it all. Even the little cookies she'd included the second time, which I'd normally leave since I didn't have much of a sweet tooth, had tasted good. Amazing, in fact.

Was it because someone else had cooked it? By that

logic, any meal I ate outside those I cooked for myself should've worked. They didn't. Only her food came alive, brought me to life, like she sprinkled it with the bereft male equivalent's version of catnip.

That thought had me shoving aside my plate and reaching for the book where I wrote. After my parents passed when I was sixteen, Gran had insisted I write down my feelings. Every six months, she gave me a new journal, and I used every page. At first, I'd let loose all the angry, selfish thoughts. But slowly, over time, the pages became a place to think and process, and to create.

Summer came to mind again, even though I knew she couldn't stay there. I thought of that smile she gave Alicia and how stubborn she was. I shook my head at the empty room when I thought of her coming on the trip to regionals.

No. That wouldn't happen—couldn't.

CHAPTER EIGHT

Summer

I sprinkled one last handful of rock salt on the sidewalk and surveyed my work. The snow had melted after the last storm, but the temps would drop tonight and usher in more snow and ice. Should be fun. So I did what little I could to keep myself from slipping on the front steps when the time came to shovel tomorrow morning.

"Summer, wait a sec," Rob Waverly called to me from his car, which he'd parked in front of Nicholas Masters' house.

I had no idea how I hadn't noticed before, but people came and went from the man's house quite often. Frequently enough, it drew my attention now. Granted, I'd been careful to observe the cars coming into our little cul de sac in case Dennin returned, but doing so made me wonder how on earth I hadn't noticed the unusual amount of traffic at the immaculate house three doors down. Probably because I kept to myself here, other than interacting with the older neighbor next door, Mr. Meier.

And honestly, it was only two or three cars most days, except weekends, which often resulted in the whole circle being jammed with cars. Like today.

"Hey. You know, you can park in my driveway next time, if you need to." I gestured to the empty space in front of my garage.

"Thanks. It's not usually quite this crazy. Nick ran a training day today because we head into rotation soon and I guess people wanted to see what he does in person—word has gotten out he trains a few of us." He tugged the zipper of his jacket down and pulled off a knit cap. Unlike when they did PT on post, none of the ten or so people milling around and filing into cars wore the Army PT uniform.

"Understandably. You and Alicia are certainly fit—I can see how his results speak for themselves." *Not to mention the man himself.*

"True enough." Something in his eyes shifted, and his brow wrinkled. "You okay? After that guy and everything?"

We'd only seen each other at a distance since then. It'd been over a week—come to think of it, more like two. See? I hadn't even kept track of the time very well. Life was good. "Totally fine. He's a creeper, but he hasn't bothered me. Hasn't even stared at my chest at work since you told him off. So... thanks."

"No need for thanks." He crossed his arms and dipped his head. "I actually have something to ask you."

He looked a little nervous, and my stomach dropped. *Oh no.* Was he about to ask me out? Not that Rob wasn't the epitome of the gorgeous American soldier dream boat, charismatic and charming and nice, but I just didn't feel it for him. Even the first time I met him, I'd thought "Wow," but not, "Wow, sign me up."

"Okay. What's up?"

"Has Alicia mentioned anything about the competition coming up?" He tucked his hands under his arms and stepped side to side. He must've cooled down enough that the chill hit him—he only wore a light jacket, warm-up pants, and gloves. I wore my full winter get-up with huge coat, hat, gloves, boots, and the cold still crept in.

"Here, let's walk to your car before you freeze. And yes, but nothing specific about it. Why?"

We cut across the circle since most people had zipped away, off to their Saturday agendas.

"The organization holding the competition requires a medical person on each team of more than two people. It's overkill, but I guess it's a CYA maneuver for them. So, we had Melanie, but she's on emergency leave."

I nodded, showing I'd heard him, but not following what this had to do with me. "Okay..."

"I'm wondering if you'd think about doing it."

"Oh. Huh. Can you send me all the information and give me a deadline to decide?" I couldn't remember exactly when the event took place or even where, just that it loomed out there in the not-too-distant future.

"Of course." He flashed a big smile. "Seriously, it'll be fun, not just work for you. In fact, if everything goes well, there'll be almost nothing for you to do."

Not exactly the right thing to say to a woman who liked to stay busy, but I could appreciate the sentiment. "I'll think about it. Do get me the details."

"Perfect." Then he put a hand on my back and angled us toward the sidewalk where a man approached. "Have you met Nate Reynolds?"

"I have. Just once, very briefly." Yes, I'd met Nate. He had an unforgettable air about him—charming and funny, but extremely capable. Totally attractive, if you liked that kind of thing. I'd seen enough to size him up and be desperately curious about his true feelings for Ariel, who was his close friend.

"Nice to see you again, Ms. Applegate."

"Please, call me Summer." My voice wobbled on my name because Masters stepped up beside Nate. No idea how I didn't see him in the first place considering he had an inch or two on Nate and Rob both.

"Okay, Summer." Nate gave me a charming smile. "You ever get tired of the hordes of people parking here, taking over the neighborhood?"

"I'm guilty of the same every other Sunday. I don't mind, and fortunately I know Mr. Meier doesn't care." I nodded to one of the two houses between mine and Masters'.

"I've heard about your feast nights. Ariel has raved about your cooking," Nate said genially.

"She's amazing," Rob put in.

I glanced at Masters to find him staring at me—intense blue eyes just *staring*. My stomach dropped when he held my gaze but didn't speak.

"Thank you. Uh, actually, that reminds me." I broke the trance-like connection between me and the towering, somber man. Somehow, I remembered—I'd taken Masters food, but I'd gotten caught up in other tasks and hadn't settled my debt with Rob. I turned to him. "I did want to invite you to feast night. As a thank you. Next Sunday? Of course, you're all invited."

"Oh, I wish. Rotation starts this week," Rob said, truly dejected.

"Then maybe the next one? I guess that'd put us at the end of February." I could feel eyes on me. No need to guess who, since I was looking at Nate and Rob, alternately.

"Works for me. Should I bring a date?" Rob asked, raising his brows.

"If you like, sure. Just let me know so I have a good count." I turned to Nate and gestured to him and Masters. "And you're both welcome as well, of course."

Nate nodded, smiled kindly. "Thank you. I'll look forward to it."

"Good. Well, gentlemen, I'm going to head back inside and warm up. Hope you all have a great day."

My eyes flicked up to find Masters staring back at me. Then he nodded, ever so slightly, a gesture I'd already come to find familiar and mildly infuriating because it gave me so little.

"Think on what we talked about, yeah?" Rob said as he pulled open his car door.

"Will do. Send me the info."

I held up a hand to him and Nate, who'd already jogged across the street to slip into his car. Masters just stood there, hulking and silent and so stunning in a T-shirt, sweats, and sneakers, I did nothing but turn and walk home.

Why hadn't I just said *bye* like a normal human? More particularly, why hadn't he? He was stubborn and... stingy. I had no feel for him in person—at least not a *friendly* feeling. Whatever I got from him in person was stern and quiet. His silence and spare words screamed introvert, so that gave him a little pass. But the man was my neighbor! And the letters he wrote were so different. They were... lovely.

I leaned against the door after shutting myself safely inside and turned the locks. I couldn't get Masters out of my mind, and seeing him every few days had done nothing to keep him out. We never spoke, and I doubted he saw me, but man oh man, did I see him. I'd caught him at the commissary more than once. I saw him at the clinic almost every time he came in. I'd noticed him on jogs several times, and resisted the urge to pull over and ask if he'd been cleared for that after the accident.

Because that would be a weird invasion of privacy and would indicate a breach in the personal privacy act, so no. I didn't do that. Also, it should be noted that he looked really good running. *Shocker*.

I banged my head against the door a few times, then pushed off, seeking something to banish that serious face from my mind. An elaborate recipe, something time-consuming. Maybe I'd make puff pastry from scratch. Or croissants.

Sucker that I was, I agreed to accompany Rob's team to the competition. I couldn't resist a chance to help when needed —really needed. There was honestly nothing better. And they needed me, bad. They had to submit the names of their team that week, and they wouldn't have much time to do it after the rotation started since everyone else on the team would be participating.

So, in just over three weeks, I'd be traveling to the UK to act as the medical supervisor for the team of three. I already knew Rob and Alicia, and I knew who Arturo was, though we hadn't been introduced. Plus the coach.

My stomach fluttered at the mental mention of *him*. Rob had listed Nicholas Masters as the coach of their small team from Kugelfels. I knew Masters coached them, but I hadn't seen him in action. I couldn't reconcile the stern man with my experiences of coaches—warm, effusive people shouting at teams, pushing them to do better, achieve more. The idea that I might get to see him do that work appealed to me far more than it should have.

After a long week, I turned into the neighborhood just before dusk. Like always lately, I glanced at Masters' house as I passed, and my heart leapt upon seeing him standing up from where he crouched over what looked like his cat. His gaze met mine, and I sucked in a breath as I slowed—more like jolted—then looked away. He looked dangerous in his dark camouflage uniform, patrol cap low over his eyes, and camo paint streaking over his face.

During rotation, the soldiers got to come and go now and then, depending on what their commander and the schedule allowed. Every few days, they'd pop home for a shower, maybe a few hours of sleep, and food.

The idea hit before I could swat it away, and the moment it did, I knew I wouldn't think of anything else until I'd fed him.

I had warm, hearty beef stew burbling in the Crock-Pot, waiting for me. More than enough to share. I'd finished the last of my six weeks of meals for the men who'd been injured two months ago. I hadn't shared a meal with anyone other than Mr. Meier next door in far too long. And there stood a man who'd likely been out in the field since the rotation started four days ago.

After dumping my things and stripping out of my jacket, I hustled to the kitchen, grabbed a two-quart plastic container, and filled it with stew. Dang, it smelled good. I tore the baguette I'd grabbed on the way home in half and stuck it in a bag with the container, then all but ran to the front door and out, sans jacket and all warm things.

No matter. I'd be quick. And—*yes!*—he was still out. He

was looking down at the white ball masquerading as a cat, and only as I got closer did I realize he held a bright blue leash that he'd hooked to a harness of the same color around the cat's little body.

Oh. My. Cheesecake. He had his cat on a leash. I chuckled under my breath, unable to stifle it. The sight was just too unexpected. This giant beast of a man in black camouflage and war paint holding a skinny leash leading to the daintiest cat I'd ever seen.

I ignored the answering zip that shot through my chest.

"Masters, hi." The words felt awkward. I wouldn't normally call a man I'd interacted with more than a few times, who wasn't my superior, by his last name. And if there was a power disparity, I'd refer to the person by rank or title. But saying *Sergeant Masters* seemed too formal.

"Hello."

Somehow, only one word held all kinds of meaning. *Hello* actually meant *What are you doing here?* And *What do you need?* And *What kind of fool leaves her coat when it's thirty degrees outside?*

I held out the bag while approaching, but I stopped a good five feet from him so I wouldn't spook the cat, who simply lay on its side, tail flicking, watching me with those judgy feline eyes.

"I brought you some food. I'm guessing you've been out in the cold, and I had some stew in the Crock-Pot, so I just thought—" I broke off, the adrenaline from seeing him earlier and my good-idea-fairy visit flagging at the unchanged expression on his face.

Foolishness kicked at my ribs. The familiar feeling of trying to get someone to like me, to approve of me, and failing miserably, slipped around my neck and cut off any other words I might've said. I didn't come here for that. I'd come to feed him. I'd come to help.

"Thank you. That's very kind."

I blinked up at him, and the humiliation eased just a little. I swallowed but didn't speak.

He studied me another moment, then said, "I'm just home for a few hours. I was going to heat up something frozen. This will be better."

"I hope so," I said, my voice weird and shaky.

He walked toward me, giving the cat's leash slack so it wouldn't have to move. If I hadn't been completely overwhelmed by his approach, I might've laughed again at the oddness. But nothing in me laughed when he came close, especially not when he stopped inches from me and covered my hand that held the handles of the food bag with his own.

I stopped breathing. Despite being outside in the cold long before me, his hand still felt warmer than mine. And big. Maybe rough? Hard to tell in this scenario.

"You're freezing. Better get back in." His breath came out in little clouds, the edges of which nearly kissed my face.

"Yeah. I didn't want to miss you if you were heading back. I ran out without my jacket."

Looking at his face at close range, even in the waning light, proved to be a more affecting experience than I'd anticipated. The planes of his cheeks and jaw were hidden thanks to the dusk and the camo paint, but his eyes nearly glowed back at me.

"I'm glad you caught me," he said, then his eyes flickered and he seemed to remember he still held onto the bag over my hand. His hold loosened, and I slipped my hand away.

"Me too."

Neither of us stepped away. We stood there another minute, and then he said, "Your feast night is next weekend?"

Apropos of nothing, but okay, at least one of us could make conversation. Who'd have thunk it'd be him? "Yes. Are you coming? Are you—are you bringing someone?"

If I hadn't already been studying his face, I might've missed his mouth pull to one side in the barest hint of a smile before he spoke. "I'll be there. Just me."

I pressed my lips together, suppressing what felt like what would've been a gigantic smile. "Good. I'll make a note of it. See you then."

He nodded, and I stepped back, then turned and jogged to my house, refusing to look back despite desperately wanting to.

I leaped inside and slammed the door, kicked off my boots, and stepped into my slippers. I went straight to the kitchen and got my own soup, refusing to think about how much I wished I'd just invited him over here. Or how I should've asked him about the cat. Or how ridiculous this crush had become on exactly zero encouragement.

Well, zero encouragement until the following letter. He'd left it on the porch sometime in the night before he went back to work, and I found it the next morning.

Ms. Applegate,

May I call you Summer? It feels too familiar to say your name, but it also feels a bit odd to continue insisting on being formal. I hope you'll call me Nick. I'd like to hear you say my name.

I'm not sure what compels you to feed me, but whatever it is, I'm thankful for it. The stew was a dream in a bowl, as I knew it would be. To say my anticipation for the upcoming feast night is incessant would be a failure of imagination. I am hungry for it—for a night at your table. And, admittedly, the fellow guests, even the food, hold a secondary draw for me.

Stay warm and safe, Summer. See you soon,
Nick

CHAPTER NINE

Nick

I have been wandering around missing you. Your ideas packed up their bags and left you long before you would've let them. I do hope the reunion was sweet.

The rotation had felt grueling and long. So much of life felt that way lately.

"Masters, will I see you at the feast later?" Nate Reynolds asked as he shrugged into a jacket he'd ditched during the sprints.

I'd started offering weekend training at my house, but I'd wanted to do measured sprints, so today we did the whole workout on post at the high school's track. Some of the soldiers needed to improve their run times, and sprints were a part of that. Granted, none of those soldiers showed up to these sessions, but the men and women who did seemed to enjoy them.

"I'll be there."

"Bringing a date?" Reynolds asked, sounding casual as can be.

I stood with my arms crossed, nodding to everyone who left with a wave. I eyed him and answered. "No, sir."

"Is Rob dating Summer? Or, are you?" He fiddled with his phone, again seeming too nonchalant.

"You interested, sir?" The cold air burned my lungs a little on the next inhale.

His head popped up, eyes surprised.

"Me? No. Just figured one of you were. I'm—er, well. You know me. Never get tied down, ha." He forced a chuckle, but it ended in a cough.

The major was a good leader, a good guy. He had a reputation as a bit of a ladies' man, but it never clicked for me. Yet again, his words didn't add up. Not the first time public image didn't match the reality, but what did I know?

I didn't respond, because what would I say? Reynolds slapped me on the shoulder as a farewell. He couldn't continue to dig and not be obvious, but clearly, he felt the need to connect with me. I'd been through it a hundred times over the years. As a quiet, introverted man, I kept to myself. Sometimes, it'd been a deficit. Other times, a true asset. And very often, a maddening puzzle for my outgoing, well-meaning peers and leaders.

I hauled myself, and the equipment I'd brought, home. I'd need to order some new stuff or see if the unit wanted to bulk up its collection of portable tools. Sometimes, novelty engaged reluctant people effectively—bands, weights used in a new way, weighted balls, things like that.

By the time I reached my house, the sky was heavy with

snow, and all I wanted to do was curl up by a fire and read. I genuinely loved motivating people, pushing them, but when the time came to an end, I felt completely drained. I'd used my full measure of words for the day, the complete stock of extroversion I could summon.

The horror of going to a dinner party later loomed in front of me. What a stupid thing to feel for something I'd been anticipating, genuinely looking forward to, for weeks. Ever since Summer had mentioned it.

Summer, who'd fed me when she saw I'd made it home from rotation. Unexpected, kind, generous... no one watching. There'd been no audience, and yet she'd insisted on the kindness. The idea that she did it for accolades or attention just didn't make sense. And maybe that had something to do with the letter I'd given her that night before I headed back into work.

A little jump in my chest had me shaking my head at myself as I pushed into the door. As always, Butter didn't greet me. He only chose to dart for the door, barreling toward freedom like a maniac, when someone else came knocking. He'd escaped a few times but became so overwhelmed with the outside world, he'd made it ten feet from the door and slumped down on his side. I'd given the leash a shot, but same response.

The cat lay stretched long on the back of the couch. He curled his head around, then ducked his nose and eyes under his paws and left his chin exposed, the small purr motor in his fluff-covered body whirring. I scratched his smooth little throat for a minute, but left off before the switch flipped and his nature forced him to bite me. Too much of a good thing drove him into madness.

The day slipped out of my hands. After a shower and getting Alicia and Art set up for a workout in the garage, I wrote and meal-prepped the food I'd bought the day before. The time for dinner at Summer's inched closer, and with each minute that passed, my dread multiplied.

I didn't want to sit around a table with a bunch of people I didn't know and make small talk. I'd never figured out why people like doing that. I understood friendship and deeper connection. I understood wanting to truly know someone, and that in order to get to that place, one had to endure the nastiness of a first date or get-together. But damn, I hated the process and couldn't wrap my mind around how Summer did these things twice a month.

Luckily, it sounded like she rarely invited the same people. She had a come one, come all approach, but she did have to limit numbers. At this point, so many people in the Kugelfels community had heard of the meals, she probably never had repeats. So I could count on this being my one and only feast night.

That thought didn't provide the comfort I expected. I finished buttoning the dress shirt and rolled the cuffs at my wrists. I didn't want to seem overly dressed up, so I wore a gray button-up with jeans, and I'd toss a wool coat, hat, and gloves on. It had started snowing half an hour ago, and though the walk was short, I'd be glad for the layers on the way back.

Out in the night, not quite fully dark thanks to the days getting longer bit by bit here at the end of February, two cars pulled into the circle and parked. My stomach turned over and my jaw pinched. A flash of nervous heat shot through me—damn, I'd probably start sweating at this rate.

Before I backed out and ran home with my tail between my legs, I accelerated my walk and reached the door in time to open it for Nate Reynolds and his date.

"Masters, do you know Ariel Wolfe?" He gestured to a

striking woman who preceded him through the doorway. He followed her, and I followed them.

"We haven't met." I shook her outstretched hand, struck by the blue of her eyes. Dark lashes, dark swoopy hair all kinds of pretty around her face, pale skin. Good for the major, albeit curious he'd date the colonel's sister so casually.

"Ariel, this is Nick Masters. He's the beast who runs the workouts for the battalion and who's training Rob. He's also an excellent NCO and a man of few words." Nate smiled charmingly, then looked at me. "And this is Ariel Wolfe, as I said. She's Eric's sister and nanny to his two kids. She's also put up with me as a friend for over a decade, so feel free to cast her pitying looks all evening."

We all chuckled. I resisted the urge to raise my brows at *friends for over a decade*. So, not his date? Reynolds struck me as a man who'd shout it loud and proud if this woman was his in any way, for now or forever, and he'd said friends. Well, again, good for him for having someone who'd known him so long and stuck around.

Right on time, a cruel flip of sadness caught in my throat. I cleared it, then said, "Pleasure," so I didn't come off rude. Despite some opinions to the contrary, I didn't try to come off as a jerk. I did, however, have one of those faces that, when I wasn't actively smiling, evidently came off like I thought I was better than people. *"You've got to smile so people get to know who's in there."* Gran's admonishment applied just as well now as it did two decades ago after my parents died and I'd started at a new school.

"You're here. Good work," Rob Waverly said, a cheerful pat on my back.

I nodded. "Made the long trek."

He laughed, and we walked farther into the house. I

took in every detail—the white couch and the cozy chair, a wall lined with bookshelves filled with cookbooks, the small touches that brought warmth to the room like a nice rug, a shelf with a candle. Stuff *she'd* chosen for the space, so it made me want to get closer and memorize it. Also, if I looked at her stuff, I could escape some of the small talk.

I started at the bookshelves since reading the spines of books was less invasive than sniffing candles or even taking a seat in the well-worn chair before I'd even seen the hostess. Speaking of, I'd heard her say, "Dinner's in five, just give me a minute!" from the kitchen when someone walked in there, so I wouldn't intrude on her now.

Even though I desperately wanted to see her. I'd had more than one daydream about what she looked like in her kitchen. Did she keep it meticulous or make a huge mess? Did she wear an apron? I didn't know the woman *at all*, but the last few weeks had built a need in me to know her. *Curiosity.* When was the last time I'd been curious about someone? So long. And that interest had been a beautiful distraction from the loss that clung to me most days.

Plus, my last letter had put me out there in a way I hadn't planned on but couldn't resist. Now she knew I thought of her, at least beyond just what she could cook for me.

I left my post at the shelves and wandered to the dining room, an intermediate space filled with a large buffet on one side, a huge table with chairs around it, and a doorway into the kitchen. I walked to the far wall so I could see the back of her—a knot at her waist and her back revealed the answer to that question: she did wear aprons. Her long golden hair swirled neatly high on the back of her head, leaving the long line of her neck unobstructed except for the apron tie.

The strangest impulse to pull at the ribbons and undo the knot flashed through my mind.

"Please have a seat," she said, whirling around with a spoon in her hand. Her gaze slipped over me in one quick beat, then met mine before she turned again to grab something.

My heart raced in my chest, the visual contact with her as good as any HIIT work. This kept happening—the rush just looking at her. It felt like... living.

"Sit over here by me, Masters." Rob pulled a chair out next to him, near the middle of the table. It seated ten and would be full tonight.

I sat, realizing I knew every person in the room to some degree or another. Rob, obviously, Major Reynolds and Ariel, two other officers from OPFOR and their wives, and Summer. One seat left across the table at the right of the head for one last guest.

Just then, Summer walked out with Mr. Meier, our elderly neighbor, at her arm. She held him firmly, then released as he slid into the seat, gently patting his back as he settled. When she slipped back into the kitchen, I studied my plate.

Something about her gentleness with the neighbor struck me just below the ribs, my breath now coming up short. The care she showed the man, even the way she held his arm, shot me straight back to Gran's caregivers. I'd idealized those people as angels with no hint of humor—their jobs a kind of service few could understand and no one could repay. Seeing her treat him with the same concern cut through more than one layer of incredulity about her I'd harbored.

I'd wondered if Summer was a superficially nice person. Did she do all this for some kind of odd show? But that moment, more than anything I'd seen from her, told me no. She was actually this caring and kind.

"Please forgive me for being a minute late. I had technical difficulties. Tonight, we have roasted lemon chicken, roasted root vegetables, a winter greens salad, and of course, something sweet for dessert. Please enjoy!"

Immediately, exclamations of how good everything looked came from every corner of the table. I stared at the food—the stuff itself and the presentation on the platters—and permitted myself a glance at the chef.

She now held a tray of food near Mr. Meier, and he scooped roasted vegetables onto his plate. Her eyes flickered up to mine, and the moment they met, my stomach dropped.

She was pretty. So damn pretty, and nice, and she could cook.

What is this? Some kind of 1950s fantasy? Get some food!

Gran's sarcastic, grounding voice pulled me out of the dreamy moment and shoved me back squarely into reality. Miraculously, the heady grief that normally followed such a moment didn't come.

Rob started talking about the last two weeks of training before competition. Luckily, we didn't have a rotation until after the trip. Nate and Ariel sat across from me and asked questions about training, most of which Rob answered. He made an excellent date.

He laughed and talked with Summer, too, and the dawning realization that he might actually be *her* date struck me cold in the sternum. He sat at her left side. They chatted easily, laughing and clearly comfortable with one another.

Good for him. Good for *her*, for that matter. Even if the

sight and the news made the very thin threads of hope I hadn't fully realized I'd spun snap, good for them.

CHAPTER TEN

Summer

Nothing could've prepared me for the shirt. I'd peeked out of the kitchen just as he shrugged out of his black wool jacket to reveal a gray shirt rolled at the wrists, and my brain decided to go on a vacation.

It hopped on a jet plane with the man in the shirt, destination somewhere tropical where we wouldn't even need shirts. Me and the man sans shirt would spend days running around in the sand and nights doing... well, other things.

See? What had happened to me? I was a medical professional. Bodies were bodies, and yes he had a fine one, but that stupid gray shirt shouldn't have fried my brain.

Normally, I'd greet my guests and be charming while helping them find seats. I'd ask for a few volunteers to serve the food to the table and everyone would sit to a spread already in place. Normally, I wouldn't hide this completely.

But the letter. *The letter.* I hadn't been able to put it out of my mind for the last ten days. Not to pulverize a cutlet too thoroughly, but his words made me butter-in-a-hot-pan melty.

I also hadn't seen him. He'd been on rotation, not even home most of the time. I'd seen his car pull into the driveway yesterday, and I'd stood watching him gather bags of groceries like a creeper until I got worried he'd see me spying on him.

I am hungry for it—for a night at your table.

Sigh. I'd read the letter no fewer than twenty times. I'd reread all of his letters at this point and could happily say he'd effectively wooed me, whether he wanted to or not. That was only mildly pathetic considering his first two were mostly full of entreaties to stop feeding him.

Poor fool. Didn't he know that now that I'd started, I wouldn't be able to stop?

But this evening, he was quiet. Of course, that seemed to be his very nature, and yet tonight, he felt closed up. I wondered if it was the group dynamic, though I'd done my best to include people he'd know so it wouldn't be a bunch of strangers. Not that he needed me to baby him, but I understood that group settings were unlikely to be his preference.

What he did do? Eat. Since he and Rob had RSVP'd yes, I'd designed a healthful menu that hopefully wouldn't throw them off their eating plan or schedule or whatever it was. I'd gathered Rob's was far more strict, but when I looked at his plate, he'd taken some of everything. In fact, they both had, and now both plates were empty.

Nick—yes, *Nick*, as I'd started calling him in my head thanks to his request—wasn't the only person I needed to keep an eye on, though. I watched Nate Reynolds like a hawk—like I would a soufflé in the last five minutes of cooking. Well, like a one-eyed hawk who tried not to be too obvious.

And honestly? So far, the jury was out. He was friendly and solicitous. He held plates and bowls for her so she could serve herself. He refilled her water when it got low without asking. I'd seen him help her out of her jacket when they came in. My girl looked *great* tonight, so if he needed a nudge, *voilà, sir, feast your eyes.*

I didn't know what Ariel thought of Nate other than she cared for him a great deal. They'd been friends a long time, though I gathered they'd lost touch while she was married. As a bit of an introvert herself, it'd taken her a while to warm up to me, but we'd had some fun nights together around the new year that pushed us into real, true friendship zone. Once a level of comfort developed, she'd opened up a bit about her past.

By the end of the meal, I was exhausted. I'd been on alert for any comments from Nick, chatting with Rob which had been fairly nonstop, enjoying Reynolds' charm and watching every little move he made next to Ariel, and also trying to engage with the Farrells and Hanovers at the other end.

Ten was just a touch too big. If I had my way, I'd make it eight. But ten allowed for me to invite Mr. Meier, and he could be my date, and then we'd have four more couples or a nice handful of singles. I'd been doing this for the better part of a year and had only had one or two where the group fizzled and the night dragged. With Rob and Nate Reynolds at the table, everyone seemed happy and entertained. Oh, and if I did say so myself, stuffed with good food.

Once everyone had surrendered their forks to the sides of their plates, I began collecting dishes. "Thank you so much for coming. I know everyone has busy weeks coming up, so please go on home safely, and come back again sometime soon."

With my back to the entrance, I couldn't tell who approached until Ariel spoke.

"What can I do?"

"No, no, didn't I tell you before? You just go. That way, everyone can get home, especially with the snow piling up outside."

I always mentioned this to people ahead, but every few times, someone would balk. I appreciated that, and I understood it, but I didn't budge on this. A Sunday night dinner was only fun if you didn't have to spend an hour helping the hostess clean up. I never wanted to be a burden to the people who came, and I refused every time, even my friend.

"That's crazy. There's a ton to do. I can stay ten minutes and help clear, at least." She smiled, her bright blue eyes sparkling. Good food, a handsome man, and a glass or two of pinot noir could do that for you.

"Seriously, no. Plus, I'm pretty sure Reynolds over there is more than ready to get you home."

An unexpected furious blush brightened her cheeks.

"He's a friend," she said in a low voice.

I studied her, wondering if that was all she wanted, or... what. Maybe she still wasn't ready for a relationship. I didn't know what it was like to be divorced, and I definitely didn't know how it felt coming out of something that, from what I gathered, had been abusive on at least one level. If I had the timeline in my head right, she'd been divorced about two and a half years. Who knew what the healing process was like?

"Okay. But you're *my* friend, and I say that tonight, you

go home. I'll have just you over for dinner sometime and you can do all the cleanup." *Over my dead body.*

She smiled, then squeezed my arm since my hands were scraping plates in the sink. "All right, stubborn. I'll see you soon. Thank you for a glorious meal."

"Thanks, Summer! This was amazing!"

"I loved that so much, I'll be thinking about it all week."

"You should open a restaurant. Thanks for the invite."

The friendly farewells gave me soul-deep satisfaction. I'd been helpless to feed myself at times, and I certainly hadn't been any help to my family in that regard. As an adult, I found myself driven to feed others. These feast nights were an outlet for that need, and I relished them. I did my best to clean as I cooked, but the cleanup was always significant. I used the time to review the meal, the conversations with people, and simply come down from the high of hosting. This became a habit early in my military career—I used my own dinner cleanup to calm down and refocus on the day. Plus, there was no room for disorder in the cramped exam rooms of a military clinic, so orderliness at work naturally translated at home.

After everyone had left—and only a little disappointment Nick hadn't popped in to say something—I wiped my hands and leaned out of the kitchen to check on Mr. Meier. I expected to see the usual sight—the old man sitting and quietly sipping tea. What I found sent my pulse into a tripping sprint.

"Oh, hi," I said to Nick, completely inarticulate in the face of him still at my table.

"I'll walk Herr Meier home when he's ready."

"I normally do that."

It may have even sounded weirdly defensive. Not that I thought he was suggesting I wouldn't. I just... he made me...

"I'm sure you do. But you're cleaning up, and it'd be my pleasure."

He pinned me with a look that said a handful of things at once, just like he'd done that first time he'd answered his door.

"Okay. Is that all right with you, Mr. Meier?"

The gent nodded. If Nick was a man of few words, Meier was one of none. He'd only spoken a few times, in short English phrases heavily accented. Of course, he most certainly spoke better English than I did German. Sometimes, I stumbled my way through talking with him in his language. Other times, I spoke English. Either way, he sat quietly, letting me chatter and eating whatever I presented him.

I didn't know his whole story, but his daughter had visited him at some point and told me his wife had died a year before I moved in and that he was very lonely. She and her siblings had moved away for work, and they only got to visit every so often. I'd taken to feeding him, invited him to every feast night, and occasionally helped with other things when he let me. He wasn't infirm, probably in his early eighties and healthy, but so quiet.

He was a grandfatherly figure like I'd never had. My own grandparents passed away before I knew them, and no one else in my family sat quietly, without judgement, like he did. We'd formed a kind of loners' bond. Guilt streaked through me at the thought of someone else walking him home, but he seemed perfectly comfortable with Nick doing it.

"Well... thank you."

Mr. Meier stood, then set a hand on mine. I smiled at him and dipped my head. He then led the way out of the dining area to the door, where he removed his coat from the hanger just inside. Nick sent me one last piercing look, something I couldn't decipher, and then followed him.

I ducked back into the kitchen, my ears full of a rushing sound I didn't understand and my heart tachycardic. I steadied myself on the counter, feeling unaccountably hot and mentally fuzzy. What had he done to me with that look?

Returning to the sink, I rinsed dishes, loaded the dishwasher, filled a pot to soak, then grabbed a rag to wipe the table. Folding it in a neat square, I nearly collided with Nick, who was walking into the kitchen just as I planned to exit.

"What are you doing?" I asked, less accusatory and more surprised. Breathy and silly, if you want honesty.

"I'm here to help clean up."

His words in the space sounded rich and deliciously masculine. There were only ever women in this place after a certain time. Only me, really. That voice in my kitchen made my stomach clench.

"I know I mentioned before—I do all the cleanup. It's a rule about coming to feast night."

He stepped closer. "I'm not leaving all of this for you."

I didn't budge. "Yes, you are. That's the rule."

"Consider it a broken one, then."

I sucked in a breath, something about that sending a thrill straight through me, even as I knew I couldn't allow this. "No."

He stepped closer. We stood only a foot apart.

"Summer."

I swallowed. He'd never said my first name before, except in writing, and *oh, hi,* it sounded so good coming from those lips in that voice.

His gaze flickered over my face, snagged on my lips, but

then returned to my eyes. "I'm here. I'm not leaving until you let me help."

That firmed my resolve. My house, my rules, no matter how flambé-hot a given guest may be. "Really? If I ask you to leave, you're going to stay here without my consent?"

His face didn't change but for a slow blink. "If you genuinely want me to leave, I will. Say it now, or let me help."

Indecision warred in me. I hated the idea of him helping me. It broke the rules. It went against the whole concept. But I most certainly did not want him to leave. He and his gray shirt needed to stay as long as possible now that they were here.

I took a breath, clenching my jaw and promising myself this wasn't a terrible idea. It also didn't have to be a big deal, even though the pit in my stomach, a confusing mix of antic-ipation and dread, told me otherwise.

"Fine," I said, then walked around him to the table so I'd have something to do with my hands.

CHAPTER ELEVEN

Nick

In the water where I tread, the mud slipping beneath my feet, it cuts through. The first pale beams press past thin skin stretched over muscle and bone. Rays sear the ragged places, hidden deep. Light singes every dark place in me. I am pulled out to sea, and go under. I am reaching, one cold-hardened hand, back to the surface.

Summer had arm's length down to a science.

She invited people over, all warm and generous, but didn't let them *in*. I wondered if she did that with her friends—she and Ariel seemed to know each other fairly well. But the rest of her guests were forbidden from helping to do anything. I admittedly hadn't attended all that many dinner parties, but the lack of both socializing post-meal *and* not letting people even help clear the table struck me as odd.

Not unlike the woman herself. She was charming and warm, but this little scene in the kitchen? Definitely stubborn, pushy, almost irritable with me. Granted, I'd surprised her by staying and flouting her instructions.

But when it came down to it, she'd let me stay. More than a little pleasure snaked through me with that victory. I scrubbed the last remaining pot—she'd cleaned like a tornado in here, and there really wasn't much left by the time I'd returned from dropping Herr Meier back home. I had no plan for how this would go, but I couldn't pass up a chance to be alone with her and to say thank you for not only this night but also all the other meals she'd given me.

She'd been so friendly and warm with Rob, I'd had to cut down the shoots of jealousy growing with each little joke or story one of them told the other. They were friends, but tonight I'd wondered if it was more. If the reason Rob hadn't brought a date was because Summer was his.

I'd walked out with him, wandering slowly into the sparkling, snowy night, working to tamp down the riot of disappointment and embarrassment forming a leaden ball in my gut. He reached his car, which he'd parked in my driveway. Before he climbed in, he stopped me.

"Masters."

I turned back from the steps of my porch.

"You like her."

My brows rose to ask the question—*so?*

"I mean, I don't know if you do, but I wanted to tell you Summer and I are friends. We get along great. We went out, did a few group things last fall, didn't click like that. Never kissed her or anything. I just thought I'd mention it."

Snow fell so aggressively that it'd coated his hair and shoulders already. Shoveling would be fun in the morning.

I nodded, and he turned to go.

In my chest, buried at the very center, something unfolded, like a map flattening out from a small rectangle into a plan. I watched him pull onto the road and follow the trail of cautious drivers leaving the cul-de-sac. Instead of harassing Butter by going home and leaving again, I turned and trudged back to Summer's.

Whether she had any interest in me, I didn't know. Of course she found me physically attractive on at least some level, though she didn't look at me quite as much or the same way as other women did. But she seemed persistent enough that she might eventually know me. That stubborn, pushy tenacity might be just what I needed.

What could I offer her? No idea. But I wouldn't know unless I tried, and for the first time in what felt like forever, I wanted to.

After escorting Herr Meier home, I returned, and now here I stood, rinsing the last pot as she bustled in and out of the kitchen, returning small things to the fridge or counter. Everything in the kitchen was colorful and homey. Her top-of-the-line stainless steel cookware hung from a pot rack above a small kitchen island, all except three enamel Dutch ovens in different sizes—the largest of which I now held.

Finally, the movements I'd become so attuned to—the swish of her black dress, the gentle pat-pat of her silver shoes—came to a halt behind me. I set the pot onto the drying rack, dried my hands on a nearby towel, and turned to find her leaning one hip against the counter and eyeing me, arms crossed.

"Summer," I said, because she was breathtaking this close, and I couldn't think of anything else.

"Nick."

I swallowed down the sound of my name in her mouth. I would've asked for seconds if I'd had the words. I certainly couldn't speak, so I waited.

She huffed. "You've done enough. Th-thank you for your help. I'll find a way to repay you soon."

Startled by her stilted delivery and her words, I nearly laughed. "Repay me? You hosted the dinner and made all the food. There's nothing to repay. If anything, I'm still in *your* debt."

How could she think for a second she owed me for washing one pot?

She opened her mouth like she might argue, then acquiesced. "Do you want me to walk you home?"

I pressed my lips together to stay the smile. She was cute, too, on top of everything else I already liked. "No. I'll make it okay."

I moved past her to retrieve my coat, reluctant to leave. Wishing she'd ask me to stay for a drink or... or say anything. But I had no confidence in my ability to suggest it without sounding *suggestive,* and we didn't know each other well enough for her to know I certainly wouldn't be coming on to her like that. Plus, she'd had the run-in with the idiot at her door not a month ago. She'd need to give me a sign she was interested before I pursued her.

I'd become aware of how much larger I was than most women as early as high school, but since then, I'd packed on forty pounds of muscle and even grew another inch in my first few years in the Army. I never wanted to be a source of physical intimidation and often found that, whether I liked it or not, my face, my body, my general demeanor, intimidated. There were times when that became particularly loathsome, and in this moment, I needed to be sure she felt no pressure of any kind from me. It was one thing to nudge her on letting me help clean up. Beyond that, there couldn't be anything.

Shrugging into my coat, I pushed my arms through the sleeves, ignoring the irritating sensation of rolled cuffs inside. I'd be home in minutes and could be back in sweatpants and a T-shirt seconds after that.

"Here," she said, one small hand pressed against my right pec over the jacket, and the other reaching up and flipping the lapel of the coat out from where it'd turned under.

That first press of her hand made my breath catch, all systems stalled, then my pulse sprinted. She'd fixed the lapel but hadn't moved—just stayed there, one hand resting against me, one gripping the jacket.

My chest rose and fell under her touch. Her blue eyes looked darker in the dim light of the entryway, and she had little wisps of hair springing out around her face ever since she'd started cleaning. The connection between us, the proximity, it all expanded and filled the space with thick anticipation.

A few persistent strands brushed her cheek, and before I knew what was happening, I reached up and tucked them behind her ear. My gaze followed the progress of my hand behind the delicate arch of her ear, noting how her long, makeup-darkened lashes fluttered when I did. The pad of my index finger trailed down her neck to her shoulder, where I pulled away.

My voice came out low and quiet when I leaned in and spoke into the miraculous curves of her ear. "Thank you for dinner."

"Thank you for coming."

Hers, a whisper.

Sleep eluded me for much of the night. I slept a few hours after writing late. In the morning, after a quick breakfast and cleanup behind me, I layered warm clothes and pushed out into the cold. I could use the shoveling to replace a jog.

CHAPTER TWELVE

Summer

The notification for a late call woke me. This meant the storm must've turned out to be bad enough, or the snow melted and then refroze so the roads were treacherous. Sometimes, the clinic had to open at the normal time, but today, they'd said we'd be opening at nine thirty. I stretched and smiled at the news. Bavaria didn't tend to stay locked in a frozen wonderland for very long, so I wanted to enjoy it while it lasted. It didn't let up from the cold, but snow wasn't all that common.

I pulled on layers and made an espresso to wake me, then started the coffee brewing to have with breakfast. After mixing up some blueberry bran muffins, I pushed them into the oven, pulled on my boots, and set a timer. I should be able to shovel most of the walkway and driveway, at least enough to get my car out, in twenty minutes. I could incentivize doing it quickly with the muffins, and then when I came in, it would be all warm and cozy with something baking instead of cold and quiet.

Imagine my surprise, then, when I quietly shut the door, shovel in hand, and found the snow cleared of my whole sidewalk and drive. Even the walks between my house and Mr. Meier's. And his house had been done. And—ah, that explained it.

The scrape and slide of a shovel over pavement, the slump of snow into a pile, nearly echoed in the small circle of houses. Nick's back was to me, and he worked with a machine-like pace. He had obviously started with me and worked his way over to his own house.

My heart glowed. *How sweet. How lovely.* After last night's stubborn insistence on helping—and then that moment with the hair-tucking and the eyes—I'd thought about him nonstop until I passed out. Fortunately, after a feast night, I always slept very well, so even Nick's gorgeous, somber face, his gray shirt fitting him like perfection, and his general appealing presence couldn't keep me up.

But this? This was too much. He shouldn't have done all this—not for me at least. I was happy he'd helped Mr. Meier, of course, but here he went again, tipping the scales in his favor. And again, I had no real way of paying him back. Did he *want* me to feel indebted to him? Was this some kind of game, or did he feel called to be a man who drove me to insanity?

"I'll help you, no problem. The question is, what're you gonna do for me?"

The memory flashed in my mind, and my stomach turned to lead. I'd had so many instances like that—someone offering help, then expecting something in return. That *something* varied from asking me to let them cheat off tests in high school to expecting more physical benefits, some-times with attempts at taking without consent. My junior year math tutor had been the one to attempt that, and I'd kneed him just like I'd planned on doing to Dennin.

I'd avoided any truly terrible assaults, but even in my military career, I'd had superiors abuse situations. Sadly, so many of my female military members could relate—a staggering number experience at least some kind of harassment, and a shocking number actual assault. Though I'd shed some of the expectation that the tit for tat would come at some point, being surrounded by people who'd faced similar issues on even a small scale served to confirm what I'd been learning all my life: if someone helps you, they're going to cash in. And more, whatever the person wanted wouldn't be something good.

On the outside, I could recognize that not everyone, and not every *man*, wanted something from me when they offered help. I believed those people existed. Nick might even be one of them. And maybe someday, my gut response wouldn't always be suspicion.

I'd gone a little off the ledge with that stream of thinking, but I practically stomped along the sidewalk. I marched up to him, maybe a little more peeved than I should've been. "Hello."

He jolted, then his shovel dropped. He definitely hadn't heard me coming.

He turned toward me. The early morning light was still dusky, but I could see his cheeks and nose were red from cold or exertion—probably both. He wore no hat, only an unzipped jacket, gloves, and what looked like utility pants with boots.

"Hello."

I'd planned to grill him about shoveling my snow, but his

gravelly voice and the way his gaze hit me knocked the words out of my mouth. Instead, I said, "You should come over for coffee when you're done. I have muffins in the oven, too."

His eyes flickered back and forth between mine for a moment before he nodded. "Okay. Should be about ten minutes."

"See you then."

I turned and shuffled back to the house, now intent on cleaning up before he arrived.

But... what had happened just there? I'd failed to address the favor, the newly piled-on debt, but those eyes hit me and I blanked. Then I invited him over.

So that went well.

My empty head kept me from picking a fight and railing against his doing something for me without my asking. And my gut spoke for me. I knew it, and maybe he did too—I wanted to feed him again. Somewhere in me, I *needed* to. Probably that innate sense of wanting to balance things out —he shoveled, so I'd feed.

Despite knowing fairly well that this was not the main reason the invitation had jumped from my lips while my heart raced and my mind flat-lined, I'd cling to that logic anyway.

With fifteen minutes to muffin time, I had maybe eight minutes to shower, change, and look a little less haggard before the most gorgeous man I'd ever seen darkened my doorway again. And he did literally darken it, because he was something like six foot three with shoulders nearly as wide as the doorframe.

I rushed through a quick shower, thankful I'd worn my hair up yesterday and all I needed to do was pull it back again—that way I'd be ready for work later. I didn't feel like having this interaction in scrubs, so I pulled on joggers and a long-sleeved tee, then a cozy cardigan. Hopefully, he liked cat-lady chic. Although, frankly, if one of us was a cat-lady, he obviously owned that title.

One benefit of having served in the Army, and later working in military hospitals, was that I could go from sleeping to making rounds in fifteen minutes if need be. Fortunately in my current life, I didn't need that kind of get-up-and-go, but times like these, I could appreciate that my getting ready routine could be extremely quick when necessary.

The knock came seconds after I'd swiped on a little makeup. Made it!

My stomach somersaulted all over the place as I approached the door. Between his letter and his helping me, and the moment at the door last night, I knew he liked me. For some insane reason, this odd, beautiful man wanted to spend time with me or... or *something*. Honestly, I didn't know what he wanted, and I wished I did. Maybe I'd just ask.

The other odd half of the equation? Our dynamic seemed to be what I'd call *lightly antagonistic chic*. We squabbled and disagreed constantly, even in letter form from the very start.

If you don't want to fight with him, maybe you should chill out.

The inner voice spoke loud and clear, and I couldn't deny the fair point. I had been the one to make things worse. So, maybe I could just enjoy him today. If I fed him, we'd be even, or close, for the shoveling. I wouldn't owe him, and we could be friends.

"Come in, come in. Wow, it's somehow colder than

when I went out there," I said, chuckling inanely, anxious energy pressing at my lungs.

"Probably the missing coat." He halted just inside the door and leaned down to untie his laced boots. After stepping out of them, he pulled off his jacket and hung it, leaving him in only a black waffle knit shirt, utility pants, and black socks.

I shouldn't have been so affected by the sight of him, but I was. And it seared embarrassment onto my skin. I felt sensitive and sweaty, and suddenly my head had gotten too big for my body.

"Summer?"

I blinked up at him, disoriented. "Uh, yes? Did you say something?"

"I asked if you rested well last night. Are you okay?" He dipped his head to inspect me.

My cheeks burned, so I whipped around. "Come on in. Sorry, just still waking up."

Yeah right. Just busy mapping the magnificence of your shoulders in that shirt.

In the kitchen, I pulled down a mug, then turned to find him lingering in the doorway.

"Come in." I waved him forward. "Do you like espresso, or brewed coffee?"

"Both. Either."

I laughed. "How definitive of you."

His eyebrows popped up and one side of his mouth rose in a slight smile.

I felt like running around, hands up screaming at the top of my lungs. *GOALLLLLLLL!* My lungs did a do-si-do and my head started beatboxing. Just that tiny little lift and I was completely and utterly twitterpated. No need to worry about antagonizing him. If he'd give me little mini-smiles like that, I wouldn't be able to think clearly enough to start a fight.

"You'll have to decide. Or, well, of course you could have both, if you want—"

He held up a hand and stepped closer. "No, no, just brewed coffee is fine."

I swallowed, my nerves an absolutely ridiculous riot this morning. We'd been in this same room together not twelve hours ago. He'd sat at my table all night. Granted, he hadn't spoken much, but still.

Before I had to come up with something to say, the oven beeped. I grabbed an oven mitt and busied myself with retrieving the muffins, thankful for a reprieve from him. In the meantime, I gave myself a talking to because this could not continue. I'd invited him for coffee, and I needed to thank him.

And kiss him.

Whoa, baby. That's a leap.

And like the little devil she was, my mind raised its little eyebrow with an attitude and gave me a look that said she knew I wanted to.

Cause yeah. I did. I wanted to get close to him and see what it'd feel like. Plus, it'd been two years since I'd been kissed, so I should probably plan to break that streak, right? That fleeting thought sent lightning bolts of nerves through my belly.

"Let me put these on the cooling rack real quick, and then I'll get it for you." I popped the muffins out and set them on the rack, doing my best to avoid the steam. They smelled so good—earthy and cozy from the bran with a little bright blueberry sweetness topping the scent.

Still not looking at him, I grabbed a mug and filled a cup. When I finally turned to face him, he stood slightly hunched over the cookbook I'd left out on the counter. I always got out the book I'd use to cook dinner so I could read through the recipe at breakfast and make sure I had everything. It wasn't a perfect system, but after years of cooking for myself, I'd discovered this to be the best way to keep my excitement up. If I planned too far ahead, I got bored, but I did make meal plans around what I found on sale when possible.

Of course, when I had others to feed, that necessitated planning ahead, and I did my best to work in recipes with affordable ingredients. I loved hosting people and sharing food, but it cost money. Food made up a huge portion of my budget, and a not-small part of me relished spending money on food for *other* people. That would've enraged my parents —they'd see it as a luxury or even as being taken advantage of, which was a sin second only to the trespass of accepting help.

It'd taken me a long time to embrace the side of me that wanted to be financially stable because it was so opposite of how I was raised. It shouldn't have been a surprise, but even things like my luxury car and hosting people for regular dinners were ways I could be *opposite* the stingy bitterness that had marked most of my childhood memories. One more way getting the new job would contribute to my happiness and my quality of life—a pay raise. Simple, and not particularly noble, even, but true.

Anyway, I meal-planned. But for myself, I liked diving into the recipe the morning of.

That it also provided me an unconscious comfort during the day added to the appeal. As a kid, I'd get breakfast and lunch at school during the year, but rarely dinner at home. I was always hungriest at night, and some part of me had started promising myself dinner as soon as I had the means to make it happen. This habit, the reading in the morning what I'd eat that night, was a small reminder of that. It was a promise I made to myself—I wouldn't go hungry, and neither would anyone I cared about.

"Here. Sorry for the wait," I said at his side, holding out a large white mug swirled with ornate filigreed detailing in the pottery. Italian pottery, my preference over Polish since food just looked better on white dishes. But they had the loveliest little details. I had a dining set of two in this style, but my dishes for larger gatherings were plain white and totally nondescript.

His gaze jumped to mine immediately, and he shifted so his hip leaned against the counter. He reached for the mug with both hands, wrapping his much larger one around mine at the handle, and cupping the other around the opposite side.

I swallowed, the warmth of his hand and the rough brush of his palm against my knuckles somehow the most sensual thing I'd ever felt. I internally stamped my foot at myself—I was finding everything about him far too appealing and thus becoming ridiculous. Slowly and with heaps of regret, I released the mug to him.

"Why'd you invite me here, Summer?"

His deep voice was a little gruff but rich, and so, so nice.

"I—to thank you for shoveling my driveway." My breath came shallow, and I felt a little dizzy.

"Unnecessary."

"Completely necessary. It must've taken you at least fifteen minutes, if not more since you did every single part that's paved, and you did it before I even woke up."

"It was quick—I got through all three houses in about forty minutes. Made a good workout to do all three in a row." One of his eyebrows inched up a millimeter.

I hadn't considered that element. There was a reason people died shoveling snow—it shot your heartrate through the roof. He'd done the equivalent of an hour's work in forty minutes which meant he must've been shoveling at an inhuman pace.

"Forty minutes? How are you not still breathing hard right now?"

I may have sounded awed and mildly horrified. As much as I loved the stuff, I hated shoveling snow. It was an excruciating exercise in lifting from the legs even though you had to bend to scoop. But the first time it snowed here, I'd decided I wouldn't complain because I had a healthy body and I wasn't about to be one of those obnoxious Americans with a snowblower out at six a.m. breaking the noise ordinances.

"I was until we got inside."

He studied my face, and since I could actually see his now, I did the same.

Something jabbed at my side. Oh, that's right, the awareness that this man was heartbreakingly handsome. I mean, I would've liked to say I could take or leave him, but I would've been lying. *Take, take, take!*

"Should you even be shoveling? Is your hip healed completely? Don't you still have a few more weeks of physical therapy?"

I would've winced at how overtly I'd displayed the fact that I'd obviously asked about his injuries, but I couldn't. He was too close. He'd set the mug on the counter and now leaned against a hand he'd placed even with my body.

"You're worried about my hip?"

"I—I just don't think you should be exerting yourself like that so soon." I tried to sound like a healthcare professional and not like a breathless, fluttery girl.

"It did just fine. I appreciate the concern."

My heart was a herd of wild mustangs in my chest, storming through the moment. I could hardly think or move or stand there any longer. I was completely jumbled, and honestly? It freaked me out. I didn't respond this way to men. This wasn't me. What weird broody voodoo had he done on me?

The lack of response didn't seem to concern him, but he did prompt me. "Why am I here, Summer?"

"I—"

I started to tell the same lie but stopped. His blue eyes searched between mine with an expression I had seen last night and more than once already today.

Suddenly, it clicked. It was *hope*. There was hope in his eyes, and it spread over my chest like glaze over a warm bundt cake.

So, I spoke honestly. "I wanted to see you."

He stepped closer so our bodies nearly touched. Those warm, rough hands reached up and cupped my head, thumbs at my cheeks. He leaned down just as I rose on my toes, and our lips touched. A light, tentative press, then again, and once more before he pulled back to study me, hands releasing my face, much to my regret.

My brain finally registered what had happened, and I reached out to hold him at his biceps. Funny how people talked about women having curves—this man had *curves*. I would've said bulges, but that sounded crass. More like smooth stones carved with relentless hours of work. Here, there, everywhere.

My hands didn't even begin to span his arms, but I gripped what I could and urged him toward me again.

CHAPTER THIRTEEN

Nick

My quiet lets me see people. When I catch the quality of a person, I'm usually right. Then you stormed up to my door and shoved your dishes at me, pressing morsels into my hand and sustenance into my soul. You've fed me far more than you realize. And me? I thought it'd be pyrite, but there you are, pure gold.

I never imagined this moment would come so soon. Not that I didn't want it—let me be clear on that. But I didn't think we'd be here, kissing in her kitchen, her hands on my arms and the soft curve of her cheeks under my thumbs.

I no longer wondered whether Summer was interested.

At least on this, the most basic, physical level. And I took that news and ran with it.

We naturally came up for air, the dizzying slide of wanting pulling my mind in all directions. Her gaze inspected me as mine did her, relishing the color in her cheeks and the expression she wore—desire? Satisfaction, even? Couldn't quite be that, as we'd only kissed for moments.

"Would you like a muffin?" she asked, her voice sweet and melodic, as always.

"Yes." *No.* I didn't want a muffin. Muffins were useless, and I didn't eat much grain, typically. But right now, I'd eat anything she set in front of me.

Her brow furrowed. "Actually, I could make you something else. I made the muffins to take into work later, but I have eggs. I could do an omelet?"

A smile tugged at my lips. "You don't have to make me something else. You've already made muffins, and they'll no doubt be the best muffins I've ever tasted."

The way we were standing, talking in low voices just inches apart, must've looked ridiculous from the outside. But she hadn't taken her hands off me, and I wouldn't do anything to jeopardize a moment of her touch. I hadn't been touched like this in too long—far too long. And it wasn't just fraught with heat and seeking pleasure, but with a warmth she brought along with her. The *life.* Even the care of offering something other than a muffin, which I would've eaten just to please her. Somehow in the last twelve hours, the thought of doing something for her had consumed me.

This need of hers to feed me, it spoke to me on some kind of primal, desperate level. The part of me that hadn't been cared for in so long. Gran had cooked for me when I was kid, but since then, I'd been on my own. And after that, she'd been my support—maybe odd for a twenty- and thirty-something man, but she'd been my ally in life after I'd lost my parents and she'd lost her son and daughter-in-law. Being taken care of by Summer, even in this small way she had no intention of meaning so much to me, shook me.

I dropped my hands, so I stood just looking at her, wondering what she'd do if I slid my arms around her waist and pressed her to me fully.

"That's kind, but I forgot about your meal plans and stuff for a minute. Would an omelet work better? Tell me honestly, please. I don't mind making one—it'll take ten minutes, max."

Her bright blue eyes blinked back at me, and a familiar longing jumped in my chest.

"Yes. An omelet would be good." *And yes, I want ten more minutes with you.*

She nodded, what I hoped was satisfaction pulling those kissing lips into a lovely, soul-stealing smile. My God, everything she did, I liked. I'd never gone from hardly knowing a person to thinking like that. Not once. *What a damn fool.*

"One condition—you put me to work."

She raised a brow, attempting an irritated glare. Trouble was, I'd seen the real thing and this one didn't hold a candle to an actual irritated Summer. "Fine."

For the next few minutes, we worked together. I cracked eggs into a bowl while she chopped part of an onion, a tomato, some red pepper, and mushrooms. After sautéing them, she poured in the beaten eggs, and I hung by her like the rapt audience I was.

"What makes you love cooking so much?" I asked, resisting the urge to trace the shell of her ear. I'd done it once before, just last night. I'd *just* kissed her, and yet I couldn't assume a few kisses meant I had the right to touch her however I wanted.

Wouldn't that be nice.

She nudged the side of the pan, adjusting the heat just a bit, before answering. "I find it satisfying. I like the process of taking a bunch of disparate things and making it one delicious dish. I also like variety and sticking to a budget, so embracing cooking my own food is something that facilitates both of those things."

Something about the way she ended made me think there might be something else. I waited and watched her maneuver the omelet, hoping she'd tell me. I didn't want to prod, but I knew whatever else she would say would be the real reason—the most important one.

"Cheese?" she asked, not quite meeting my eyes.

"Just a bit."

A few minutes later, we'd settled into seats at the dining table. She sat at the head, just like last night, and I sat at her right, where Mr. Meier had been. Another thing I wanted to ask her about. But first...

"What else were you going to say? About why you like to cook?"

Her fork paused halfway to her mouth and she leaned back. She pressed her lips together, thinking.

Now I knew it mattered, whatever it was.

"Growing up, my family was what they call *dirt poor*. We didn't always eat, and when we did, it was whatever we could get. I could count on two hands the kinds of fresh fruit and vegetables we had before I left home."

My chest constricted at the image of a small Summer without enough to eat. I shifted in my seat, grasping for something worthwhile to say, but she continued.

"I'm the fourth of five kids. I did a fair amount of

scrounging, but there were a few years when I didn't eat at home at all. I had breakfast and lunch at school, and on weekends the librarian and pastor took turns feeding us."

Her cagey look sent my hand for hers. I covered it and squeezed. "I'm sorry."

She raised one shoulder, then let it drop. "No going back. Being hungry taught me a lot, and not just about food. But I hate the feeling now. And I hate the thought of other people feeling it."

It clicked. "That's why you feed people? It's your mission—part of your purpose?"

She chuckled and cast her eyes down like the idea embarrassed her. "I guess it is, in a way. I'm sure most of the people I feed wouldn't go hungry without me, but that's the root of it. I recognize that. But I also really do love cooking and doing it for a group—or even one other person is so much better than doing it just for me."

The sensation in my chest brought to mind a lit fuse burning, sparkling from one end of me to the other. What sweetness and light. What pure, caring goodness. "That's lovely."

She laughed, a disbelieving sound. "You're nice. I never would've expected it."

I frowned at her, then sliced a piece of the omelet with the side of my fork. "Why would you think I'm not nice?"

"You're just so straight-faced and serious at first. Or maybe all the time. But it's not... *mean*." She smiled at me like this revelation genuinely pleased her.

For my part, I was mildly horrified. Had she thought I'd be *mean*? Or had I been mean to her? I'd certainly had my fair share of uncharitable thoughts about her generosity. "Have I treated you in a way that was mean? If I have, I didn't realize it, but I need to know. Please tell me."

"No—no. I mean, I didn't love you rejecting my food." She inserted a *look*. "But I think it was more a first impression kind of thing. At the fest last fall—that was the first time I'd been introduced to you, and I'm not sure you even met my eye. Then you didn't speak to anyone and left early. It struck me as rude then, but in retrospect, after knowing you even just a little..."

Her probing gaze unsettled me. I didn't remember meeting her. I only vaguely remembered the fest—Thatcher Wild had invited me, and since he and Rob and a few others I knew would be there, I'd said yes. I'd needed an escape from the shroud of anxiety that'd plagued me. "My grandmother had been sick for a while, but she took a turn for the worse right before that. I shouldn't have gone out but hoped maybe it'd distract me. I'm sorry I was rude."

"I'm so sorry about your grandmother. Is she okay?"

I sucked in a breath, and let it out. "No. She passed just before Christmas."

"Oh, I'm so sorry." It came out low and full of regret.

Maybe because of her earlier admission about how she grew up, or maybe because I desperately needed someone to understand, hope feathered through my mind, wondering, if I said these things aloud, would it remove a bit of the ache? Could sharing this reality and seeing the truth register in someone else's eyes make the situation less isolating? I hadn't done that in years now—shared a burden. Sometimes, I'd tried, but talking to someone who didn't remember you didn't quite have the same effect as sharing with a loved one. Even though it didn't make sense, I wanted it to be her I connected with, poured out to. "She was my last relative. My last... person."

Her mouth dropped open just slightly, and she grabbed my hand. "Your parents?"

"Died in a car crash just before my sixteenth birthday. I went to live with my grandmother then."

"Siblings?"

"Only child."

To my parents' regret, too. They'd tried for more. I didn't remember much about that except a snippet of conversation when I was about ten. My mom had said something about how they were going to "stop trying," and even though I didn't understand anything about infertility or pregnancy, I knew it meant I'd never have a brother.

"Can you stand up, please?" she said and shot out of her chair, still holding my hand.

I set aside my napkin and stood, cautious and curious even as the brutal mix of nostalgia and grief and horrible loneliness sloshed in my gut. She took my other hand in hers so we faced each other.

"I'm going to hug you now, unless you have objections."

My heart skipped. "No objections."

And then she released my hands, stepped right to me, and wrapped her arms around me. She squeezed, and the pressure reminded me to return the gesture. She'd shocked me, but only for a moment. My arms surrounded her small frame, but it felt so good. God, how long had it been since I'd been hugged? Months and months. No, actually. Over a year.

I let out a ragged breath, and she rested her head on my chest. The action held purpose, like she'd imbue me with every drop of consolation, every ounce of respite, through this connection.

Eyes shut, I inhaled the moment. I committed to memory every perfect thing about it. I would write this moment and read it ten times a day for the rest of my life.

Your small hands at my back push away the grief, urging it to move. Your breath at my neck whispers away the sorrow, magic in the air. Your body pressed to mine steals the hollow and fills it with ease. I will never set you away.

You pull back and look at me with your sapphires, your soul. Your fingers on my jaw and your lips just touch mine, but you have given everything in this moment. You have given me a memory worth keeping.

CHAPTER FOURTEEN

Summer

I'll be your person. *I'll be your person!!!*

My whole being screamed the thoughts in the wake of his confession. No family. No one left. The genuine and lasting grief etched on his face as he spoke told me his childhood had been different from mine. He'd loved, desperately, his parents and his grandmother. And they were gone. My mind raced with questions—what about aunts and uncles? Cousins? No other grandparents? But if that were the case, he wouldn't have said it that way—she was his last person. His last relative.

I could see that idea—being the only one left—haunted him. I wanted to understand more, talk more, but hugging him seemed right. And it had felt right. He'd melted into it, and I didn't think I flattered myself by saying he felt genuinely comforted by it.

He'd left not long after, both of us needing to move on

with our mornings so we could get to post safely and on time. Somehow, before I left, he'd slipped a note on my doorstep. I only knew this because I'd looked carefully while leaving the house, half a hope in my mind for the very thing.

Summer,

Thank you for a delicious breakfast and for yet again catering to my preferences. It should be said that the omelet tasted better than any I've ever eaten, but I'm not surprised.

What I'm writing to thank you for, more than the food, is your company. And to ask your forgiveness. The night of the fest, I wasn't myself. My mind and heart were cloudy, and I couldn't take in much. I know this—I know I wasn't myself —because if I had been, and I'd met you, I would remember. As it is, I routinely catalogue every interaction we've ever had, so the fact that I don't remember what is evidently our first encounter plagues me.

I bet you were lovely. I know you were beautiful—this is fact, and true at every moment, so it must've been then.

My apologies for the unfocused thoughts. I couldn't leave for work without telling you how thankful I feel to have spent this morning sipping your hot coffee and kissing your perfect lips.

Have a good day,
Nick

~

By two that day, I was dragging. But not in the way you'd think—not that afternoon lull, I've-been-here-forever-and-I-still-have-miles-to-go feeling. More like, *all I want to do is go kiss Nick Masters' face off, but I can't because we both have jobs.*

The letter! *Kissing your perfect lips.* I mean, really.

The clinic had been pretty slow—probably due to the snow. People who would've come in for something minor decided not to, plus we had to reschedule everyone who would've shown up for an appointment during those first few hours when the clinic was closed.

Every time I saw Major Hall lately, I couldn't help feeling a little fizz of excitement. She'd asked me to apply for the job. That had to be a good sign. No—it *was*. I could embrace that and run with it. I'd also come up with a community project to help develop my credentials as a manager. Of course, no amount of volunteering would designate me as a capable manager of a group of nurses in a clinic—that was a practical qualifier only on-the-job experience would nail down. But I could beef up my general leadership experience. Typically, I jumped into events or projects that organizations around post created and did whatever they needed. This was my chance to facilitate and have a more recent, community-specific example of managerial action on my resumé, and hopefully a few good talking points for the interview.

I had two months to get it together, execute, and then take the results and all the rest of my professional experience and lay them at the committee's feet. So far, thinking about that impending change was the only thing I could shift my focus to that would get my mind off Nick.

Mostly because I didn't want to get my mind off of him. He made me feel like my heart was walking around on tiptoes. It didn't make sense, but I felt all fluttery. In fact, I felt that so much, I'd taken my pulse and BP—normal. Maybe slightly accelerated because I sat there, counting, remembering how Nick's calloused hands felt on my cheeks.

"Hello there, Nurse Applegate."

Rob's voice brought me back the moment. I stood outside my office door leaning on the frame, staring out the window at the beautiful, glittering snow, and turned to find my friend grinning at me.

"Hey. Why are you here?"

Not that seeing people I knew while at work was at all unusual. In fact, working at the clinic in a small community like Kugelfels meant I got to know almost everyone, whether they ended up my team's patients or not. I liked that.

He smiled widely. "Glad to see you too."

I started to protest, but he waved me off with a laugh.

"Just getting a physical. You have to have one within two weeks of the competition, and then of course you have a general check there. I don't think they do blood tests at this level yet."

"It's coming up quick. I read through all the regulations and everything I could find on what I'm supposed to do, but there isn't much." I'd scoured the organization's website and all the information Rob had sent.

"You'll do great. Plus, none of us are getting hurt, so you don't have to worry." He wiggled his brows, the cheeseball.

"Fine then."

He looked left to right in a dramatic gesture, then dipped his chin. "So, how's Masters?"

I stood straight, no longer leaning on the doorframe. The sound of Nick's name from someone else sent a jolt of happy nerves through me. "Just fine, I'd imagine. Why do you ask me that?"

He raised a disbelieving brow. "Well, let's see. When

we left your house last night, I made sure he knew you and I weren't dating."

I reared back. "Why would you even—"

"He'd been wondering. I could tell. And he's a man who wouldn't do anything to harm someone else if he could avoid it. I wanted to make very sure he knew that spending time with you, should you happen to also want that, wouldn't be stepping on my toes."

My stomach twisted. I couldn't quite tell why—anticipation? Embarrassment, even? "Do we act like we're more than friendly? Has that ever been an issue for, uh, for you?"

"No. Oh, goodness, no, honey. Please don't look upset. *No.* I damn sure would've asked you out in the fall, but after we hung out a few times, I figured out we just didn't click like that. And honestly, that's great, because I get you as a friend, and I get to see Masters all tied up in knots over you."

His dark brows raised and lowered a few more times. What a ham.

"I wouldn't say he's *tied up in knots*, but... he's nice."

Rob blinked a few times, absorbing that. "Sure. *Nice.* That's how I'd describe him—"

"He is! But whatever. He did come back, and he insisted on helping me clean up." I made a face.

Rob's smile practically sparkled. "I'm so sorry. That sounds terrible."

I rolled my eyes and gave him an unimpressed glare. "I make it very clear before people come that they are to leave, no cleanup. It's one of my rules, and I don't have many. Should you be so happy that he wouldn't obey my simple rule?"

Even as I said it, I had to admit that in the end, I was glad he had.

"I think there are few people who can truly stand up to your level of determination. I also think the same is true for Nick Masters. So for me, I'm just going to sit back and watch you two out-stubborn yourselves and see what happens." Then came another smile that brightened the hallway.

"We'll see. In the meantime, you need to tuck away your charm assault before half the population of the post collectively swoons and things start shutting down."

He loved that, based on the grin. "Delightful to see you, Summer. We'll be training a ton until about two days out, so I may catch you in the neighborhood. But if I don't see you before then, I'll see you at the airport."

I waved him off, watching him go. As he pushed out the swinging doors dividing the waiting room from the hallways where exam rooms and offices were, I thought I caught a glimpse of Dennin. My stomach immediately sank, but by the time the door swung back the other way, he was gone. Must've been my imagination.

Shaking off the slimy feeling that seeped in anytime I thought about or saw the creep, I focused on Rob's words. Could Nick really like me *that* much? I mean, he wasn't shy about showing interest. I appreciated the very clear absence of game-playing and trying to seem aloof, especially for someone who had a resting expression that screamed mildly irritated at best.

I didn't know where it could go. He was introverted and taciturn, and I was... not either of those things. He was pushy, and while I liked parts of it, I didn't know if I wanted that all the time. Like Rob said, I was determined, and I could admit I preferred to be the one in charge in a lot of situations. Would I want Nick, in all his beauty and unexpected kindness, to be there countering me?

I shook that off too. So far, we'd kissed a small, delicious handful of times, and he'd written me letters I couldn't imagine ever getting rid of. We seemed to get along... kind of? Almost every interaction we had began with a disagreement, then melted into something fizzy and sweet. We hadn't talked about all that much—well, other than a few deeply personal, hard truths from our lives. But who knew if we even had something in common?

I also didn't need to be assuming that because we kissed, we were now a thing. I needed to chill out and focus on developing my community engagement plan and prepare for the London trip.

And if I happened to see Nick Masters out and about or, you know, around... I could talk with him, and it'd be fun. We were friendly, and we could keep doing that without it meaning something huge and life-changing.

CHAPTER FIFTEEN

Nick

I can't look away—won't. Unless you tell me I'm mistaken.

I had not fully appreciated Summer's stubbornness. Frankly, *stubborn* didn't do her justice.

"You realize if you were a man, people would call you pigheaded. You know that, right?" I said this in a frustrated mumble, pacing across my garage gym space.

"That's incredibly rude."

She spoke from the place she'd glued herself to when she came in. She'd slipped inside the door while Rob and Art were midworkout. At least she hadn't insisted on getting directly in the way of one of the guys.

This was our last Saturday to do much of anything, and

we'd been at it all day, mimicking the competition. We'd ease way off in the next few days, but most athletes didn't take too many rest days the week of because it just didn't help them mentally.

"If I'm being rude, I apologize—"

"*If?* It's not a question. Calling someone pigheaded is definitively rude."

I couldn't look at her while she was this frustrated, because looking at her face did things to me. It made me weak and melty, like I'd been left in a hot car and then had to get out and walk, boneless and gummy. I needed sharpness, an edge, to talk some sense into the version of Summer who'd shown up minutes ago, seething.

"I'm not sure why we're even arguing. Are you?" I asked, tapping Art's quad, reminding him to increase range on that side of his squat.

"You're not sure—" She threw her hands up and walked in a tight circle before blowing out a long breath. "Can you just come over here and talk to me? For just a minute? Then I'll leave you to do your work and move on with my life."

I wanted to smile but tucked it behind a frown instead. No way could I let her see she had me smiling and expect to go toe to toe with her. It'd be hard enough to be close to her. I hadn't seen her since Monday morning, except at a distance. We'd both been running around crazy this week, me training and prepping for the trip, her doing whatever she did, and even seeing her for a minute without instantly kissing her with all the pent-up desire felt like a small form of torture.

But on the point we were arguing, I would not give. I left Art to his work—he was in the zone now anyway—and traversed the fifteen feet or so to where she stood. I stopped and crossed my arms, mimicking her stance.

Her eyes flickered over me from my head, to chest, arms, and slipped all the way down to my feet, then bounced back up and rolled. She accompanied this with a sound of mild disgust.

I raised a brow at her.

"You just—of course I come in here all mad and ragey and then you finally come close and it's like—you're like—"

"Yes, Summer? What am I like?"

Yes, I poked the bear. But the look she'd given me was pure fire, so I couldn't resist. I wanted her to speak, to give me all of her words. I wanted everything from her, and I had no idea what she wanted from me. I wasn't above collecting the scraps that fell from the table of this conversation.

She groaned, exasperated. "You're driving me insane. Look. You're not paying for the plane ticket to London. That was never part of the agreement."

She held out her phone to display what looked like an e-mail—likely the plane ticket confirmation I'd gotten earlier today and forwarded.

"False. It was always part of the agreement. It would've been when Melanie was our medic, and it's the same now that it's you."

Her lips pressed together, and she slowly moved her head side to side in an exaggerated shake. "Nope."

"Yes."

"*No.*"

"*Yes.*"

I matched her vehemence, though I didn't feel it the same way she clearly did. Her cheeks were flushed, and she looked genuinely bothered. I didn't want to upset her, but this insistence on paying her own way when she was doing *us* a favor—nonsense.

"Nick! Why are you being like this?"

My name out of her mouth, even in that tone, slipped under my frustration and forced out a smile. When she saw it, she stilled.

"Why on earth are you smiling when we're arguing?"

I sobered, erasing all traces of the stupid, simple joy of her saying my name. *Good grief, what a sucker.* "No reason."

"Seriously."

I said nothing, did nothing, and avoided all possible *anything* that would further stoke her ire.

After a beat of silence between us and only the rough breaths from Arturo and a periodic clinking from Rob as the soundtrack, she sighed. "I'm paying you back for this."

"No. You're not paying *me* anything. The team bought the ticket."

"What? I—I thought that..." She ran a hand through her long hair. "Never mind that. I'm going to earn it, then."

"Of course you are. You're acting as our medical person, and depending on how things go, that could be pretty involved. This isn't a handout. It's part of the contract you signed."

I waited, hoping maybe this—the news that it wasn't from *me* that her ticket had come, but from our team— would quell her upset.

She blinked rapidly, then looked around the gym. Anywhere but at me, until finally, she gave me her eyes. And like every other time she'd done it, my stomach flipped. I swallowed, then stepped closer and spoke in a low voice, uninterested in Rob and Art getting any more of a front row seat than they already had.

"We're glad you're on the team. I hope you can accept the ticket as a part of the agreement. You can review the contract, and you'll see we're obligated to provide travel and accommodations. You can't argue that, either, because we're all sharing a rented place." Might as well cut that argument off before it started.

She opened her mouth, then snapped it shut. My attention hung there, on the upper curve of her lip, her cupid's bow. When my gaze found hers again, the temperature between us had risen out of the sub-zero depths. I clutched at the self-control I'd carefully cultivated over a lifetime in order to refrain from backing her up against the wall of the garage and kissing her.

She cleared her throat. "We'll talk about this some other time."

I shook my head once. "We're done talking about this."

She huffed out a small breath. If she had something else to say, she left it unsaid, to my regret. She turned and departed out the side door, leaving me full of questions.

After a beat, I inhaled focus, then exhaled distraction, working to recenter myself on the here and now. On Art and Rob. On everything we had to do to set them up for success next weekend.

I wouldn't allow myself to think about the odd dynamic of that argument—the thrill of disagreeing with her. The strange pleasure I got from seeing her flushed and irritated. What did that say about me?

That evening, once the guys had left and I'd cleaned up, I knocked on Summer's door. I knew before I did that she was gone—I'd heard the distinct sound of her car's engine about an hour ago. I wondered where she'd gone, but we weren't communicating at all unless in person. I couldn't text her and ask her—we hadn't breeched that social barrier.

Since I'd guessed at her being gone, I'd written her a

letter. Maybe it made me weak or cowardly, but I found it easiest to share my thoughts with her this way. It might also give her a chance to process things so that if I'd been moving too fast, she'd know she didn't have to worry. After dissecting the conversation slowly and painfully over the hours after she'd left, it occurred to me that maybe she thought *I* bought her ticket. Like, as a date. Or something.

So I wanted to set that record very straight. After mentioning the contract, she seemed to get it a bit more clearly. Still, I didn't want her feeling pressured or like I had expectations of her just because we'd kissed.

So I left her a letter on her porch and wandered back to cuddle up with Butter for the night.

~

Summer,

After we talked, I realized you might have been thinking I personally bought you the ticket. I can understand how that would be upsetting and create an uncomfortable dynamic between us and also for the team. I want to be very clear: we purchased the ticket, like we would have for anyone acting as our medical team member, as a team. The same is true for the rented apartment where you'll have a room and a certain allowance during the trip to cover food. This is partially funded by sponsors of the team and partially by dues, so please don't fret over these details. You'll be able to come with us feeling obligated only to do the job you agreed to do. You will not be beholden to me or anyone else for anything else.

I apologize for taking so long to understand the implica-tions of the ticket sent from my e-mail. As coach, I make the travel and accommodation reservations. Please forgive me for causing any confusion and for failing to immediately address your concern—I truly did not realize you might've thought I'd purchased the ticket personally.

I am planning to drive to the airport and am happy to have you join me. The other three live in different towns, so they'll be getting their own transportation. That said, if you're more comfortable driving yourself, please do so.

I've listed my phone number below. I hope you'll use it now, or later—whenever you like. Please let me know if you'd like a ride before Thursday at 20:00. Until then, have a great week,

Nick

CHAPTER SIXTEEN

Summer

Girls' night out came at the perfect time.

I'd spent the rest of the day rocking back and forth between thrilled that Nick clearly wanted to kiss me again and dread that he was slowly stacking up things I'd owe him for. When the time came for me to drive to the train station and meet my friends for a night out, I was more than ready. I wanted good food and company, and I didn't want to think about Nick or his stupid huge biceps or that baffling, mind-blowing smile he threw at me.

We were meeting in the small city of Regensburg, less than a half hour from Kugelfels and the surrounding towns where most of us lived. I'd caught an early train so I could grab a few items at the Asian market before our reservation. The commissary on post often had a nice selection of Asian cooking ingredients, but nothing like an Asian grocery store.

The snow hadn't completely melted, but it would be gone soon. The air was chilly, but thankfully, not terribly icy. For the very beginning of March, I'd take it. Sometimes, wintry weather lasted another month, and sometimes, we'd have warmer days breaking through—much like anywhere else, I supposed. I'd only been here for two winters before this, but so far, this one seemed to have more snow but less lethally cold days.

"There you are," Bec Jones said, clutching her purse close to her body in a way that gave the impression she'd snuggled with it. Her high heels made her only an inch or two shorter than Katie Miller, who stood next to her.

"Ooh, what's in the bag?" Emily Wender asked with a flick of a perfectly manicured nail, eyeing the sack I carried.

"I ran to the Asian market—I'm doing some Korean dishes for the next feast night." I'd already decided since I'd be gone for this next weekend for the competition and wouldn't have my normal time to prep.

Bec raised her hand. "Me. Please me. And Thatcher. Can we be on the list?"

"You know, I haven't ever been to one of your feast nights," Katie Miller said, a sweet smile on her kind face.

"You can all come. Maybe this should be a girls' feast night," I offered.

The resounding *yes* made me laugh, and I warmed. All of me. It'd been years since I'd had a group of female friends like this. Not since my time in the Army, and even then, it had been more situational—work colleagues who became friends due to forced proximity of life. Maybe that was how all friendships started, but I loved that these women had become my friends over the last few months because we'd prioritized spending time together.

"Where are Ariel and Livie? I was thinking maybe you guys were coming together," Emily said, holding the door to the restaurant open.

"Ah, Livie can't come tonight—she's under the weather. Ariel's on the way. She had to take a later train than she'd planned on—something about her mom? Not sure, but she's coming. She'll be like twenty minutes late, so she did give me her order if we want to go ahead." I swiped my phone open, double-checking the note she'd sent.

"Nah, we aren't in a rush. The whole point is to relax and be together. Plus, you know the waiter won't be in a rush." Bec gave me a smile, and we chuckled, no doubt both thinking of the same thing.

We'd traveled together this past Christmas, just a quick trip to Croatia, but we'd encountered one of the slowest restaurants of all time. A three-course meal had taken two and a half hours. No lie. While Bec and I both appreciated a slower approach, that'd been a stretch. Had it been a meal with more courses? Sure. This was not one of those luxurious, dreamy ones.

Service in Europe was always a huge adjustment for Americans. By now, I was fully adjusted to the slow, leisurely pace of dining out, and I knew it was something I'd miss if I ever moved back Stateside.

Even thinking about moving back made my spirits plummet. It wasn't like that was a risk for me—I had a job, all my paperwork was in order, and I had the chance for advancement which was incredibly rare at a small post like Kugelfels.

Sometimes, I wondered if being in Germany gave me an added layer of freedom from my past. Like, if I was nowhere near the small town I grew up in, it somehow meant I was that much healthier and happier. And on some level, that might be true.

But I'd never been happier than in Germany, and in many ways, in the last few months. The distance from home was one thing, but I wanted to believe that, more than that, it was that I'd grown and matured. I'd left home more than twelve years ago. I wished I didn't have to even think about it anymore, but I did, and inevitably, moving back to the US brought up the thoughts of visiting.

I'd be guilted into visiting, even though at one point during college, I'd been officially disowned. Then somehow, that'd been changed—I suspected thanks to my younger sister Jenny. The first time, I'd visited for approximately two hours, and I'd prearranged that. My mother was only fifty-five and my dad sixty, so they still worked. I'd gone on a Saturday, drove up in the car I had then, a used Honda sedan I'd bought in my first year of active duty.

The questions about the car came immediately. The criticism about taking out a car loan first, then the explanation of paying it off—one would think that'd be good news, but instead it made me *uppity*. They reminded me how little I did for them, how much I owed them for raising me, how I should be grateful they taught me to fend for myself. At twenty-seven years old, I got in the car, drove twenty minutes out of town, and then pulled over and bawled my guts out. And honestly, that'd been one of the more pleasant visits since Jenny had been there, and most of the time had been focusing on her and her new baby.

I breathed deep, reminding myself that moving back to the US would happen eventually, but I had nothing to worry about. If I did move, I'd deal with it. Fine. Done.

I shouldered the yucky feelings out of the room and

shut the door on them. No time or place for any more of that nonsense right now.

The host seated us at a carved wooden table, the bench seats built into the wall creating a horseshoe shape. Perfect for chatting with everyone, and fortunately, this place offered small cushions, which helped the comfort factor significantly. I never wanted to own or even work for a restaurant, but I liked to notice things like that—how the seats might influence the dining experience. If you had the best meal in the world, the food of your absolute dreams, but your butt was numb from sitting on a hard, cold seat? No thanks. No one needed that kind of distraction from the food.

Soon enough, Ariel arrived, and everyone peppered her with questions about Livie, her brother, her niece and nephew, and her mom. Then finally, Emily asked what all of us always wanted to know.

"And how's Nate?"

Ariel kept her attention pinned to her menu. "He's been gone a lot—long hours, rotation, and busy with work right now. They have the rotation starting late next week so I—" she cut herself off. "So last I saw... much of him... was at Summer's feast night." She turned her brilliant blue eyes to me.

There was something pleading in them that made me perk up. Before I could ask her what was going on, she kept talking.

"The food was so good. I expected nothing less, but we couldn't stop talking about how good it was. I think you might need to plan to invite Eric and Livie soon, or Livie is going to die of jealousy."

Emily set her straight. "Well, we just decided the next

night is going to be ladies only, so Livie can come. Eric will have to wait a while."

"He'll be fine," she said, then took a long drink of her wine. We'd ordered a bottle of red, and I'd filled her glass as soon as she sat down.

The conversation moved on, and I could see some of the tension slowly seep out of her shoulders. While Katie and Bec watched Emily telling a story about some encounter she'd had with the garrison manager, I leaned in and whispered, "You okay?"

She tilted her head toward me but kept her eyes on Emily. "Yeah. Just frazzled. We should have dinner sometime soon."

"Yes. Let's. Maybe this week?"

I didn't typically share my feelings easily. It gave me a sense of restlessness, and I didn't like burdening friends with the ups and downs of whatever silly things my mind had grasped onto. But I'd also never had friends like these, and I felt particularly drawn to Ariel. I wanted her to be able to confide in me, and somewhere in the halls of my heart, I understood that only worked if it went both ways.

Plus, I wouldn't mind updating her on the whole Nick thing. Especially before we went to London. It'd be good to check in.

She turned to me and smiled. "Perfect."

"Well, if you two are done whispering, I have something serious we need to discuss." Emily raised a brow, and we all chuckled.

"Let's have it," I said, curious. You never knew what to expect with her.

Her face sobered, and she nearly glared at me. "I heard you're organizing a community food and shoe drive. I heard you have finagled a way to donate out into the community, somehow getting around the kilometers of red tape that entails, and I heard you're doing it *all by yourself.*"

I swallowed. "It's just a little side project. The drive ends right after spring break, so it's not too much longer and then it's out of my hands anyway."

Nerves shot through me. *And then we'll see if that's enough to make me look like I know how to manage.*

"That sounds amazing, Summer."

Katie's soft words made me want to hug her. I didn't need constant accolades... or at least, I normally didn't. Something about these last few months had me feeling like a colt just learning to walk.

"What can we do to help?" Ariel asked.

My throat tightened. "It's kind of on autopilot now. You can spread the word so people do actually donate. It's been a little slow, but I think the weather hasn't helped. There are drop-offs at the commissary, PX, and chapel."

"I love it. You're just the most aggressively generous person I've ever met, and I'm in awe." Bec's compliments never fell flat, and this one was no different.

I wasn't sure I liked the idea of being *aggressively generous*, but I understood it. In fact, the phrase did sound like me, and frankly, how I wanted to be viewed. I didn't want to be subtly generous or lackadaisically generous. What was the point of serving people if it was *easy?*

"To our amazing Summer. Generous to a fault, and the best chef I've ever had the pleasure of knowing." Emily raised her glass and winked at me before we all clinked.

A mix of joy at her calling me *our amazing Summer,* and discomfort for all the attention on this part of my life, swirled around in my mind. Or could be that was the wine. I needed to eat something and steady myself. Then maybe I wouldn't feel this odd... guilt, for lack of a better term. I loved these women, but something about the conversation left me feeling unsettled, even as we moved on and everyone pestered Katie about how she liked her master's program.

By the end of the night, I'd eaten everything on every plate served to me, laughed until I cried, and teared up more than once. We all took the same train back, doing our best not to be the raucous Americans. When we parted and I got in my car, the sudden muted quality to the air came as a jolt to my senses. I breathed slowly, feeling my way through the odd sensation—full, happy, sad, heartened, lonely.

Why did I feel lonely after all of that delight and fun? I didn't like ending an evening like this in such a pit of self-pity. I didn't want it, and it had no business, no space, in this night. I jammed the ignition button on the car, then briefly petted the poor thing in apology because I did push it too hard, probably. I drove home carefully, wondering how late Nick had worked, if he was still awake, if he was angry with me for not wanting his charity with my ticket.

When I saw the tell-tale envelope, my heart leapt. I would've liked to have been less desperate for something from him, but the frustration from our conversation earlier today lingered, and this cloying, crushing sense of loneliness had me needy for it. All in all, pretty pathetic, but maybe he was to blame since he'd trained me to have a Pavlovian heart-leap every time I saw he'd penned me a letter.

Imagine my surprise when nothing inside spoke to me like he usually did. It was formal and stale. It felt distanced. Purely apologetic and courteous. I tossed it onto the kitchen table but plugged in his number since I would take him up on the ride to the airport. No need for me to leave my car parked outside for four days if I didn't have to.

~

Knowing I would be gone for a long weekend and taking two days off work wouldn't normally stress me out. But doing so with Nick, whom I hadn't seen or spoken to since our discussion about the ticket? Yeah, that was getting to me. I felt clumsy and off. I'd texted to tell him I'd gotten the note and that, yes, I'd like a ride to the airport if he still felt comfortable with it. I did caveat because his entire letter had felt like a giant *yeah we kissed but now I'm putting you firmly back in your place* notice.

He sent back *"See you Friday at 09:00."* Well. How typically verbose.

Irritation climbed up my neck—the same feeling I got when I broke a fried egg too soon. Not horrible, but definitely more irritated than I should've been for something small. Just fry another egg, Summer! Just move on from the text, woman!

I'd promised myself I'd tell Ariel about everything with him on Tuesday when we had dinner, but that afternoon, she'd regretfully canceled. Livie still wasn't feeling better, and actually considered going to the hospital. Ariel wanted to stay with her mom, who'd just arrived from the US, and the kids to help out. I honestly didn't understand how they could all stand living together in one house, but I did love how important family was to her.

I couldn't relate. I'd walked away from my family—at least that was how they said it. Leaving the state by going into the Army after college had sealed the fate of my relationship with my siblings and parents—they wouldn't speak to me for years, and so I didn't speak to them. I still called at Christmas and on birthdays. Every once in a while, one of them would answer the ancient house phone line and give me a clipped response, but most times no one picked up.

But something changed after Jenny got married, and I'd been invited home for a Fourth of July barbecue. That was the second of two visits in my twenties before I moved to Germany. Strangely, I'd hoped maybe the occasion of a holiday, and belatedly celebrating Jenny's marriage, might make it all better. It was filled with reminders of why I'd been encouraged by my therapists over the years to put in sturdy boundaries. I had, but I'd always felt like maybe *this* time, they'd be proud of me. They'd see how I worked so hard and advanced myself, paid back anyone I owed, and did well. After the second visit turned out so much like the first —and a stockpot worth of heartache—I gave that up and never really looked back. I started reveling in things that went starkly against their grain—like my big dinner parties and nice cars.

The idea of wanting to stay connected to basically anyone other than Jenny was pretty much unfathomable. She and I texted every few weeks to check in, but otherwise, we all just lived our own lives.

I didn't hate that. I just... didn't like it either. And seeing Ariel being so close to her family made me see how lovely an adult relationship might be with parents or siblings. At the same time, I had no desire to go back home. Fortunately, I didn't have to, and I was about to make life here even better with this new job.

But Ariel canceling wasn't the worst happening of the week, though I did really regret that I couldn't spend time with her. The thing that made me spitting mad was happening upon Dennin after he'd torn down my flyers for the food and boot drive.

The best space for advertising where people would pay

attention was at the community post office, and I walked through the doors to check the donation box just as he was exiting, hand full of both the flyers I'd posted. They were bright, fluorescent green, and sure enough, missing from each board when I went to check.

He slammed into my shoulder on the way out, hard enough that the soldier behind me steadied me. "You okay, ma'am?"

"I'm fine," I said, rubbing where he'd run into me.

Apparently, my lack of romantic interest in him made me the enemy or some nonsense? I hadn't spoken to him since he'd come to my house, and I'd only seen him at a distance. We didn't typically work together, and I thanked God for that.

He hadn't acknowledged me in any way other than the shoulder-check. I didn't know whether to be relieved he hadn't said something or even angrier because of it. In the end, I could post more flyers. No problem. But did this mean he was going around pulling them all down? How did he even know it was my project, and who wants to stop people from donating to a canned food drive?

If I hadn't already felt beaten down by the week and just *done*, I would've reacted more. As it was, once I got my mail and made it back to the safety of my car, I didn't rage or cry or feel scared like I might've. The countdown clock ticked away toward morning when I'd see Nick, and the closer I got, the more anxious and focused on that event my mind became. Dennin's childish destruction and running into me couldn't hold my attention.

By the time morning came, I'd slept very little. I'd reread all of Nick's letters because I liked to torture myself, especially since that last one seemed so very different. The one just before it had felt like a beginning, a door opening. This latest one read like an ending.

Letter aside, I was ready to help Nick and his team. I could do my job, and hopefully see a bit of London since I'd only ever been for a short trip early in my time in Europe. And I wouldn't obsess over the quiet man who now held me away from him when all I wanted was to get close.

CHAPTER SEVENTEEN

Nick

If I say you are perfect, will you know I mean it? Will you understand your perfection means nothing like flawless and everything like flawed and messed up and scarred and so damn beautiful I can't breathe when I think of you?

London greeted us like an angry cat, hissing and spitting and gray.

Funnily enough, it seemed to both mimic my mood and Summer's.

The ride to the airport had been silent. We exchanged half-hearted hellos when I knocked on her door and took her suitcase—much to her chagrin, and yet she didn't say a word—and that was it.

She chatted with Rob, Art, and Alicia here and there as

we all waited for our flight, but it was as if she'd muted me. True, I didn't speak much, but I'd commented once or twice and she gave me nothing. No acknowledgement.

I could tell I was being punished, but I didn't quite know why. Maybe she was still angry about the argument, though when I'd gotten her text saying she did want to ride with me to the airport, I'd foolishly taken that as a good sign.

I'd have to address it at some point, and soon. Normally, I'd avoid something like this, leaving the person to stew and me to not engage with whatever was going on there. But ignoring the tension between us, and absolutely not the good kind, wasn't an option. I wanted to enjoy having her here, and for us to have time together. There were breaks in the schedule. I'd figured out some things for us to do, if she was up for it, but I couldn't very well go from barely speaking to *Hey, let's go out for a gourmet meal, my treat.*

I corralled everyone before they dispersed into rooms. "Grab a room and settle in. We've got registration at the convention center in two hours, and I've got a meal coming for us at six."

Everyone took their bags and found a room. The rented apartment had five bedrooms, two bathrooms, a small living room and dining room, a decent kitchen for Europe, and no frills. It didn't have the charm of a typical vacation rental, and I suspected it was used for events at the convention center rather than hosting tourists. But what it lacked in charm, it made up for in separate bedrooms, more than one bathroom, and proximity to the hall.

I hadn't traveled much at all, and when I did, I tended to stay in hotels. But I could count on one hand the number of trips I'd taken anywhere but back home. Anytime I had block leave, I went back to see Gran—or I had. Spring break would be the first extended leave since she'd passed at Christmas.

So easily, grief slipped in, coating me in a thick, aching sadness. I cleared my throat like that might help.

My stomach dropped when Summer's eyes met mine, but hers flicked away before I could do anything. Not sure what I would've done, but it was the first time she'd made eye contact since this morning. Of course my stupid gut would take it personally. At least it'd momentarily distracted me from heavier thoughts.

She padded down the hall in jeans, a shirt, a warm jacket unzipped, and sneakers. Her long blond hair disappeared into the collar. That detail had caught my attention, gripped it relentlessly, because all I wanted to do was gently pull it out, let it hang free and run my fingers through. *What an idiot.*

I followed in her direction since the others had gone down the opposite hallway. Two rooms sat on one side of the living room, and the other three were down the far hall. So I'd be close to Summer.

I blew out a silent, annoyed breath. I had to get this hopeless feeling gone or I'd endanger everyone this weekend. I needed focus. But I had to clear the air with her. She ducked into the first room, so I took the one at the end, the bathroom situated between us. I'd give her a few minutes before making an attempt to navigate this weird dynamic between us.

I puttered around in my room, setting out my clothes for later and tomorrow, arranging my toiletry bag so it would be ready to grab for the bathroom, placing a book, journal, and pen on the nightstand. The bed looked comfortable and clean, so in the end, that, working bathrooms, and a decent kitchen were all we needed.

After reviewing the schedule, all the plans, the documentation we needed, and anything else I could think of, I knocked on Summer's door.

"Come in," her voice said from behind the panel.

My heart skittered as I turned the knob and found her crouched low over her suitcase where it sat open on the floor. *Good hip mobility.* I slapped the thought away, rolling my eyes at the observation. Hard to take the coach hat off, especially on a weekend like this.

I stood for a beat without her acknowledgement before she glanced over, a brow raised to prompt me to speak.

"Hi."

"Hi."

Screeching, horrible, record-scratching silence stretched between us. For a big city, the place had almost zero ambient noise—that, or all sound had been pulled from the air between us, nothing but awkward, repulsive distance filling the space.

But I had no idea what to say. I should've been thinking about *that* this entire time, but between worried glances at her, I'd been trying to focus on the weekend. And that was why we'd come, so I couldn't fault myself too heavily there. Except for now, standing in front of her, wishing I had words to speak to her instead of feeling a tightening in my gut that told me I wanted to close the door to my room and sit down to write this down rather than be forced to stand here and muddle through them in real time.

"I—I'm glad you're here. That you came. Thank you."

Her lashes fluttered. I'd surprised her. *Huh.*

"I am too."

Those three words helped. A lot. Because even if they didn't convince me she actually wanted to be here, she could've said anything else. But she chose that. So maybe she was trying to figure out what the hell had happened in the last week to make this so strained too.

"We'll, uh, all go over together. You need to come to this to get your badge and so they see your credentials."

She nodded. "I figured."

"If you need anything, let me know. Not that you will. I know you're incredibly self-sufficient and no doubt prepared, I just... you know. Let me know."

Oh, why? Why had I let this fool mouth run?

"Okay. Will do."

She shifted something in her suitcase, then glanced back, likely waiting for me to say something else or leave. But I couldn't bring myself to do either.

Summer, not being shy or one to mince words, spoke into the awkward void. "Did you need something else?"

"No. Sorry. See you in a bit."

With that brilliant parting shot, I ducked out of her room, shut the door of mine, and fell face first into the bright white comforter.

"Bridger looks good. My money says he'll take it." Art shoved a large forkful of food into his mouth and chewed. He and Alicia had done a lot more competing than Rob, and they were both in the running to pick up some attention at this event.

"I'm starstruck. I would feel a little stupid, but I never expected some of these people to be at this event." Rob had a dreamy look on his face and had since we'd walked into the convention center. Some of the biggest names in FitCross had been standing around chatting—some had come to judge, some to compete, and some were there with sponsors. Most didn't travel just for fun, but this London event had draw.

"Bridger will take men's. Jonsdottir will take women's," Alicia put in.

Three of us nodded. Both guesses weren't really guesses. For this region, Jonsdottir was by far the top female competitor.

Across from me, Summer ate quietly, a faraway expression pulling her brows together just slightly. We hadn't spoken again, but she'd been close by all afternoon as we toured the center, saw where everyone would compete tomorrow, and signed in. We were a small, relatively unknown team, but since Art and Alicia had gained traction, we'd garnered some attention.

I'd never been good at the glad-handing as a competitor. I could do it for my people, but not so much for myself.

"What's going on in that head, Summer? You look like you've got some deep thoughts happening."

Rob's question snapped her out of whatever trance she'd entered. "Oh, sorry. I'm super tired. But..."

"But?" Rob nudged.

She smiled then, something sweet and pleased that hit me low in the belly.

"This is going to sound terrible, but I was thinking about how I was probably the least fit person in that entire building today. It was an interesting experience." She scooped up some food and took a bite.

"What? Nah. Plus I can genuinely say that only the idiots are scoping people out that way."

Art's cheery reassurance was kind, but he was wrong. Everyone evaluated everyone else's fitness at all times. It was one reason I prioritized being as fit as possible myself, even though I wasn't competing. It reflected better on my team if I looked the part.

"I don't mean it in a *poor me* way at all. I'm happy with what I look like and—"

"You should be."

The words punched out of me, unbidden. But I couldn't have held them back for a thousand dollars. I didn't think of her as someone who'd have low self-esteem or be self-conscious, but being in a room full of people who worked out like it was their job—*because it was*—could do things to people that they didn't anticipate. I hadn't even thought about that side of it because, well, I couldn't imagine anyone seeing her as anything less than exquisite.

Her lashes fluttered and she pressed her lips together.

"I am." Her eyes flicked up to me, and she gave me a warm look that made my cheeks heat. "I just mean, it was interesting to be aware of. Not self-conscious in a bad way, but in an *I'm noticing this* kind of way."

Rob piped up. "I get that, for sure. It's overwhelming. The smaller events are full of normal people, but this is intense. I've watched enough of them online that I knew what to expect, but still. I'm definitely second-guessing—"

"No. No more of this. What do we talk about?"

This kind of thinking could get under an athlete's skin fast, especially someone new like Rob. He was here as an amateur, and his military ambitions would ensure he didn't go far, but in typical Rob fashion, he'd wanted to push himself to get to the competition, and here he was.

Rob gave a chagrined smile. "No comparing. Do your own workout, do your own work."

I nodded.

"Don't forget *I can't do this workout for you.* That one always really motivates me."

Alicia gave me a playfully annoyed look, and I shook my head. One of the first times she'd worked out with me, I'd said that, and I could tell it had irritated her. Of course she didn't want me to do the workout for her—the woman was a beast. She had a drive no one I'd ever trained or trained with had, and I couldn't respect her more. But she'd showed her hand with that one, so I used it when needed.

Out of the corner of my eye, Summer stifled a laugh.

"Ah, yeah. That's a good one because it's stupid obvious and also doesn't really make sense. But it's okay, Coach—we still love you. Someday, you'll have a whole packed gym full of adoring little workout nerds, and we can say we were your first." Art patted my shoulder before helping himself to another large serving of the hearty salad that came with dinner.

"Yeah, where do you want to retire, Masters? Where do I need to haul my old, decrepit body to workout with you once I leave Uncle Sam?" Rob asked like he didn't know, and I wondered if it was for Summer's sake.

"Back home. I hit twenty and I'm done. Coming right up."

Man, was it. Not soon enough, and yet terrifyingly soon. I couldn't say whether the feeling I got when I thought about life after the Army was an even mix of antici- pation and dread, or just dread highlighted by inevitability. Whatever the case, thus far LTC Wolfe and Sergeant Major Allen's efforts to get me to stay in had been futile.

"You're old enough to retire?"

Summer's voice drew my attention back to where she sat across from me.

I nodded. "Just about."

"Huh."

That was all she said, as though that wouldn't haunt me all night. What did that mean?

Alicia snickered. "Surprising, right?"

Summer's eyes cut to her. "Yes."

"I thought the same thing."

"What's this? What are you saying?" Art demanded.

I thanked God for his pushy insistence on clarity in that moment, because I certainly couldn't ask.

Alicia finished chewing, and Summer kept her eyes on her plate, sliding around the few last items left. Finally, Alicia spoke.

"You just don't look old enough to be ready to retire, is all, Coach. Don't stress it."

"It's your pretty face, Masters. It's just aging too well to tell your secrets." Rob gave me a giant grin.

I blinked slowly back at him. I may not have looked thirty-seven, though I thought I looked right about that and was perfectly happy for that to be the case because I *was* thirty-seven. I'd joined the Army right after finishing high school. When you enlist at eighteen, sure enough, twenty years fly by and you hit retirement age at thirty-eight.

"I've got to go start my sleep prep or I'll be a zombie. I'll see you guys bright and early." Art stacked his dishes and got to work on them in the sink.

No dishwasher, but we'd make do. Art and Alicia both had very specific evening routines, and all the more the night before competing. Rob's was less specific, but all three of them needed to get to bed in the next few hours.

"I'll take care of the dishes. You guys go do your thing. See you at seven." I waved them off and took a load into the kitchen. Rob and Alicia wandered away with *good nights* and Art let me take over his scrubbing after my reassurance that I didn't mind.

I didn't. The energy a competition day like tomorrow took was exponentially more than what a normal day of working out at home did. The adrenaline hit the moment you woke up if you weren't careful, and it wouldn't flag until long after the events had ended. The biggest challenge would be day two, but in the meantime, we could get them all set up for a good day one.

Summer moved quietly into the kitchen and set down a pile of containers. She silently placed lids on the few that still held food and put them in the fridge. When she came to stand next to me and held out a hand for the sudsy plate I'd just scrubbed, I had to speak up.

"You too, Summer. You go relax. I've got this."

"I can help you."

"Of course you *can*. But I've got it tonight."

Her lips flattened. "It'll be done so much faster if you let me help."

I raised a brow, the irony of her pressing me to let her help clean up glaring between us.

She made a regretful sound. "I know. I get it. But I let you help, so you can let me."

We stared at each other for another moment, and though all hadn't returned to how things were before, this back and forth felt a little more familiar. It should've set me at ease, but instead, I found my pulse ticking up to race. I blinked away from the trance she'd set me in and focused on the task. I wanted rest tonight too.

We worked without speaking, and in less than ten minutes, we'd washed all the dishes, wiped the counters, and I'd checked the food we'd take with us tomorrow. And then we were walking down the hallway to our rooms. Words collided in my throat but wouldn't come out. I made an odd, mangled sound.

She turned to me, worry creasing her brow. What an idiot—rather than speaking to her, I'd loosed a garbled, pained sound, and she probably thought I was dying.

I cleared my throat.

"Sorry. I just..." Nerves crawled around my belly, making me mildly nauseated. "I wanted to say you shouldn't worry about... your fitness. You know. Like you were saying earlier."

"Oh. Okay. I'm not *worried*, I'm just—"

"You're perfect.

Her mouth hung open, her shock evident. I could understand. I felt the same way—I hadn't planned on saying that aloud.

"I—I mean you shouldn't think anything about yourself except kind thoughts. It's too easy to get wrapped up in appearances at these things. I'm sorry I didn't mention it sooner."

The dim hallway light hid the full color of her face, but her cheeks looked darker. I'd embarrassed her. *Perfect*.

"I'll let you get to bed. See you in the morning."

And with that, I ducked into my room, cursing my stupid mouth for shooting off in the moment. *This* was why I didn't speak much. This was why I wrote letters when it mattered. As was my habit, I sat down to journal and prayed I wouldn't find Summer standing outside in the hallway come morning, still stunned in place.

CHAPTER EIGHTEEN

Summer

Nick Masters had to be the most confusing person I'd ever met. I got a letter from him last Saturday essentially saying *Let's keep things between us about business* and then... *what?!* He came to check on me when I was unpacking—nice. Then, seeing him at dinner interacting with his team created all kinds of new awareness. He encouraged them, knew them well enough to know what each of them needed. He'd shooed them off to bed and done the cleanup himself. If I'd ever felt a kinship with someone, it was in that moment.

Nick Masters was a helper. Perhaps that should've been obvious since he was both a soldier and a coach, but neither of those things explicitly meant a person had that helping gene. But Nick did. He did it in an unassuming, quiet way, but he evidently did it well. And Art, Alicia, and Rob clearly loved him. Everyone else I'd talked to who worked out with him thought the world of him, even if it was paired with a kind of dread-fueled awe, knowing whatever workout he'd foist on them would be brutal. But that was the job of a fitness coach.

I swiped on mascara, then inspected myself. I'd rested well, which surprised me. I'd expected to obsess about his comments the whole night—our entire odd history of interactions, really. But instead, I'd passed out. Today, I looked and felt a little more like the Summer I expected myself to be—eager for the day, ready to help the team, excited to see the competition. I hadn't actually thought through what the events would be like, but I had a basic understanding, being vaguely familiar with the sport.

And if Nick's voice saying *"You're perfect"* happened to float around my head the rest of the day, I wouldn't be mad. Because that had been one of the sweetest things anyone had said to me. Not so much because he was saying I was physically perfect—I knew he didn't mean I was *actually* perfect. But in the moment, it emerged from him like he couldn't *not* say it, like it was a biological imperative the words be spoken to me. What he meant was that I'm perfect as I am, that I shouldn't compare, and while I hadn't really been doing that, his need to tell me made my heart ache.

I didn't know what any of that meant, but I felt less wary. Thank goodness, because I'd be standing with him all day, watching him encourage his people. It would've been painful if things had continued like they'd started yesterday.

I stepped out my door and heard bustling in the front room. I arrived to see bags piled next to the door and Rob nodding while Art spoke. Alicia swiped at her phone while she sipped something steaming from a mug, and then Nick walked in, plate full of food in hand. Our eyes met, and my stomach flipped. He gave me a small smile, and I returned it with one of my own.

Yes, good that things had relaxed a bit, even if that meant I'd spend the day with heart palpitations every time he so much as glanced in my direction.

Nick ducked his head and looked Alicia in the eyes. "You come out even—not too strong. Just like we practice. This is yours."

Alicia nodded, touched her fists to his, then jogged to the starting area. The event, like so many I'd seen today, seemed absolutely grueling in a way that didn't appeal to me in the least. I liked exercise and I stayed fit, but holy crap. Alicia was about to do a series of pull-ups, then dead lifts with increasing weight, and finally, a twenty-meter handstand walk. *Yeah.* Handstand walk.

Each event that came clarified for me that Alicia and Art were exceptional. They'd both placed in the top five of each event, and both had won at least once so far too. Rob had done surprisingly well according to Nick, placing in the top ten for most of his.

I couldn't pretend that I wasn't fascinated by it all—it was incredible to watch. But my favorite part? Watching Nick. I tried to be inconspicuous, but it was a sight to behold. The full force of his concentration centered on his competitors. So far, the events had been staggered so he hadn't missed anything, and of course that made my job easier too. Granted, I hadn't had to do much other than wrap a callous that got ripped open, but still.

The best part of the process came at the end, when whoever competed had completed their work. He didn't say much during the event itself, but when the end came, he always nodded, made notes in a little book he carried, and then patted his people on the back in approval. My favorite was when they did something amazing, which to me seemed like every time, but so far had been exactly four times—Art and Alicia's two first-place wins, Rob's first event completion, and Alicia's hitting a PR, a personal record. He'd clapped, whistled, and joined the general mayhem that happened at the culmination of events—and he'd smiled. Like, full-out, gorgeous teeth, perfect happiness on that serious face. It. Was. Magical, y'all.

You know that feeling when you bake a cake from scratch and the middle doesn't sag once it cools? That smile was better than that. I felt like a triumphant cake-baking fool after every event.

I couldn't explain away the stomach flip, either. I liked him. I did. I certainly didn't understand him, nor what he wanted from or with me, but my oh my, was he pretty to look at. And spending the day watching him be so darn capable and proficient didn't hurt. Capability, self-sufficiency, and excellence were a covert turn-on, and Nick Masters had all his *see what I can do* cards out today.

Alicia moved through the current event like a machine. Art, Rob, and I cheered wildly when she reached the handstand walk. Nick watched with so much concentration, I wondered if he might be casting a spell. When she crossed the line first, we all jumped—even Nick—because this put her in the lead. We jumped around, Art, Rob, and I hugging each other and then Alicia when she made it over. Nick cupped the back of her neck and patted her once, then released her and loosed that smile on us.

My heart fluttered in my chest, the sight too beautiful to ignore. He turned it to me, and I could've sworn that smile broadened a bit further. When a man like that smiled like so, it was a sight to behold. It was rare and precious, and it made me feel a little weak.

Breathe. Breathe, you idiot. You can't lose it right now.

"Time for you to go," he said, still beaming.

It took a moment to absorb what he said. "What?"

"It's time for you to go. There's a cab outside for you."

He said this like I should understand what he meant.

"There's still one more event. Why would I—"

"You're covered."

Rob piped in. "A friend of mine is covering down for the last one. It's just me, and I'm unlikely to place in this one. I'm too freaking tall to compete with these shorties on some things, and this is one."

That, I believed. Lengthen the levers of your body and almost all things became harder—pull ups, most lifting, etc. The only real advantage could be endurance, but even then, you had a larger body with more resistance to drag around. Most of the men were closer to Art's height at five foot nine or shorter. Rob's six-two was a downright disadvantage. Good thing he wasn't trying to make a career of it.

"And where am I going?" I asked, not doing much to mask the upset. Where were they sending me off to?

"Trust me," Nick said, eyes boring into me.

I blinked and bought time by taking a sip of water from my bottle. Did I trust him? I guessed I did, at least on some level. I had no reason to suspect he'd do anything to harm me, and the fact that the others seemed to know what this was and were excited for me to go do it... *okay then*. I could play along. I could pretend like an unplanned thing on my to-do list that I didn't see coming was completely fine and I welcomed the adventure. *Suuure.*

"Okay."

He nodded and gave me a card with an address on it. "Cabbie knows where you're going, but just in case. Call me if you have any problems, and see you in a few hours."

Someone shoved my purse in my hands, and then off I went, walking through the halls, down the stairs, out the exit to find the black cab waiting.

"Applegate?"

I nodded, and he opened the door for me, then jogged around to his seat. I got the impression he didn't normally exit the vehicle, but the sun was out, and maybe he'd been waiting for a while. Inside, he confirmed the address Nick had provided and then pulled onto the road.

I didn't know quite what to feel as the streets slipped by. I'd visited London before and done most of the must-do touristy things—saw the landmarks, visited the Abbey, took a tour of the Tower of London, saw the changing of the guards at the palace. I liked getting those classics out of the way in favor of the less obvious things, and tomorrow after-noon, we'd have a little time for that.

For that matter, I'd planned on some sightseeing this evening, maybe in conjunction with a dinner out, but who knew where this little journey would take me, or for how long.

Twenty minutes after leaving the event center, we pulled up alongside a nondescript-looking building to a side door. Good thing I trusted Nick, because otherwise, I might suspect I was about to get murdered here in the warehouse district of London.

I exited the cab, thanked the man, and was just about to knock on the only door in sight when it swung open. "Ms. Applegate?"

My eyes widened and my confirmation stuck in my

throat. I nodded instead so I wouldn't seem like a total dunce.

"Great to meet you. I'm Paul. Come join us. We're just getting started."

Still unable to speak, I nodded again and followed, total confusion and glee and starstruck wonder bursting in my belly. I, like so many, loved a certain British baking show, and here was one of the famed judges. I'd just shaken his hand… the hands that'd shaped a thousand beautiful bread loaves. And *wow*, he was handsome on TV, but in person, he looked even more like a silver fox. And yep, there were those glacial blues. Whoa.

What the heck is happening?I

I followed behind the man, still struggling to comprehend what was going on. Through a hallway, we entered a large room that looked very much like the set of the show itself. Twelve butcher-block covered work stations outfitted with KitchenAid mixers and crocks of utensils sat waiting, each occupied except one at the front right of the room. My spot.

A bolt of pure excitement shot through me.

"I'm sorry I'm a little late. My friends signed me up for this, and I didn't know about it until you opened the door." If I sounded a little breathless, I couldn't be blamed. The man was a legend, a TV star now, and I was about to take a class from him.

"Not at all. Find your spot, and we'll get on with it." He gestured to the empty station, and I quickly took my place.

He centered himself at the front of the space and clapped his hands together. "So, everyone ready?"

Heck yes, we are! I stopped short of cheering, but the glee had to have been showing on my face. I knew I was beaming, just like everyone else there. And while the bulk of that joy came from being here and having this opportunity, there was one more source. I'd felt it bubbling up with the curiosity and excitement from the moment he'd sent me out to the car. And now, he'd clinched it.

Nick had set this up for me. *He knows me.*

Truly reveling in that reality right now would take away from the incredible experience, so I wouldn't. But tonight— tonight, I would let myself simmer in the reality that a man I only barely knew had done something like this for me. A man whom I wanted to know me even more, and who I hoped would, very soon.

CHAPTER NINETEEN

Nick

I would give you stardust. Say the word, it is yours. The incandescent beauty of you both will outshine all the darkest places.

The rest of the day went smoothly. Rob's last event was brutal, but we'd anticipated that. His spirits were high, and I had to give him credit for that. He'd been able to keep the sense of wonder and excitement of just being there rather than expecting himself to perform beyond what he'd trained for. He was new, and his ambitions weren't ultimately for competition. I admired his tenacity and his willingness to compete even when he had far less experience than many of his fellow competitors.

Art and Alicia had both killed their days. Art held

second place overall, and Alicia led the women. They were both incredible, especially considering quite a few of the top athletes here were already sponsored and working out a lot more than they were.

All that said, I didn't have quite as much fun once Summer left for her class. I'd done my best not to let my mind wander to her and wonder what she thought of it. Maybe it was too obvious? Too commercial or basic? Maybe she'd be upset I hadn't talked to her about it so she could choose how to spend her time.

Rather than dwelling on those concerns, I stayed mentally in the competition. But by four, three hours after she'd left, I couldn't ignore the nervous energy. The events were done and my people were ready to recover back at our temporary home.

Once I got them settled, I went for a workout in the building's gym. It'd been expanded and well stocked thanks to the competition being nearby, so I was able to push myself and therefore banish thoughts of Summer's eyes, lips, voice, hands... *everything* from my mind for a bit.

By six, I'd showered, changed, and would've helped with dinner but Art and Alicia refused. In the past, we'd traded off who cooked, and since I'd ordered last night's meal, I guessed they counted that as me cooking. Not quite fair, but if they didn't want me hovering, I couldn't blame them.

At six twenty-three, Summer walked in. Just the jiggle of keys at the apartment door made my heart start sprinting because everyone else was already inside. But rather than jump up and look like a puppy whose owner had returned from work, I stayed put on the couch, book in hand, feet up on the ottoman. So relaxed and chill, I impressed even myself.

"She's back! Our star baker has arrived," Rob said, greeting Summer with a big hug.

I was knotted up enough that I didn't even feel ashamed of the whisper of jealousy that slipped through me. I wanted to hug her. Sure, fine, let Rob hug her too because they were friends, but I wanted that as well. Enough it made my stomach clench and my throat burn until I doused it with a drink of water.

Alicia and Art cheered and peeked their heads out of the kitchen, clearly both midstep in their dinner prep. "How was it?"

Summer smiled at them, a dreamy, sated look on her face. And that—*that* made my stomach drop.

"So good."

Her voice, too. It emerged breathy and sweet.

Then her gaze found mine. Try as I might to seem anything short of completely rapt, I'd set aside the book and turned to face her, to study every gesture and breath. The electric shock that came in that glance, the pure happiness, shook something loose in me.

"Did you bring anything home?" Rob asked hopefully.

She smiled brighter, somehow, and produced a bulky canvas bag I hadn't noticed.

Rob grabbed it and peered in, then clutched it to him. "This is all mine. Art and Alicia won't eat this anyway."

"Neither will you—not until after tomorrow." I couldn't suppress the coach in me, not even in this moment. The last thing any of them needed was a bunch of bread and pastries right before they tried to sleep.

"Don't worry. I have recipes and techniques I'll be practicing. I'll need to give away some of it or I'll die in a carb coma on my kitchen floor."

"What did you make? Tell me everything and I will mentally consume it all for now." Rob shot me a dirty look.

Summer rose to her tiptoes to speak, her excitement bursting from every pore. "We covered so much ground in six hours, it's not even funny. We made... oh man, bread—like four different kinds of bread. We did cookies. Of course we did a Victoria sponge, an Italian sponge, and meringue. We did some chocolate work and made caramel, which I've never done. And... gosh, I know I'm forgetting so much already. I have a whole booklet of recipes, thankfully."

"Okay, yes. Sinking into a baked-good-and-sweets coma now." Rob pretended to faint.

She laughed, and Rob said something, but I didn't hear. My mind had narrowed the entire apartment to her.

Then I realized I was probably staring like a weirdo and turned back around. I didn't want to crowd her or pressure her, but every ounce of me willed her to come talk to me. *Come tell me how it was. Did it make you happy?*

Instead of asking, I picked up the book I'd been staring at and continued the good work.

"That was a very mean trick, Nick Masters."

Her voice arrived before she did, then the cushion next to me slumped as she sat down. Close, but not touching me.

"Mean trick?" I asked, gobbling up the sight of her so near. She'd pulled her hair back into a ponytail, and little wisps of hair haloed her face. Her eyes were bright, her cheeks pink, and her lips eminently kissable.

She smiled, and her eyes flicked back and forth between mine. If I hadn't become familiar with the feeling, I might've worried that the tightness in my chest was due to a medical condition. No, just Summer. Just looking at her made me feel empty and overfull all at once.

"I had no idea what I was walking into until a very

famous man greeted me at the door and led me into a warehouse outfitted just like the set of a certain British baking program. I cannot believe you didn't tell me ahead of time." Her words sounded frustrated, but she hadn't stopped beaming at me.

"A good surprise? Not too..." I couldn't pin down the right word.

"Not too what?"

"I don't know. Mainstream or something? Like, you watch the show?" I asked like I hadn't gathered solid evidence at her house the times I'd wandered her living room and skimmed the wall of cookbooks.

She attempted to stifle that blazing smile, but I knew it lurked behind the more serious face she'd put on.

"I think you know very well I do. I'm guessing you saw my cookbook collection and knew exactly how much I'd enjoy a class like that." She blinked a few times, then hit me with a knowing look.

Even her eyebrows were pretty. I'd never really thought about someone else's eyebrows, but hers... they were just right. A few shades darker than her blond hair and arched in a clean, smooth curve that tapered off at the edges. I quite desperately wanted to place a kiss at the corner of each.

"It was an educated guess."

Her smile returned, and she set a hand on my arm. Her skin was cool from being outside. She hadn't even taken her jacket off yet.

"Thank you. It was a wonderful surprise and an amazing experience. I don't know how I'll ever thank you enough."

I looked down at where she touched me. I hoped she wouldn't move away just yet. "You don't need to."

"How did you pull that off? I'm just—shocked. I

couldn't believe I was standing there in a room with him! How did you get that ticket? How can I make it up to you?"

I smiled at that. I'd hit the jackpot, and I knew it. "A buddy in charge of the competition this weekend has some friends in high places. Long story short, I got you that ticket. And you don't need to make it up to me. It's a thank you for being here, helping us out."

Her lashes fluttered. "It was a thank you from the team?"

I could tell her yes. I *could*. I'd never meant to outright admit otherwise, but now that she asked me point blank, I didn't want to lie to her. What a stupid thing to lie about.

"Uh, no. Just me." I may have mumbled it a bit.

She released a breath, and her fingers flexed lightly against my skin. "Nick."

The softness. The hint of a plea and surprise. My name coming from her, again. I wanted to close my eyes and remember the sound only slightly less than I wanted to take her face in my calloused hands and claim her mouth. My heart thundered—she had to hear it.

She leaned toward me. "What made you—"

Alicia interrupted her. "Are you ready for dinner? We'll dish it up if everyone's good to go."

Summer straightened, pulled her hand away, and swallowed. "Of course. It smells delicious."

Her eyes didn't leave mine.

"Great. Two minutes." The voice retreated and left us to the moment.

On the surface, the conversation seemed normal. A person thanking another person for a gift. But here, between us, it felt fraught with significance. I regretted my inexperience, the lack of knowledge about interacting with women gaping like an unfortunate chasm.

"I'm glad you liked it."

Those long lashes fluttered again. I smothered a smile, enjoying the small detail I'd become familiar with in our few meetings. She did this when flustered or when thinking. She did this when I said something she found irritating or nice. It was adorable.

"I did. I..." She sighed, then smiled a small, almost regretful little move. "I really did. Thank you."

Her eyes flickered over me then, and she stood. Another man might've reached out, stayed her, attempted to gather back the moment. It'd been a while since I'd wished to be a different kind of man, but the thought flashed through me.

"Dinnertime!" Art hollered from the kitchen, cutting through my pointless musings.

I stood, stretched my spine and rolled my shoulders, and walked into the kitchen to help dish up the meal. I didn't let my eyes trace over Summer and promised myself I wouldn't try to talk to her again. As much as I'd been anticipating seeing her, tonight I felt gummed up. I couldn't speak, could hardly think near her, and stood on the edge of expressing that simpleminded madness with lips and tongues in another language. Until I knew with certainty she'd welcome that, I needed to keep my distance.

Completely doable. Two more nights in a room across the hall. One more day standing next to her during the competition. Another half hour or so eating dinner across from her. Not a problem.

CHAPTER TWENTY

Summer

During the class, I'd blocked Nick from my mind. I'd promised myself I could think about his thoughtfulness after. So on the cab ride home, I'd inspected the gesture and come up with a clear answer. Though not dictated by the contract, signing me up for a baking class must've been part of the team's thank you to me. Delightful, but unnecessary.

Then he'd admitted it. Right there on the apartment couch. Like it wouldn't melt my insides completely to know the class was from him. Evidently completely. Maybe Rob had given him the idea, which I'd considered since he knew me best, and yet Nick had been in my house. He'd seen my shelves. And honestly? He'd seemed a little shy, almost embarrassed to admit the class hadn't been from the team.

Now that dinner was wrapping up, a delicious, simple

meal courtesy of Alicia and Art, I couldn't keep the restless, anxious feelings at bay. I needed to get Nick alone. I wanted to pin him down and make him speak to me—tell me what he thought of me. *Why* had he done something like that, and what did it mean? If I read into what I *thought* it meant, then it meant he... he... well, it meant he more than wanted me.

And the way my stomach dropped through the wood floor every time he spoke or looked at me, or I looked at him, well... *Yeah.* I more than wanted him, too.

By the time we'd cleared plates and wiped counters, washed dishes and covered leftovers, the apartment had fallen quiet. The athletes were clearly exhausted and already mentally gearing up for the next day. They said their goodnights and left me and Nick to the last few to-dos in the kitchen.

Though I kept my eyes studiously *off* of him, carefully polishing a glass I was drying, every bit of me tuned to him. The sound of an occasional deep breath. The strong and warm feeling of him only feet from me in the small space. Nerves twisted in my belly, and I shut my eyes against the crush of anticipation that rushed me as I carefully placed the last glass in the cabinet.

The force of his gaze hit me as soon as I turned to face him. My goodness, the man could convey a thousand words in a glance.

"Looks like we're finished here," I said, a little impressed that my voice sounded solid under the circumstances.

He only nodded and held out a hand like *after you.* I hung the towel I'd used on a small hook and moved to the doorway. Impulse drove the next action more than anything else. Once standing even with him at the entrance to the kitchen, I reached across him and flipped the light off. When I brought my hand back, it grazed lightly against his chest. It was all I could do to keep from flattening it there against him, but good girl that I was, I didn't.

The small catch of his breath made me meet his eyes. If my breathing hadn't already been shallow, seeing his blue gaze would've sent me there easily enough.

"Thanks for your help," he said, like I wouldn't have assisted with the cleanup.

"Of course."

He followed me out of the kitchen and down the hall-way. Each step closer to the doors of our rooms tipped the anxious, eager energy, the need to *do* something, higher. By the time we reached my room, I'd decided.

I turned to face him, and placed a hand on his arm. His eyes flitted over me, taking in every movement as I leaned up on my toes and pressed a kiss to his cheek. His clean, laundered scent made me want to stay right there and breathe against the smooth-shaven jaw, but I resisted that urge and returned to flat feet.

"I'm glad you liked the class." The gruff, low voice was quiet and almost... tender.

"I loved it."

The words hung there between us for seconds that felt like minutes, but then he moved. *We* moved, and as though we'd choreographed the motion, came together in an embrace so perfect, I'd never forget it.

His hand on my shoulder, the other one at the back of my head, my hands on his arm and the junction of his neck and shoulder, our lips met in a kiss both frantic and needful. This wasn't a sweet, gentle kiss exploring each other. This was kerosene on a slow-burning fire.

He devoured me, and I him, the delicious slide of his

tongue against mine something I'd never imagined could feel so utterly essential. His hands stayed put, gentleman that he was, and so somehow, I managed not to map the majesty of his chest and arms like I wanted.

A door opened somewhere in the apartment, and we broke apart at the sound. My breath came fast, and looking at him did nothing to calm it. Our eyes met, and my body became magma from the visual of him looking at me like that, let alone his lingering touch.

Instead of retreating, his hands moved—the one at my head slipped around to my neck and the other slid up the line of my shoulder. He cupped my face, stepped fully into the space we'd made moments ago, and took my mouth again.

This kiss felt different—no less heated, but the pace was a kind of circling hypnosis, slow and lulling rather than borderline crazed. My hands fisted in his shirt, and I could only think of him. *Nick.*

He pulled back, searching my eyes.

Oh. I'd said that aloud. "Sorry, I—you're just..."

A smile tugged at one corner of his mouth, and he released me. I reluctantly let go of his shirt.

"I'm just...?"

His eyes were bright as he waited, and my heart kicked. He looked happy and relaxed, and as always, heartbreakingly handsome. "You're just full of surprises."

He chuckled low. Just that rough, spare sound sent little bolts of lightning down my arms.

"That's funny?" I asked, my voice just above a whisper.

He shook his head, a ghost of a smile on his lips.

"Not funny. But I feel the same about you." His eyes narrowed, then relaxed. "Hang out with me tomorrow, before the kids are out celebrating."

I'd noticed he called Art, Alicia, and Rob *the kids*. He couldn't be that much older than them, but he had the coach vibe going on strong, so I didn't fault him for it.

"You don't think you'll want to go with them?"

Even as I said it, I internally cringed. I didn't want to sound anything but enthusiastic. Yes. *Yes.* I definitely wanted to do whatever he wanted.

"I will. We'll meet up with them. They'll have some stuff to do and they'll want to clean up and probably nap. We can go enjoy the city for a bit and then do the requisite toasting." He reached for my hand.

"That sounds good. Just tell me where to be and when, and I'm all yours." I said the words to be jaunty and fun, but spoken at a near-whisper in the darkened hallway, his calloused palm against mine, they seemed weighty.

"Good." He raised our linked hands between us and kissed the back of mine all while those blue eyes watched me.

Air left me in a rush.

"Yeah," I said dumbly, not even sure why I spoke.

"Sleep well."

I kept my mouth shut then, just nodding and reluctantly letting go of his warm hand so I could stumble through the door to my room and gather myself.

I heard his door shut seconds after I closed mine. I leaned against the wood and indulged in a moment to just breathe in the last few hours. He'd arranged for me to go to the class, taken care of every detail along the way, and then admitted it, albeit only after a little prodding.

And then, the kisses. I let out a full-on sigh. The man could kiss, and yes, I'd already known that, but still. First kisses were always kind of hectic—so much *new* that it didn't all sink in. Granted, I remembered every second of our first kiss, or I had until tonight.

Now, my mind had been flattened out and seared over the heat of our most recent interactions. And all I could think was how I looked forward to doing it again. I searched my mind and felt nothing but pleasure and a lingering sense of disbelief that the baking class had ever happened—no anger. No bitter frustration that now I had to pay him back. Now *that* was a revelation.

I didn't know what any of this meant, but Nick wasn't someone to play games. I needed to address the last letter he wrote, the weird business-like tone it'd taken, and how very *not* businesslike he'd just treated me. I didn't mind that, but I didn't want to wake up to another letter like the last one.

I did wake up to a letter. It wasn't like the last one. It said:

Dear Summer,

There is nothing about you I don't like. I know very little, though, so I'm anticipating our time together today. I hope we do it today and then again and again. Forgive me, because now that I've tasted a few minutes with you, I want to feast on your time. I want to collect your minutes and hours and hoard them, miserly and mean to everyone but you.

Fear not—my greedy tendencies will be held in check, if not by my larger sense of reality and that the world is more beautiful with you out in it, then also by the reality that we do have jobs to do today.

But please know, with every bit of me, I am ready for you.

Nick

~

After reading that, I had to take a moment. I'd honestly never thought about letters being some kind of sneak attack heart-battering foreplay, but *hello*. I wouldn't have imagined that because I didn't remember ever getting letters from men I dated. I might've had a note here or there, but mostly it was texts and the like. And that fell so far short from seeing handwriting scratched into paper, knowing the writer had held a pen and shaped each word *for me*.

Plus, he had a really nice way with words, to put it mildly. I liked his turns of phrase. I'd never been big into poetry or English or any of that, far preferring the sciences in school at all levels, but I could appreciate his style. He certainly painted vivid pictures, and there was always such a clear sense of *him* in the sentences—a bold, sweet version of him.

I didn't want to walk out into the living room and be weird. So I took a few breaths while looking out at the dawning London spring day and steeled myself. I could be around the man and not be obviously muddled. That was possible, and I would do it right now.

I marched out of my room, ready to greet everyone and offer to whip up some eggs or whatever they wanted, and stopped dead in my tracks. Any sense of cool composure I might've had drained away, right through my shoes, and my cheeks flamed with the rest of me. My stomach clenched, my jaw slackened, and my throat dried out. All the air in my lungs left me in a rush, and I made a sound, something endlessly delicate and normal, a little bit like, "*ughuh.*"

Nick sat on a chair just inside the door, head bowed slightly over his phone in one hand, his brow furrowed in study. His other hand tugged at the laces of one shoe, the other already off and sitting next to his opposite, socked foot.

Oh, and he was shirtless. He'd obviously just gotten back from a workout, and I couldn't help the physical response I had to him. Yes, I'd seen him before, imperious and bare-chested when he answered the door holding his fluffy white cat, but not since... not since he'd become *real* to me.

He must've heard my odd sound, because he shot to his feet. "Hey, sorry. Did I wake you?"

"N-No. No. No." *Oh, Lord, stop it.* I hadn't been this tongue-tied around him since that first time either. I didn't plan to start now just because he flashed his perfectly carved pecs and arms and abs and... *everything* at me.

"Do you need something?" he asked, taking a step closer, one foot in a shoe, one out.

"Uh." I laughed, just one elegant *ha*, then went on. "I wanted to be up early in case anyone wanted breakfast. I haven't cooked at all and thought I could help."

A smile lit his eyes. "That's nice of you. I'm sure they'd love it. They'll probably be out any minute. I was just checking the schedule."

He held up his phone.

"In your running shorts?"

Because that was the other thing. The shorts weren't quite what I'd heard people call *ranger panties*, which were super short, minimal running shorts. But they definitely showed off a great deal of his extremely muscular quads.

Like, the kind of quads that probably didn't even fit in jeans. Or, maybe now, in the modern world, they did, thanks to technology and super stretchy denim.

Are you seriously standing here thinking about the fiber content of jeans that would fit over his leg muscles? I shook my head to clear it.

He chuckled, and amazingly, flushed.

"I just finished working out. No one else was up and I overheated." He gestured to a pile of clothes that looked like a sweatshirt and T-shirt, clearly hastily tossed on the floor. "I'm sorry if I—"

"Don't be sorry. It's... I mean, I'm about to go spend the day staring at shirtless men and women in sports bras and boy shorts. That's—you're—it's fine." Mortification poured over me from head to toe.

He squinted then looked down at his toes.

"Okay." He glanced back up at me tentatively, a wry smile pulling at those perfect lips. "I'll go get cleaned up."

I nodded, then kicked myself into action. I did not need to watch him prowl toward me, muscles hanging over him like plates of steel under skin, and I did not need the temptation of watching him go.

A small part of me wondered if the disparity between us might be a problem. Like, could you enjoy grilled cheese made with white bread and a Kraft single paired with a fine red wine? I mean, I could. If the grilled cheese was made right. It was all in the way you toasted the bread—had to have butter to—oh, good grief. He'd addled my mind with his abs and his little grin.

I wasn't anywhere near *that* kind of fit. He'd said I was perfect, which was lovely, but would he really want to be with someone so comparatively... soft? Not to mention, I'd probably always be acutely aware of how beautiful he was. I had decent self-esteem and believed strongly that looks were only a part of the equation, but this man...

I shook that off, banishing the hazy, hot feeling that had arrived the moment I'd caught a glimpse of that bowed head and the broad caps of his shoulders.

Eggs. Omelets. *Food.* I'd feed everyone, and hopefully, the process would help me move past the devastation that was Nick Masters wearing nothing but shorts, socks, and a blush.

CHAPTER TWENTY-ONE

Nick

I have wanted few things in life, and all of them slipped through my hands. I will keep myself from wanting you so you'll last a little while.

Day two of competition went well. I couldn't say I was proud of myself, but the athletes performed at the top of their games. Alicia took first overall, Art came in third, and Rob managed to place in the top ten, which really was incredible considering his limited experience. But me? I'd been a distracted jerk and could hardly focus on the events right in front of me.

Actually, no. I hadn't been a jerk. I'd done my best. Really, I had. But standing next to her all day after the night we'd had... not a simple task. I'd never thought of myself as a person who needed physical touch. I'd lived alone for years, and my only surviving relative had lived half a world away for the last two years. Now she was gone. I'd grown used to existing in my own space, my own body, without anything else factoring in.

Now, I found my corporeal, solo existence unsatisfying. I'd felt her hands on me, if only for a few minutes. I'd tasted her lips and felt her breath. I only wanted more. Standing a foot from her without touching her smooth skin resulted in a feeling of such waste, it made my hands shake.

At the same time, I suspected all of that would be a bit much to admit to Summer. She liked me, yes. And she wanted to spend time together, so we would. But she had not been starved for affection and for someone to care for like I had. She had not lost the only person who offered such outlets for her like I had.

It didn't feel like too much of an exaggeration to say that when I was with her, I felt more alive. It was that feeling I hadn't realized I was missing until I'd felt it spark with her—life. Sensations and moments to store away in memory. Things I'd catalogue on paper so they'd survive, whether they evaporated into illness at the end or not.

And so my natural intensity paired with the loss of Gran could very well create an overwhelming situation I needed to keep under wraps. I'd hinted at it in writing, but in person it would be too much. I felt far more than physical attraction to Summer already, and it wouldn't be fair to expect her to return that level of feeling. Not yet.

Perhaps not ever. Realistically, what could I possibly offer her? I was as close to an island of a man as a person could be. I led a solitary existence so contrary to her social, generous one, it was laughable. I'd had the thought before but brushed it aside in favor of enjoying whatever came of our next encounter. And now, after leaving the event and traveling back to the shared apartment, after changing clothes and tamping down nerves, I would do the same. I wouldn't think of the myriad of things I wanted from Summer or for how long I wanted them. I would think only of this afternoon. I would do something I rarely successfully did—I would enjoy the moment.

"Ready to go?"

Her cheery voice and a double knock on the open door to my room made me turn.

My stomach flipped when she met my gaze and smiled, genuine happiness beaming off of her. That. *That* drew me in, every time. She could be stubborn and even pushy, but she had this light, this golden beauty that lit up the space around her. I'd never been her patient at the clinic, but I could only imagine how soothing and delightful being treated by her felt. Watching her bandage one of Rob's callouses earlier today had told me enough about her surety and gentleness in such moments.

"Yes." I grabbed my jacket and patted my pocket to confirm I'd remembered my wallet. "You up for walking?"

"Sure. No rain today, which seems miraculous."

She walked next to me down the hallway. The three athletes were either sleeping or resting, so we exited quickly and quietly. We'd already made plans to see them later.

"How about we walk through Hyde Park and figure out what else we want to do? I have a few things on my list I wouldn't mind, but I'm up for whatever." London was one of the few places I'd been before, as it turned out.

"Perfect."

We took the stairs to the bottom of the building, then pushed out into the bright gray day. The low cloud cover hid the sun, but somehow it was still bright enough to make me wish I'd worn sunglasses. That'd easily tag me as an American, or at least not a European, since rarely did I see sunglasses before April over here. Still, I missed them, and I squinted over at Summer, who snickered.

"It's not *that* bright, is it?"

"I'll adjust. I'm a big boy."

She chuckled as we crossed the street with the walk signal. Though I'd been here before, looking the "wrong" direction before I crossed the street still took reminding. I'd avoided renting cars and driving in the UK for the same reason.

We stepped onto the graveled path of Hyde Park, the *crunch crunch* of our shoes oddly satisfying after standing on carpeted floors in the conference center for the last two days. We quickly discussed our plan, and then I dove in. If I only got this afternoon, I had to make it count.

"So, what'd you think of the weekend?"

Her cheek curved, and I realized the disadvantage of walking and talking. I couldn't look at her. I couldn't enjoy her lips or the little wrinkle in her nose when she thought about something before speaking. I had too many other expressions and gestures to catalogue to be able to imagine them while we walked. I'd have to work in afternoon tea or something so I had at least a little time face to face.

"It was amazing. I knew people did this, obviously. I've heard of the sport, and I even knew people at Kugelfels competed. I knew Alicia was a beast, and I've gathered Rob's schedule with you was insane. And you obviously look completely ridiculous, so I knew it was intense and borderline supernatural, but witnessing the athleticism and determination... it was so inspiring. Like, I may need you to teach me some of this stuff."

My heart kicked. "I will happily teach you anything you want to know. Why do I look ridiculous?"

I wouldn't normally fish, but the word choice threw me. She'd gotten an eyeful this morning, but as she'd pointed out, she'd been looking at half-naked people all day. Forgive me for wanting her to declare her thoughts about me, particularly.

She glanced at me, then back at the path in front of us. "You look like a fitness model. Like you're paid to have muscles."

"I am."

She raised a brow. "As a coach?"

"No. In the Army. I have to pass PT tests and be fit enough to do my job."

She made a disbelieving sound. "I'm sorry to tell you this, because I don't want to sound like I'd ever discourage you from looking like an anatomy lesson on well-developed male musculature, but there's a long way between passing a PT test and you."

I chuckled. "True. Obviously, my interest goes beyond simply passing. I've always liked exercise, and after my parents passed, it was one of the ways I processed the world. It's hard to imagine a life where I don't coach people more and more, especially after I retire. With that, for me, comes walking the walk, so to speak."

We'd slowed to a stroll, but at this, she stopped and turned a little toward me. A look of something small, light, and pleased made my pulse tick up a notch.

"I like that about you."

She moved again, so I followed, though I would've been happy to stand there and look at her. I didn't know what to say to that, so we walked quietly side by side, looking out at the early spring version of the park. Last I'd visited had been July the first year I lived in Germany. The vibrancy of the grass and trees was missing, but it still felt like a lovely little manicured version of nature in the midst of the city.

"So you think you'll coach when you retire from the Army?"

"Coach, train, yeah. I'm not sure I'll end up with anyone who wants to train the way Art and Alicia do, or even Rob, but if that works out, I'd enjoy it. If not, just training people to work hard safely and to meet their goals sounds good to me."

Lately, it sounded better and better. I was fully aware I might be suffering from some *grass is greener* mentality, but the Army drag had gotten to me. I couldn't keep my mind off the countdown to when I'd hit twenty years and be able to walk away, retirement fully vested and the rest of my life in front of me. I'd inherited everything from Gran, too, so financially I wouldn't have to worry.

At the same time, that prospect of *the rest of my life* filled me with so much emptiness, sometimes it took my breath away. What kind of future did I really have? Leaving the Army after twenty years—more than half my life at this point. I didn't want to stay, but would working out, training people, and just existing be enough? *That* was not a topic to consider right now.

"How long until retirement for you?"

Her voice brought me back to the moment.

"Not quite fifteen months."

She whipped to me. "I know we talked about this with everyone, but really? Retirement after twenty years?"

I nodded.

"But you're—you... how old are you?" She looked so perplexed, almost troubled.

Interesting. Wouldn't have guessed that. Also hadn't

anticipated that I might be too old for her. I hadn't even considered that aspect.

"I'm thirty-seven."

She swallowed. "I'm thirty."

The tone in her voice didn't sound good. I'd call it disappointed, but that didn't quite hit it. Pensive, yes, but with a twinge of regret for some reason.

"Is that a problem?"

Might as well get that out of the way. I certainly didn't see it as one, and I hoped like hell she didn't either. But if she did, I needed to start the process of winding myself back onto my safe little spool. I'd already unraveled more than I could've imagined, and if this—

"No. Not—I don't think so."

Not exactly an effusive endorsement of the age gap. I didn't know what to say to prompt her to talk more, but she pivoted toward me, her hands tangled together.

"It's just, what do you mean when you ask that?"

"When I ask if my being thirty-seven is a problem for you?"

She swallowed and nodded.

Nerves crackled. *Okay, just say it.* "I mean, are you uncomfortable dating someone seven years older than you?"

The beaming smile that blossomed on her face made my heart leap in pleasure. The words that came next all the more.

"You want to date me?"

I exhaled on a soft laugh. "Am I all that cryptic?"

She bit her bottom lip, almost like she wanted that to subdue her grin. But nothing could contain it, still. "Actually, you are."

"Really?"

"Yes."

"What, in my last letter, could be construed as anything other than that I want to date you—often and repeatedly?"

She huffed, but the stubborn set of her jaw kept her from smiling again. "Maybe not this most recent one. But the one before that? The one that was the equivalent of a business-like handshake?"

Ah. Yeah. "That came on the heels of you seeming very upset by the prospect of my having purchased your plane ticket. I was worried you found that abhorrent, and the assumption wasn't far off."

She sighed, and even though it was a kind of frustrated, long-suffering sigh, my stupid gut tightened at the sound. I wanted her sighs, yes. All of them.

"It wasn't that *you* had particularly. Or that wasn't all of it. I just..." She trailed off, eyes traveling across the open expanse of grass to her right. "I hate feeling indebted to anyone, and I didn't want to go into this weekend feeling I owed you or anyone else. I just wanted to come and help with the competition and cheer everyone on."

Interesting. This made perfect sense in the context of almost every one of our interactions. Anytime I did something—anything—for her, she reciprocated. Usually with food.

"I'm sorry we weren't clear from the very start."

And I'm sorry for whatever happened to make you hate that feeling. I didn't say it, but something about her tone, and the interactions we'd had in the past, told me whatever this was had roots deep in her. It wasn't just disliking debt in the way most people did.

"Thanks. And I'm sorry I freaked out about it." She stopped just before we reached the edge of the park. "I'm glad I came. I'm glad Rob asked me. And I'm glad you want to date me."

CHAPTER TWENTY-TWO

Summer

His eyes heated as they roamed my face, and my stomach did a handful of backflips.

"That, I do."

"Good."

My chest rose and fell like I'd just finished a jog, all from him looking at me and being so clear about what he wanted. Being the person he wanted, I was finding, proved to be a heady experience.

He nodded, pinning the thought in place, then grabbed my hand and laced our fingers together. Butterflies released into my chest, fluttering so fiercely I would've thought this was our first contact.

"So, tell me about your work, and life, and everything."

I huffed to release a bit of the pent-up tension. "No pressure, huh? Just lay it all out there?"

"Not anything you don't want to tell me. You know my

plans, and you've seen me at work the last few days. You have a feel for one of the things I love. I want to know that about you."

My heart pulsed. Here he was, folks. The literal dream. Physically astounding and emotionally almost too keen. I'd never been around anyone like him and definitely hadn't dated anyone like this.

"I love my job." My heartbeat jumped. I knew the words that wanted to escape, but telling him put me at risk. If I told him, and then failed, I'd have to admit to that. But I wanted him to know, and to know me. "I'm going to interview for a promotion. I've been hoping for this chance, and I'm not all that competitive for it since I don't have managerial experience at this level, but I want the job so bad."

"How do you not have managerial experience? Isn't half of what you do managing patients and all that comes with that?" He steered us around a corner, and we stopped at a crosswalk.

"Not of other people, technically. And it's specifically a managerial position. But I'm running a food and boot drive in a few weeks, and I'm having to coordinate with a few different entities. I figured out how to coordinate with the local city governments to allow the donation to go to the local refugee center. It's not anything major, but it should be one more little bullet point I can slip onto the resumé that shows I've made an effort."

I hoped. Goodness, how I hoped and prayed. If I missed this opportunity, it was unlikely I'd be able to wait out the next person who took the job. Then I'd have to settle for no advancement, or move, and I didn't particularly like the idea of either of those things.

"Eventually you'll come crawling back, begging us for our good favor."

Though I tried to ignore the voice, I heard my father's parting shot from all those years ago, and the few times I'd seen him since, it'd been something similar. Anytime I faced potential failure, they rang loud and strong. I'd never have a reason to live with them again, but the threat had been real at seventeen when I'd left on a college scholarship, and I'd never managed to shed the feeling of that moment. Determination. Fear. Heartbreak.

Not only would the promotion get me a job I wanted, it could also provide that much more financial security. I'd move up on the GS scale, which meant a pay raise as one primary benefit. I wanted that raise, but fortunately, I didn't *need* it. I lived comfortably, especially since I gave away a fair amount of money in the form of donations or making food for others. But I wanted it—that boost, to see the nest egg in my accounts grow and know I'd gone so far beyond what my parents had expected of me, which was total failure.

Nick spoke as the light changed. "It sounds like a great idea. I want to help—just tell me how."

The crowd surged forward, saving me from responding. I immediately admired and felt repulsed by his offer. So nice of him, and yet I needed to do this on my own. The crux of the event's success needed to rest with me so that I could demonstrate my ability to manage the various moving pieces.

But the sincerity of his comment hung between us, and I couldn't just ignore it, despite the busy street.

"Thank you." *Keep it simple and avoid committing later.* "I think everything is pretty much set. So far, the response has been good, and I'm hoping people will do a nice push before spring break. That'll give me time to sort through everything and distribute it while things are more low-key that next week, and it's a few weeks before my interview so I'll have all the numbers ready to relay for the committee." I forced my mouth shut, realizing I was in danger of continuing to babble, and sweet as Nick was, he wouldn't interrupt me.

"Sounds like a solid plan."

"Thanks."

I felt stiff, like my work chatter had somehow derailed us, but I shook that off. He seemed to like me, and if he didn't like me talking work and organizing community things, that would change. I hated the thought, but I was trying to embrace myself as I was. I hoped he could, too.

We crossed another street, walking in companionable silence. I took in all the famous sights, appreciating how walkable London was. Not all cities were, though most in Europe had been designed with pedestrians in mind. And London, I liked. Especially on a decent weather day like this one.

We passed the palace, but we didn't stop to gawk at the guards. Eventually, we made it to the river, and lingered at the corner of a bridge to admire Big Ben.

"I'm not sure what you want to do now, but I was hoping we could go to the Tate Modern." Nick's hand— holding mine again after a brief lapse thanks to a crowd— squeezed.

"We're doing what I wanted to do—just walking. Well, and the class last night. I try to take a class everywhere I visit, and that was a dream come true. Truly."

"I'm glad. After I registered you, I had this thought that you'd think I was controlling and weird for trying to surprise you." The question in his voice was clear.

"Not at all. I did wonder how you pulled off all the details so completely—the cab's timing and everything. Plus, me joining the trip was so last minute, I'm still amazed you got me a ticket. But not controlling or weird, for sure." I gave him a sideways smile.

He shook his head, just barely. "Good."

We crossed the bridge, then slipped down the walk on the far side of the river until we came to the museum.

"What made you want to come here? I'd peg you for an Imperial War Museum guy."

"My first visit, I spent half a day there. This one was my grandmother's favorite. She was an art history buff and traveled to all the famous museums of Europe when she was younger. One of the last trips she made, she went to the Tate Modern, fairly reluctantly, and fell in love with it."

Of all the things I'd expected, that wasn't it. I needed to learn the lesson that Nick would likely always surprise me.

He inspected me, then chuckled low. "Why do you look surprised?"

I shook my head. "You keep surprising me. I never imagined you'd be so..."

He squinted, waiting.

"Interested in art, I guess. But then I say that, and I think of your letters." Just mentioning the letters made my stomach flip. "I should probably stop assuming things about you."

One side of his perfect mouth pulled up just barely. "You expect me to be a meathead soldier?"

I laughed, a little of the discomfort at my assumption easing with his joke. "Honestly, before I actually knew you, or started getting to know you, yes."

He grunted, a sound indicating he wasn't surprised.

"That happen a lot?"

I expected another joke, but what came made my heart ache.

"People often assume things about me. When you're someone quiet, there's more room to make guesses, and silence usually gets taken as confirmation of whatever assumptions. It's not my favorite thing, but *oh well*. Such is life."

Stepping to the side of the walkway, I pulled his hand to me, still clasped in mine, and held it close to my heart. "That's frustrating. And stupid."

He shrugged.

"What *is* your favorite thing?"

Though nothing on his face changed, I'd swear he smiled. No idea how he managed that because truly, his lips hadn't moved. Still, the expression made me feel a little giddy. He inched closer right there on the sidewalk, shielding us from fellow walkers by facing his broad back to the river and dipping his head. Then, he spoke. "I've got a whole pile of favorite things. I'll write them down for you. You?"

My pulse picked up, both his nearness and his low, rich tone of voice hinting that whatever would be on that list, I'd like it.

I wanted the list. *Oh, yes. I do.*

"Food. I like food," I said, flustered and blushing.

He smiled in earnest then, and my stomach tumbled. *Oh. My. Goodness.* The man was completely beautiful when he smiled like that.

"What?" I asked, desperate to know the cause of that smile so I could replicate it again soon, and often.

"Nothing at all. Let's go inside." He nodded his chin to the building we stood next to.

The brown brick building behind me was none other than the Tate Modern, apparently. We entered through a large, open end that seemed almost like a loading dock and opened into a huge space. A massive ramp led museum-goers down to the center of the space where a store waited.

"This is different," I said, sounding as uncouth and uncultured as I ever had.

"From what my grandmother said, that's a theme here."

He tugged me along, and we found a map. Apparently, the exhibits were free, so we didn't need tickets. Another rarity based on my limited experience. Soon enough, we were roaming halls filled with everything from a room of Andy Warhols to the famed Fountain by Marcel Duchamp which consisted of a urinal.

But where I might have chuckled and simply cast off the object as something that only a modern art museum would call art with a roll of my eyes, Nick leaned close and told me the story behind it. It didn't change my perspective that I wouldn't want a urinal on the wall of my living room, but it pushed me to look deeper.

And what I'd been learning about Nick took hold as we wandered, sometimes close, sometimes each stuck in our own heads. At times, I could swear he was locked in a trance, maybe thinking of his family or his grandmother. The way he thought was a complete mystery to me. I'd never met anyone like him, and though that same sentiment had come and gone a dozen times in the course of our inter-actions, I felt it clearly today. Nothing about him came as expected. Where one might expect a rough, almost toxically masculine man based on his bulk, strength, and even voca-tion, what you discovered was someone... *gentle*. Introspec-tive, thoughtful, analytical, and creative.

He intimidated me. Completely. I'd already recognized him as a formidable coach and professional, and that was outside his military job. The competition this weekend had shown me what a caring mentor and leader he could be. But now, hearing him talk about which pieces had made an impression on his grandmother, or things he'd researched and looked forward to seeing... it skewered me.

Pair the curiosity and general brain power with his propensity for hand-written confessions, and I was doomed. And that didn't include the physical elements, which need not be mentioned since cataloging his assets would ultimately just drive me insane.

"What's on your mind?" he asked as we crossed over the Thames on the Millennium footbridge, the museum at our backs.

My focus on the glinting silver metallic ropes swooping along just out of reach, I searched for something to say besides *I really like you but you're overwhelming*. I landed on, "Just digesting the day."

He didn't respond, but we kept walking, our pace leisurely but purposeful. Ahead of us loomed St. Paul's rotunda, and the sight of it struck me. A laugh bubbled out just as we hit the end of the bridge.

"What?"

His gaze felt warm and sweet. The fluttering sensation in my chest heightened, and I would've kissed him if we weren't surrounded by fellow walkers. "I'm just having one of those *this is my life* moments."

He raised a brow.

"You know, those moments where you have that sense of awareness hit you. Like, I'm actually here, walking off the Millennium bridge, staring at St. Paul's Cathedral where Princess Diana was married. I'm in London, and I kind of know my way around because I've been here before, and it's just... crazy."

I never would've dreamed of such a moment when I was a kid. I had no aspirations to get to London or anywhere but *out*. Well, out and *fed*. It still baffled me that none of my siblings had truly left home. They had no idea what they were missing.

"I haven't traveled all that much, but I think I know what you mean. It's surreal to be in places you grow up hearing and reading about."

We marched up the steps side by side. At the top, we stopped, gazing up at the towering cathedral. I glanced at him, a twist deep in my chest. "It's... wondrous."

He hummed and squeezed my hand. "Yes. Exactly."

What he couldn't know, and what I couldn't express, was the feeling of being there with him. *He* was wondrous. A person like I'd never known, and someone who I felt drawn to in a way that almost seemed dangerous. But today, after a mind full of beauty and a body striped with awareness of him, all I could think was being here, with him, was wondrous indeed.

CHAPTER TWENTY-THREE

Nick

I will look at a painting on a wall and see life. See curios-
ity. See transgression against what came before. But I will
look at you and yes, I will see truth or beauty, beauty and
truth, or a bit like Keats put it, all I know on earth and all I
need to know.

As the day wore on, I grew quieter. By the time we met Art, Alicia, and Rob for a celebratory toast and meal, I had spent all my words. My mind had filled and filled, and I didn't have anywhere to go with the thoughts until I got back to the apartment and could safely release them on the page.

Spending the afternoon with Summer had been dream-like—surreal, just like we'd talked about. Some of that stemmed from finally visiting a place I'd always wanted to go to, ever since Gran had described her experience years back. But much of it came from being there *with her*. In some ways, maybe it had been stupid to take her there. It was a memory I'd always have, and now, it'd be inextricably linked to Summer. Whenever time ran out for us, the experience would be tinged with sadness and loss.

And I'd had too much loss. At thirty-seven, I'd lost too many people, and I hadn't had many to start. I didn't want to lose Summer, and yet I recognized she wasn't mine to begin with.

She'd seemed pleased with the idea of us dating. *Good.* I wanted that, even if I didn't know exactly what it would look like. She'd proven to have depth, and to be interested in me beyond the physical—though we clearly had chemistry. Her compassion when I told her about Gran weeks ago, her reaction when I told her about the museum... it was all more thoughtful and real than I'd had with anyone before.

The positive to taking her to the museum came from seeing her adapt to something she clearly wouldn't have been interested in otherwise. I didn't mind that, especially since she didn't seem uncomfortable with the experience. She might not've visited and spent a few hours wandering through a modern art museum on her own, but she hadn't been restless or critical or irritated. I'd dated more than one woman who had no interest in the arts and simply couldn't stand that I did. I didn't need someone who shared my every passion, but I did need someone who could support what I liked without disparaging it.

These small revelations had come over time and were partly responsible for why I so very, very rarely tried to date anymore. But Summer had busted through that, with her food and her stubbornness and her showing up on my doorstep insisting on caring for me. That care had snuck by my usual rejection of any physical attraction, and lately, any desire to get to know someone. She barreled right through with her delicious, persistent offerings, and I could only thank God I hadn't been fool enough to continue refusing them.

I did my best to reenter the moment, the pub food now cleared away, and only half-empty room-temperature, dark English beers remaining on the table.

"You all did amazing. I can't believe how accomplished you are, and this isn't even your full-time focus."

Summer had been effusive and warm, as usual, but her praise for the team had served to increase the celebratory feel. She made everyone feel good about what they'd done and had drawn us all back together. Not that there had been division or awkwardness, but simply that she made the moment better.

"Thanks for stepping in to fill the med role. Pretty boring for you, but hopefully you had some fun this weekend."

Rob's comment came with a little twinkle in his eye, like he knew exactly how I felt about Summer and suspected he knew how she felt about me.

A bolt of longing jagged through my chest. I wanted to know how she felt. I needed to understand if I was alone out here in these ever-deepening waters of feeling.

After another half hour of chatting, we all wandered home. Summer knitted our hands together, and my stomach dropped low. Any touch from her sent my senses reeling for a moment before they adjusted and reoriented to orbit around the connection.

Inside, they all grabbed drinks and planned to play a game in the living room. I didn't pay much attention, because the need to be alone had gripped me, and I had no chance of shaking it loose. I said good night to everyone, but Summer caught my eye before I turned down the hallway to our rooms.

"Are you okay?" she asked, concern in her voice.

"Yes. Just tired."

Her gaze swept over me head to toe, searching for the cause of my exhaustion. She looked like she might say something, but instead leaned up and pressed a kiss to my cheek. With a hand on her back to encourage her to linger, my eyes shut and I inhaled her scent, her warmth, and the sensation of her lips on my skin.

"Sleep well. I'll see you bright and early."

I nodded and watched her pad back down the hallway to the living room. Rob's boisterous laughter filtered in from the space as I shut the door on the noise.

The mix of emotions welling in me felt like an iron singeing my chest. The day had been triumphant, full of beauty, and special. But lingering at the edges and slipping through those lighter feelings came grief.

The person who'd known me better than anyone else on Earth, who'd known me as I grew up, and as I became an adult, was gone. Gone even more entirely than she had been the last few years. Even though she hadn't known me since before I came to Germany, I hadn't thought of her as gone. I'd thought of her as missing. Parts of her missing. But now, her soul lived somewhere else, and mine felt bruised. Smashed down.

I braced my hands on the wall and breathed through the clenching rush of sadness. Not two months ago, this would've felt more like brokenness than anything else. It would've felt like parts of me were falling off and shattering on the floor with each breath. That I stood and stayed together, this signaled progress. And much of it had to do with the people down the hallway, laughing and chatting and letting me be a bit morose and lonely because that's how I was.

Rob had been a friend to me in a way few had. Many people were kind, and some made an effort, but Rob's presence in my gym had forced me to let him see a bit more of me. And perhaps his attention to detail had let him see past the stern, quiet face and into the shades of grief that'd become darker when the loss I'd known was coming finally arrived. Plus, he got credit for Butter. I never would've imagined enjoying a little beast like him, and I had Rob to thank for him too.

Art and Alicia, who'd been with me longest, provided stability and grace simply by showing up and trusting me with their training.

And Summer. My heart squeezed at the thought of her, wringing out the bloody rags of grief and brightening. She made me laugh and relax and want things I'd never actually thought I'd have.

A conversation I'd had with Gran years back played in my head.

"*I'm not sure I'll ever find someone.*" *I said this as an apology because I knew she wanted me "settled," as she called it, before she lost any more.*

"*Pish, Nicholas. You'll find her when you find her. Until then, you be a man who knows he's worthy of a good woman.*" *Her gray eyes hounded me, like she could see in my mind and all the doubts that swirled there.*

"*I will.*"

She narrowed her eyes—suspicious, but only in that motherly way she had. "*Will you?*"

I didn't say a thing.

"You will find someone, my dearest, who loves you. You'll find someone who loves the warrior and the poet. And until you do, you know I count having you as my grandson as the very best and most beautiful part of my life." Her voice shook a little, but she cleared her throat and pressed her lips into an exaggerated, large smile.

I blinked away the memory and rolled to my side—I didn't remember lying down on the bed. It hurt, so much, to think of her, and yet *not* thinking of her didn't honor her memory. The woman had been a grandparent to me first, but then she'd become a guide, friend, and in so many ways, a parent.

Could Summer possibly be the person she was so sure I'd find? I'd never cared about anyone enough to wonder. It'd only been surface-level relationships at best. With her, from the very beginning, everything had been different. But that didn't necessarily mean she even *liked* me, not in the way someone needed to in order to spend a life together.

I pushed up off the bed and fumbled through brushing my teeth and changing clothes. Minutes later, I sat with my back against the headboard and began to write. As the words etched onto the page, my chest loosened. My breathing evened out, and the sharp edge of grief softened to the familiar and ever-present ache.

What a strange pairing—the veritable elation of time spent with Summer entwined with the staggering brutality of loneliness. Not simple aloneness, but this hounding sense that I alone carried the genetic legacy of my family. And more, that no one else had known me. Knew me.

It doesn't have to be that way.

Somewhere, the voice spoke, and as it often did, it sounded a bit like Gran. My resistance to it, though, had flagged. I accepted that I wanted Summer to know me—the parts of me I didn't show others or that they didn't bother to see. I longed for that, and not just generally, but from her. As usual, my feelings no doubt outpaced hers, but maybe she'd come around.

And in order to do that, I would make my intentions very, very clear.

CHAPTER TWENTY-FOUR

Summer

The rainy day dawned a bit too early, but knowing we'd be back to Kugelfels in a matter of hours brought excitement. I had the week's meals to prep after getting groceries, and then I had work. I'd need to check in on the donation sites, and it'd be wise to review my resumé one more time.

I'd submitted my application through the government website that fielded all GS jobs here, but it wouldn't hurt to double-check what I'd put on there for skills and such since I rarely had to speak about my qualifications.

If truth be told, the main reason for the floaty feeling came down to Nick. Like cranberries when you rinse them in a sink full of water—they just bob there, buoyant and bright—that was me. Not that I tried denying it all that hard, but part of me rejected the idea that my outlook on the day or the week would be so cheery just because of a man.

The other part of me said that was stupid, and caring about someone, enjoying being with them, was plenty reason to be happy on any given day.

Brushing my teeth, I chuckled at the memory of Rob's thinly veiled interrogation of me the night before. Nick had excused himself to go to bed. I hated to miss time with him, but he'd disappeared inside himself an hour before we'd returned to the apartment. I wasn't fool enough to think that was because of me. His grief was very real, and though I didn't fully understand his relationship to his grandmother, I could see that retracing her footsteps at the museum had been genuinely bittersweet.

When I came back from saying good night to Nick, Rob's smile said everything.

"You can keep your knowing little looks to yourself," I snapped, fakely irritated. He might as well know, and it wasn't like we'd kept it a secret that we'd spent all afternoon together.

"I'm just happy. You're great. He's great. It's great." He beamed.

Art and Alicia laughed, then Alicia spoke up. "You guys are too pretty, just so you know. It's kind of mean to everyone else because you're both ridiculously beautiful people, and seeing you next to each other, let alone touching or affectionate, is just a lot. Plus, it now means you're both off the market. Prepare for hearts to break all around post."

I gave her an unimpressed look. "Yeah, okay, crazy."

"Seriously though, it's great. He's a good guy," Art put in.

A warm, pleased smile grew on my lips. "I know he is."

They all seemed to sober at once, and then Rob spoke, like he represented them. "On a serious note, go easy. He's been through a lot the last few months, which I'm sure you've gathered, and—"

"I won't hurt him." I said the words so confidently, like I *knew* I wouldn't. It made me wonder—made me hope—that I wouldn't.

I shook off the memory, and the mild sense of unease that'd arrived with it. For something that had started with me laughing, it'd turned serious, not unlike the conversation itself. I appreciated their concern for their friend. If anything, it only spoke more highly of Nick that these three would be concerned for him and his well-being. Short on words he may have been, but he had the loyalty of his people without a doubt.

The problem was, I couldn't guarantee I wouldn't hurt him. Just like I couldn't be sure he wouldn't hurt me. But I'd said I wouldn't last night because I could honestly say I didn't want to, and that no part of me planned to. Sometimes, things went south, but I didn't want that. In fact, the fluttery, restless feeling that woke me and had me more than eager to see him this morning told me I wanted anything *but* that.

I raced through finishing up packing. We needed to head out in a matter of minutes. We'd agreed last night we'd grab food at the airport so we didn't have to fool with any cleanup before we left. I was ahead of schedule, but still rushed through. I wanted a moment with Nick before we were all crammed together and asking him how he felt was out of the question.

After rolling my case and carry-on to a spot near the exit, I padded back down the hallway to Nick's room. The door swung open just before I knocked, and I sucked in a breath.

"Morning," I said, voice just above a whisper. I didn't

know why—everyone must've been awake with our departure time coming up.

"Morning."

My stomach clenched. The sound of his voice was just... delicious. Like dark chocolate ganache over a flourless cake. Dense and thick and delectable all in one bite.

"Did you sleep okay?"

Without thinking, I reached for his arm and set a hand on the warm skin of his wrist. Normal temp, not that feeling his wrist could actually tell me. His color looked good—not pale. I'd known he wasn't sick, but I also couldn't bury the nurse impulses entirely.

His eyes found mine, and he nodded. The look there instantly set my heart racing. I should've been used to his intensity and the fullness that came from just meeting his gaze, but no. I had officially not gotten used to those eyes and just how much lay behind them. Desire, yes, but also longing. I pulled in a breath through my nose, clenching my jaw shut to keep from begging him to tell me what he was thinking.

"Are *you* okay?"

It wasn't begging. It wasn't the *please tell me what that look means, or just take me here against the wall* desperation I felt, so I took that as a win.

"Yes. Thank you for asking."

"I—I care about you. I know sometimes you need time alone—that's what you're used to, what you prefer. But I hope you know you can talk to me, too. I can listen. I know I tend to be a talker." I closed my mouth and pressed my lips together as I realized I was jabbering away right then. This thought needed finishing, though, and so I continued. "Despite that, I can listen."

He smiled, all warm and sweet, and someone poured champagne into my chest.

"Thank you." He took my face in his hands and leaned down to place a soft, quick kiss on my lips. When he pulled back, he looked happy.

For no good reason at all, tears welled in my eyes. I shut them and raised onto my toes, pressing another kiss to his firm, beautiful lips. Without moving far, I said, "Guess we better go."

He released me, sliding his hands from my face, down my neck, and to my shoulders, where he squeezed, then backed away. "Let me grab my bag. I'll meet you up front."

By the time I dragged myself into my house, it was after three—two hours later than I'd planned on getting home, but such is life with delayed flights. At least it finally took off, and at least I got to ride home with Nick.

After I refused his offer to carry my small bag inside, the invitation to join me for dinner tonight had been on the tip of my tongue. Before I got it out, he asked me to come to dinner at his place tomorrow. I readily agreed and asked if I could bring anything. He said he'd like to cook for me, unless I would be happier doing the cooking.

That had shut me right up. I kissed his cheek and practically ran inside, something about his caveat about cooking for me stirring all manner of emotion in my chest. First, I very rarely got invited to other people's houses anymore. If I did, I always offered to bring something, and they always accepted. In this community, more than any other I'd lived in, I'd created a bit of a name for myself as a capable cook and hostess. I liked that, but it made his invitation to his home, and for *him* to feed *me,* all the more impactful.

Then he went and topped it off with the insight into *me.* We'd been friendly for weeks now and had been interacting for a few months by this point, but he knew me. At least, in this respect, far better than almost any of my exes had, for sure. And in some cases, better than my close friends.

As I tossed clothes into the washer, I mulled over the man. I liked him. I'd learned more about him this weekend, and each piece I found, I nestled into the puzzle of him in my mind. Those thoughts led to the inevitable physical response—butterflies and stomach flips and dippy little audible sighs I was glad only escaped when I found myself alone.

The problem with that was simple. I shouldn't feel so much for a man I'd just met and had only barely started dating. But already, I recognized that my physical response wasn't based on his physical appearance. I mean, I liked that —oh, yes, yes, and yes again, I did. But I liked all of him... even the introverted, spare-worded, quiet version. In fact, it wasn't a *version,* not like other people were. It might be that Nick proved to be one of the most genuine people I'd ever met. What you saw in any given circumstance was what you got.

Could the same be said of me?

I sighed long and loud and dramatically and punched the button to start the wash. Honestly? No. I had my customer-service-nurse face, and my hosting-feast-night face, and my smaller-group-of-friends face, and then there was me. The one underneath it all. It wasn't that I wanted to deceive people but that fitting into a given place required flexibility, and I had that skill. I'd learned it as a kid when it became clear I couldn't rely on my family for what I needed, and I'd mastered it as I entered active-duty service in the Army and began my nursing career.

What I didn't know was how Nick would feel about me as he witnessed those changes. Would he notice? Would he care?

I brushed away those questions and moved to the kitchen. I'd whip up something with whatever I had in the fridge, and tomorrow after work, I'd hit the commissary. Not ideal, but I didn't have the gumption to face going out again.

And if the prospect of being at his house, seeing inside his space, kept me completely distracted the rest of the day? Well, who could blame me?

CHAPTER TWENTY-FIVE

Nick

You have taken all the jagged edges and filed them smooth —you've brushed against the hardest parts and not surrendered. Where there is only steel and misery, you have taken your heat and light and melted me.

Feeding a woman who cooked like Summer proved to be a bit daunting. I didn't allow myself to overthink. Rather, I doubled what I already planned to eat—my version of chicken piccata—and moved on.

I did recognize that an inability to cook for a woman who loved food the way she did could potentially be a dealbreaker. Then again, she loved cooking, so maybe she wouldn't mind. I found my food edible, and so had anyone I'd cooked for, but expectations had always been low. And

I'd only ever cooked for people I coached, who were unlikely to complain. Normally, meals in that context were baked or grilled meat, steamed or sauteed vegetables, and a big salad. We kept things simple during competitions.

I dressed in jeans and a button-up shirt. My house, as usual, welcomed me home the day before with only a few items out of place—a bright orange toy mouse belonging to Butter had migrated, and he'd also sharpened his claws on a roll of toilet paper. All in all, uneventful. This also meant any preparations for Summer were focused on food prep, and of course just getting through the workday before I got to see her again.

If Captain Wild noticed my distracted state, he didn't mention it. He'd already heard the good news about the weekend, no doubt from Rob, so he congratulated me on the results. It was an excellent turn out, and it would be useful for marketing myself if I ever got around to doing that. While on active duty, I couldn't pursue coaching full time, obviously. But the clock didn't stop, and soon enough, I'd need to transition into the next phase. The only question was where, and with whom, if anyone.

By the time I arrived home, I had just forty minutes before Summer would be here. I scrambled through cleaning up and prepping, feeling more flustered than I could remember. I didn't do things that *flustered* me, and yet knowing the woman would be in my space in a matter of minutes set me on an electric edge.

When the knock finally came, I stalked to the door, took a long, slow inhale and exhale to ground myself and halt the nerves, and opened it.

She beamed at me. An answering smile showed on my lips.

"Please come in," I said, stepping aside so she could

enter. Her sweet, warm scent caught me, and I followed after her inside like a puppy.

"I'm excited to see your house. I love seeing German homes. They're all so unique." She had a small box in her hand and a bottle of wine.

"They are. Yours is cozy." Part of that was the design—the rich woods and the German stove in prime placement. Mine was utter contrast—far more modern. But hers felt cozy because she'd made it that way, too. The bookshelves, the over-sized living room furniture, the large, welcoming table for hosting feast nights.

"Yours is really"—her eyes skated around, then circled back to me "clean."

I chuckled, and she smiled, all bright and a little wry. My chest tightened.

"It's really nice," she offered, like I'd need something to appease me after her first statement.

"I've admittedly spent less time on furniture for my home than I have on the gym. This living room is big enough that if I bought couches to fill it, I'd end up with overflow when I move to a smaller home."

And I would. This place was likely double the size of whatever I'd end up with in the States when I retired. I didn't mind the space, even the places that were empty. My couch, love seat, and coffee table fit most places I'd lived over the years, and they'd be more than enough wherever I ended up eventually.

"Makes sense. It is hard figuring out how much to decorate each place, especially if you're not exactly sure how long you'll be there." She held up the wine with a raised brow.

"I'll take that." I moved to her, glad for an excuse to

close the distance. She'd wandered over into the kitchen, no doubt eager to check out the setup in there.

"I wasn't sure if you drink. I mean, I know you do, but I didn't know if you normally do or only sometimes, but I wanted to bring something, so..."

Her voice trailed off when I took the bottle and set it on the counter next to us without looking away from her. "I'll have a glass with you."

"Okay."

I wanted to kiss her. I felt it down to my toes. But I remembered my manners and instead said, "Let me take your coat."

She unbuttoned the long sky-blue wool coat. It fit her perfectly—bright, cheery, and warm. I reached for the collar and held an edge while she maneuvered out of it. She wore jeans and a creamy, soft-looking shirt. I folded the coat over my arm, about to excuse myself to hang it, when she spoke.

"Can we just..." She took it from my arms and tossed it over a chair at the nearby dinner table, then slipped her arms under mine, stepped close, and pressed into me. She hugged me.

My arms came around her immediately. My heart thumped in blissful response, and I wrapped around her more fully—my shoulders and neck curved so my whole body hugged her back.

"This is nice," she said, then let out a breath that made her whole body deflate.

"It is," I agreed and inhaled her scent, that addictive combination I'd only been able to enjoy once or twice. She loosened her grip on me, so I did the same, letting my hand stroke along her back only to nearly swallow my tongue.

My breath caught and held as my hands ran down the track of her spine, the bare, warm skin there exposed. Somewhere below her midback, my fingers met the fibrous material of the top. The pleasing drape of fabric around her neck evidently dipped much farther down than I'd imagined.

She must've felt me still and stop breathing. I only hoped she didn't realize just how completely my brain had shut down at the contact with so much of her glorious skin. She looked up at me, a glimmer of pleasure and maybe mischief in her eyes.

"Like my shirt?"

I nodded immediately, and my thumb arced over the small ridges of her spine. "It's very soft."

"It is."

My stomach dropped through the floor, into the basement, and probably through the foundation of the house. The look in those blue eyes notched my hunger for her from desperate to ravenous.

"We should eat." *Let's get that part over with.*

"Yes, please."

I swallowed and reluctantly released her. She had a pleased grin I couldn't fault her for. She knew she'd affected me, and I didn't mind her knowing, as long as it didn't scare her away. That said, I needed to get my mind off the silken skin stretching the length of her spine and instead finish up the meal. Just a few things to do and we could sit and eat, and I could distract myself from the hounding desire coursing through me.

Minutes later, I pulled out a chair for her, which she happily took. I delivered a plate to her place, then one to my own, and sat. Her face said enough, but she spoke too.

"This is beautiful. And it smells amazing."

The woman's eyes actually sparkled. Knowing I'd put that look there sent a flood of satisfaction through me.

"I hope you like it."

"Do you always plate your food like this?" She sliced into a chicken cutlet.

"I don't usually have so much garnish." My cheeks warmed, just a little, though I didn't mind her knowing I'd made an effort.

She hummed after taking a bite, then smiled. "It's great."

I took that for the high praise it was. Maybe she was just being nice, but she dove into the lemony dish with gusto. We chatted easily for a few minutes off and on while we ate. Once finished, she sat back and stared me down.

I raised a brow.

"I'm just wondering how you are. After the museum and everything."

I wiped my mouth and took a sip of wine to buy myself a minute. Something like this required an answer that I'd like to think about a while before saying anything, but that didn't work very well in normal conversation. So, I did my best.

"I'm good. *Better*, I think. It hit me hard, and even coming home yesterday, I felt a little foggy, for lack of a better word. But it was cathartic. Something in me has eased."

Her bright eyes watched me a moment before she moved. She stood and reached out a hand. I took it and suspected there would never be a time when she offered her hand and I didn't accept it immediately. She tugged a bit. I got the message and stood. Before I'd straightened out fully, she wrapped her arms around me and pressed her head to my chest.

"Thank you for sharing the experience with me." She released me far too soon and stepped back before I could even extricate my arms from hers and return the gesture. "Sorry. I just... had to do that."

The warmth kindled by her affection and nearness grew into heat. At the same time, my heart twisted in my chest—her sweetness and care felt foreign and so welcome, it scared me. "You can do that any time you want."

Our gazes caught and held. The impulse to take her in my arms and crush her to me, to claim her mouth, and as soon as possible, her body, overwhelmed me. I hammered it back down and picked up my plate, then hers.

"Have a seat in the living room. I'll be right there."

"I can help—"

"There's nothing to do. Truly. I'll rinse the plates and put them in the dishwasher and join you." If she thought I was about to let her clean up, she was wrong. Some of her own medicine.

She scowled at me, clearly recognizing the gesture, but grabbed her glass of wine and wandered to the next room. I tore my eyes from her—the smooth expanse of her back and everything else.

Retreating into the kitchen, I made a promise to myself. I'd do whatever I could to encourage her interest in me. I'd do anything possible to keep her—whatever little bit I had of her.

CHAPTER TWENTY-SIX

Summer

The aforementioned fluffy snowball with electric eyes leaned a dainty paw on my knee and stretched its neck out to sniff me. I hadn't had a pet growing up, but I liked animals well enough. This one seemed nice, though it was the first I'd seen of it tonight.

"Sorry. Is he bothering you?"

Nick rounded the couch and set his wineglass on the coffee table near mine.

"No. Just checking me out, I think." The cat still sniffed my fingers, trying to get a sense for my soul and its likelihood to bow to him, maybe.

"Butter, give her a break." He shooed the fluffball, and the cat hopped down and sauntered to wrap around his leg. Meanwhile, my mind, my heart, my entire being, was stuck back on his first word.

"Butter? His name is *Butter*?"

Nick's eyes narrowed. "Yes."

I bit my bottom lip, attempting to keep from melting all over him. "I love that name."

Understatement. More like, if I ever had a pet, that would be the name I'd choose.

"He melts. When he sleeps, no matter where he falls asleep, he just melts into a little puddle. Sometimes, he'll end up with his head on a cushion and his tail and legs down on the floor. It's ridiculous."

The expression on his face told me how much this little creature meant to him. I could've guessed, based on the previous encounters with the man and his cat, but it still made my heart *thump thump* to see him speak so sweetly about a tiny little animal. Maybe it was the juxtaposition of his powerful body and the bright white, soft little thing. Whatever the case, his affection for Butter made *me* melt.

"Rob got him for me in January. He's still growing, but he has tripled in size already." He ran a finger from the cat's nose up over the bridge and smoothed down the short, soft fur between his ears.

"Rob bought you a cat?"

He nodded, a half smile pulling at his lips as he sat next to me. "He knew I'd been through a lot. He didn't get what a big deal it was, but he knew it meant more than simply losing a grandparent might. As man-about-town as he pretended to be, he was an extremely thoughtful person, and very observant. I hadn't said much, but he knew."

"Rob is sweet. And I'm glad you weren't allergic," I joked, working to ignore the ache all of this caused in my chest. I remembered him saying, weeks ago, "*She was my last person. My last relative.*" In fact, I heard those words echo in my mind fairly often—they crushed me to think of. I didn't understand what a close relationship like they must've had would be like, not after more than a decade virtually alienated from my own family. But I could see it tore at him.

He offered a closed-mouth smile in response. "Me too."

"I've never had a pet." If he wanted to talk more about the hard things, the grief, then I wanted him to. But I wouldn't pry or pressure.

"So far, I like it. Granted, he's more friendly with you right now than he was with me for weeks. But he's good for a four-day weekend, as I just discovered. I have a pet sitter come during busier rotations and he did well with her for the London trip, so I'll do that during spring break too."

"Are you traveling?"

He nodded while swallowing a drink. "I am. I haven't done much since living here. This is actually my first trip longer than two nights. I made myself book it when I got back after the funeral."

I set a hand on his. "That will be great."

He covered my hand with this larger, warm one. "It will. I think I'm ready for it. I feel like I'm stepping out of a murky lake. It'll still be there, but I'm almost all the way out, and I won't dive back in."

"That sounds like a good thing," I said, unfamiliar with the nuances of grief.

"I think it is. I've been grieving her a long time. Some of it is thinking about my parents, too—she was a huge part of my life after they died, and my only support for all of my adulthood. The actual loss hit hard, but most days now, it's more of a low pang. These last few days heightened it because of the trip, but at the same time, I feel..." He broke off, and his eyes searched mine. He laced our fingers together. "Happy."

I clenched my jaw to press away the emotion that rose at that. "Good. That's good."

That familiar intensity thickened the air between us, and my pulse rioted. His face had struck me as painfully beautiful, but so serious. At close range, with the permission and pleasure to take in every little detail of him, he was heartbreaking.

And not perfect, actually. I'd noticed before but had never just... looked at him. Not without a sense of nervous anticipation—and trust, that was at play now, too. But my heart thundered, eager, not anxious. I could appreciate the little scar interrupting one brow, and the way his bottom teeth weren't quite exactly straight. Warmth bloomed in my chest.

The oddest thought occurred then—or, maybe not a thought, but a release. Like I'd given myself permission to want and enjoy him, fully, finally. It'd been months of crushing and weeks of our strange brand of flirtation. I'd kept myself close, not allowing a tumble into the feelings lurking so nearby. He pulled on every heartstring I had, and everything about him drew me in. Even his quiet, gentle soul, which he had shared so generously with me already.

He sat angled toward me, one arm resting on the back of the couch. When he spoke again, his voice came out rich and full of promise. "I hope this doesn't make you feel pressured, but I want you to know that you have a great deal to do with that happiness."

I exhaled, a kind of helpless sound I couldn't contain. "That's... I'm glad."

Had anyone ever said something like that to me? Not that they liked me or thought I was beautiful, though those were nice things. But that I contributed to their happiness?

Little fireworks shot off in my chest. Looking in his eyes,

at that face, after he'd said those words, pushed adrenaline to my toes. My hands reached for him. "Nick—"

Fortunately, he had the same idea. Or maybe he heard the desperation in my voice. Either way, our lips met in a joint effort, and I shuddered in relief. The kiss escalated quickly—so quickly. Like we'd lit a match inches from kindling and all it needed was a light breeze for it to catch. This was a determined gust, and Nick's mouth and hands on me caught and stoked the flames.

In moments, I sat on his lap facing him, my fingers sifting into the short hair at his nape, kissing him like I'd die if we stopped. Eventually, he broke away from my mouth and began a path along my jaw. My hands smoothed along his glorious shoulders, the muscles like warmed granite under his shirt.

"This shirt."

He spoke the words into my neck, where he kissed a line to my shoulder. His finger skated along the edge where it curved around my throat, then over the arc of my trapezius and down. The calloused pads of his fingers sent shivers of delicious sensation in all directions.

"What about it?"

I sounded breathless because I was. Completely captivated by the slide of his skin against mine on my back, tracing around the curve of my shoulder blade. My breath caught, hung up on his warm breath at my collarbone and the achingly slow progress of his hands. I wanted him to touch me now, later, everywhere.

He lifted his head, and the desire in his eyes would've lit me on fire if I hadn't already been aflame.

"It's so soft, but your skin's even softer."

He sounded drugged. Dazed. Whatever it was, it sent

heat to every part of me, an assault on every bit of reason and control I might've been clinging to.

"That's... good."

I didn't know what I was saying. My ability to communicate, to make any sense, had fled with the first press of his lips to mine.

He laughed. The sound, light and full of joy, made me smile, then join him. He pulled back from his close attentions and looked into my eyes. What he'd said earlier—that he felt happy—I could see it there on his face. I wanted to save the image, and the feeling of utter bliss it sent through me, and never forget it.

"I've never done this before," he said with an unexpected sense of wonder, his palm warm on the bare skin of my back.

My mouth opened, but no words emerged. He'd never... *he* had never... "You're a—"

"No." A blazing smile split his face and absolutely demolished my heart. "No, I've just... I've never laughed with someone like this while being... physical. I've never had *fun*."

That sobered me. Like so many things, his earnest expression, his honesty... it just slayed me. "Well, I'm glad you can have fun with me."

Deep in my heart, buried under the fears that'd kept me from anything close to this with anyone else, I heard the words. Ones that I'd never even remotely wanted to say to someone before. *You can have whatever you want with me.* And more.

Far more significant for me, someone who did whatever she could *not* to take from others, were the words: *I want everything from you.*

CHAPTER TWENTY-SEVEN

Nick

I had this fantasy at work. You'd come over. We'd sit on the couch. The minutes would tick by, and I'd just stay there, arms around you, knowing you wanted to be right next to me.

Nothing in my life to this point could compare to the night with Summer.

No, she hadn't stayed the night, not when we both had to be up early for work. But the hours we spent were so full. I hadn't realized how much of my life felt empty until she'd arrived and filled it up.

Obviously, the persistent awareness of being alone and grieving had prime placement, so it wasn't that I didn't realize how sad I'd been. I knew that well and needed only to flip back through the pages of my current journal, even the several preceding this one, to see it. Until the last few months, where new themes had slipped in.

Going about my day, some of the restlessness I often felt had dissipated. Not precisely because of Summer, but more from having something to look forward to. The sense of endless, unremarkable days stretching out until retirement, and then fumbling toward owning a gym, hadn't evaporated by any means. It still clung to my heels, nipping at my feet as I walked. But it no longer hung on my back, dragging me down. *That* was remarkable.

The high from time with Summer ebbed by midday, though I hoped to see her tonight. She'd made plans to deliver a meal to someone and had work for her food drive to do. But we'd said we'd check in after work, and I itched to get to that point in the day. Before that I had to meet with Sergeant Major Allen. Good man, overall, but I didn't relish meeting with him.

"Sergeant Masters. How's it going?" Allen waved me into his office, unusually congenial for himself.

"Doing well, Sergeant Major."

He nodded, an exaggerated movement I'd forever associate with him. "Good to hear. Still eyeing retirement next year?"

"Roger. Working toward getting things organized for what's next." For once, that didn't bring such a fall of dread.

"Good. Good for you." He squinted, eyeing me like he might puzzle out my true motivations if I sat there long enough.

I knew what was coming but couldn't fault him. In fact, I knew I should take all of this as a compliment.

"Colonel and I have been talking. We'd love to see you stay on longer."

I said nothing—didn't want to refuse immediately and sour things.

"All I'm asking is you think on it. I know I've mentioned it before, but you won't be too far from dropping your packet, then we get to out-processing and before you know it, you're on terminal leave and staring down life as a civilian."

A muddled swirl of thoughts hit me then. Relief, uncertainty, and closer than ever before, hope. *Hunger*, even. "Thank you. I'll think about it."

He held up his hands. "All I'm asking."

I nodded again, and he gave me the go ahead, so I stood. "Have a good day, Sergeant Major."

"You too, Sergeant Masters."

I left his office, wondering just how much the new feelings had to do with Summer. I couldn't pin all the emotions on her—we'd just started. But somehow, last night, our relationship, whatever it was, had progressed. Beyond the physical, we'd connected. We had been, in small ways, for weeks now, but this was more than I'd ever had with anyone, times ten. It wasn't perfect, but it was ours, and I wanted more of it.

By the time I knocked on Summer's door, it was past nine that night. She'd had an issue come up with the food drive, and of course, refused my help. She hadn't said what it was, and since she'd texted, not called, I couldn't tell whether it was something big or not. By the look of her when she answered the door, it'd been a rough day.

"You okay?" I asked, stepping into the living room as she shut the door.

She nodded, uncharacteristically quiet and clearly upset. I held up an arm, and she immediately leaned into me and wrapped herself around me. I took the hug and savored it, shutting my eyes with the feeling of her against me. After a moment, she took a deep breath and let it out slowly. Another minute, and then she released me.

"Thank you." She looked a little better—more color in her cheeks now.

"Thank *you*."

She pressed her lips together like she might not tell me what was going on, but acquiesced. "I went to check the donation boxes, and they were disappointing. But then I discovered all the flyers had been torn down."

"Who would do that?"

Her lips thinned again and she sighed. "I'm afraid it might be Kent Dennin. The guy who you and Rob chased away that morning a month or so ago? I saw him do it once before at the mail room—he had two of them in his hand right as I walked in and he was exiting. He didn't say a thing but kind of... bumped into me."

Twin bolts of alarm and fury shot through me. "Have you reported him?"

"There's nothing to report. Or, if there is, it just seems so childish. I haven't so much as seen him looking at me in weeks." She ran a hand over her face and moved to her couch where she plunked down. "I don't know what his deal is. But I'm not going to spend a bunch of energy trying to figure out some creeper with a bad attitude. I got more flyers made and hung, and I'll just have to go check them daily and make sure everything looks good."

She ran through her other promotional plans—different places she'd announce the drive, including gatherings she'd be visiting. She'd talk to groups like some of the Bible studies and spouses' events in the next ten days, as well as a possible briefing at the OPFOR.

"I'll get to see you," I said dumbly. *Obviously, you idiot.*

She shifted on the couch, scooting so she sat closer and angled toward me, our knees touching. "Yes. I have actually only seen you in uniform a few times."

Something about the way she said that told me she looked forward to doing so again. "And I'll get to see you charm everyone into donating."

She smiled, and the frazzled air about her relaxed. "I hope."

I brushed a hand up her back, and she tipped to the side until she rested completely against me. "You seem a little stressed."

One hand settled on my chest. The warmth of her palm bled through my shirt, and my heart kicked.

"I need this to go well. I need the interview to go well, and I need that job. A lot's riding on this."

The *need* sounded so particular. "What happens if you don't get the job?"

She looked up at me from where she'd nestled in. I had to work not to shut my eyes at the sight. Holding her like this, talking after a long day, felt right.

"I lose my one chance for advancement here."

"And you wouldn't move for a position?"

We hadn't talked much about future plans. Suddenly, the idiocy of not knowing what she had in mind for her future struck me. I'd already mentally jogged down that line of thinking, wondering if our lives could match up. Maybe she hadn't.

She held my gaze. "I love it here. I don't want to have to move. This job is one I've been waiting on basically since I got here. I knew the nurse supervisor was planning to leave in the not-too-distant future, and I worked my tail off to complete my master's degree as soon as I could so I'd check that box. I don't know what I'll do if it doesn't work out."

I squeezed her close, hoping to reassure her without words. I'd never been in a position where advancement was so limited. Until this moment, I'd never had to consider what that might feel like. Of course there were jobs and opportunities that I'd wanted and not gotten, but as an infantryman, the options for me were always fairly wide open.

"It's going to be great. You've been working in this community for years, not just for this one thing. This is just one more effort on behalf of the people here. The hiring committee will see that."

They had to. No one gave as much as Summer. And while I recognized that may not suit her to this job particularly, I refused to believe that a less than stellar showing of canned food and boots could keep her from achieving this goal.

"Thanks. I hope."

We sat there, snuggled close, for long enough that the hour dragged at me. I lived an early-to-bed life, especially on weekdays when I woke early to prep PT setups for soldiers at the gym. I'd do the same tomorrow, which meant I needed to leave.

"I hate to say this, but I need to get going."

We separated and stood.

"Sorry I kept you up late. Thanks for coming over for a bit."

She looked as tired as I felt. We'd both do better with a good night's sleep.

"Can I see you tomorrow?"

"Yes, please. Saturday, I'm hosting a girls' night, and Sunday is the next feast."

I shook my head. "You're a busy woman, Summer Applegate."

"You're not exactly a lay-about, Nicholas Masters. How many training sessions do you have lined up this weekend?"

One brow flared in response. Fair enough. But unfortunately, her busy schedule happened in the evenings, and mine took up most of the weekend days. The stone of that truth sank to the bottom of me. "We'll hardly see each other this weekend."

She set her hands on either side of my neck. "Are you missing me already?"

"Of course. If I had it my way, I'd be with you all the time." Ah, damn. Maybe a bit much there.

Her lashes fluttered, and before I could try to pass off my comment as a joke, she beamed at me.

"Well, that is the most adorable thing you've said to me."

I chuckled at her clear delight. "Guess that didn't freak you out?"

She slowly shook her head from side to side. "Not in the least."

My heart thumped hard in my chest. The heat in her eyes sent my arms around her, and my body pressed into her in seconds. Our kiss was sure and full of promise. It was sweet, both satisfying and maddening, because anything with Summer made me wish for more. Since we both knew now wasn't the time, we broke apart.

"I like you," she said, her voice a little rough.

"Good. I like you too."

We said goodbye, and I made the brisk walk home. I didn't voice the concern over her plans for the future or how they diverged from mine. We would talk more tomorrow—I'd savor every second with her, and I wouldn't need to rush. We had time to explore things between us, and even if our schedules made seeing each other difficult this weekend, we'd figure it out. I'd show up on her doorstep at ten every night if I had to.

CHAPTER TWENTY-EIGHT

Summer

I didn't ask the obvious question last night, and it nagged at me all day.

It would've been so easy. Just say it, right there in the moment. *Nick, what are your plans?*

He'd said retirement and moving back to the Northeast. But it'd been in the group context in London, and so much had happened in the short days since then. I wanted to know more. I *needed* to know more because I'd already invested in him more than I had in anyone else, ever. I didn't want to get wrapped up in someone who planned to leave any day. He technically had time, but often it felt like people retiring had months of leave they could take before they got out. I didn't want him to just... disappear.

My gut clenched, but I exhaled around it, determined to finish this day well and then enjoy an evening with him. We wouldn't get much time together this weekend, and part of me regretted that. But canceling girls' night wasn't an option, nor was canceling the feast—I'd already invited guests, and I didn't want to be rude. Instead of scheduling the feast night as girls only, I'd remembered I'd already extended an invite to a couple, so we'd shifted around, and once I promised to cook and host, my friends seemed more than pleased with the change.

The day at the clinic was uneventful—too much so, since I'd hoped to have a little face time with Major Hall, but never saw her. She was probably mired in meetings and other obligations—the woman worked like mad.

After work, a trip to the commissary, and checking all the donation boxes and gathering things so none of them overflowed, I finally made it home. I changed quickly, texted to confirm he was ready while rounding up dinner, and practically sprinted to Nick's.

He opened the door before I knocked.

"Hi," I said, breathless from the near-jog I'd taken, all while keeping the food from spilling—or so I hoped.

"Come in." He took the bag, then stepped aside so I could enter.

I didn't go far. I'd been thinking about this—about seeing him again, and being able to touch him—all day. I wanted my hands on him and his on me.

"Come to the kitchen," he said, a hint of humor in his voice.

Maybe my desperation for him was obvious. I didn't mind him knowing. And happily, he seemed just as eager to have me there, considering he'd answered the door even before I stood fully on the step of his porch.

His hand came to my lower back, guiding me along, and my body lit up. His large, warm palm pressed through my coat—I could hardly feel it, in reality, but the gesture was enough. And it reminded me I wanted the coat off. I removed it as we walked, but he didn't return his hand since we'd made it to the kitchen. *Fine then.*

He set the bags on the table, then turned to me. I'd already dumped my jacket over the side of a dining chair. We came together, my hands at his waist and his at my face. I loved how he did that—held my head so gently and purposefully.

"I missed you today," I admitted.

"And I you."

Then he kissed me, so much heat and longing and... *wow.* The man could kiss. And together, we clicked. It felt right to be here, in his arms. For once, I didn't feel that twinge at the back of my neck—I didn't have a nagging sensation that my care for this person would leave me weak. His instant and consistent return of my feelings whenever I expressed them went a long way in helping that.

I shoved that away and savored the brush of his fingers at my jaw, down my neck. I didn't want to escalate things too quickly, but the lure of his abs proved too strong. I slipped my hands under his shirt and smoothed them over the ridiculous ridges of his stomach.

At the contact there, his breath caught, and then he chuckled. The combination of those two sounds was basically the hottest thing I'd ever heard.

Before I could outright attack him, a light pressure against my knee startled me. I broke from the kiss and looked down to find the adorable Butter leaning up against my leg with his front paws, checking out the action.

"Are you jealous, little one?" I asked, regrettably removing my hands from Nick's abs and petting the cat's feather-soft fur on his head. His purr thrummed through his little body.

"He doesn't do this with me. He makes me come to him most of the time. I think he has a thing for you," Nick said, faking grumpiness.

"Butter and I were meant to be. Weren't we, tiny fluff?" I hunched down to better pet and love on the cat, who was more than happy to lean into my hand where I pet his head, eager for my attentions.

"Guess you were."

I glanced up, because the tone of those words was so serious, given the moment. Nick stood smiling down with arms crossed, towering over us. But his face had a beautiful smile creasing his cheeks and lighting his eyes.

My heart, though it hadn't completely slowed from the kiss, accelerated again. "We better eat or I'm going to jump you again and we'll get nothing done."

He laughed. "Then I'll stay right here."

I beamed at him. "Okay, I take it back. Feed me, please, Sergeant Masters."

He nodded once, though the smile lingered as he unloaded the bags of food on the counter. I gave Butter a final pat and moved to the sink to wash my hands. When I glanced from the sink, Nick's profile struck me. The man was utter perfection physically, and all the more so because he wasn't actually perfect. I got to see those little things up close. But what made him so completely beautiful was the heart underneath.

"What's on your mind?" he asked, glancing at me before dishing up more food on the plates in front of him.

My stomach flipped, but I approached, setting a hand on his muscular back and leaning in to watch him. "I'm not sure I should tell you."

He raised a brow.

"Don't want to scare you away," I said, then winked,

hopefully covering the real fear in that thought. He'd given me no reason to think he'd go running for the hills if he knew how much I liked him, how much I thought of him, and generally how much I wanted with him and from him. But I didn't know.

His hands stilled at my words, and he turned his focus to me. He angled his body, too, so every ounce of that Nick Masters intensity trained on me. "You won't."

I swallowed. My heart cartwheeled. "Good."

The simple pot roast, veggies, and a salad went down well. Nick devoured everything on his plate and then got seconds. The satisfaction of feeding him lit that usual glow in me, but it felt brighter tonight. Maybe because of where we'd started months ago—him attempting to politely refuse my food. Or perhaps it felt so significant because it was. Feeding someone you cared about in a personal way was fundamentally different than feeding a stranger or even an acquaintance.

Not for the first time, I wondered how feeding a family —my own family—might feel. Then I realized Nick was clearing the table, so I jumped up to help.

"No, no. You know the rules. You cooked, so I clean. Give me just a minute and I'll join you on the couch." He piled our plates and bowls into a neat stack and left me nothing to do, so I did as he suggested.

Butter had set up vigil on the back of the couch. I ran a hand over him, smiling when his purr ignited. Rounding the corner, I sat, reveling in the dual sensation of sated hunger and blooming anticipation. Oddly enough, it was a feeling I had come to associate with spending time with Nick. The sated feeling didn't always correlate with eating, although tonight it did. But I also felt satisfaction of a deeper hunger, something I'd only recently begun to recognize existed in me.

I leaned back against the cushions gingerly, hoping I wouldn't disturb Butter. Then I felt something under me and pulled out a small notebook.

"Whoops," I said aloud, though I could hear the water running in the kitchen, so he was still cleaning up. I fingered a page that'd bent when I sat on it.

Then, because my eyes were nosy jerks, I read the words while pressing the fold out of the paper. Neat, slanted writing filled two and three lines at a time with spaces between.

I never saw you coming, and it's a damn good thing.

I chuckled at that. I wasn't arrogant enough to be sure it referred to me, but if it was, I had to laugh. I certainly felt the same way.

When you press against me, the world collapses into nothing. All my concern circles the contact, the slip of your fingers in my hair, the slide of your tongue in my mouth. The hitch of your breath is a beat, a moment, a thousand seconds I hang on. The pull of a smile at your lips is melody and song.

Oh, wow.

And I shouldn't have kept going, but I did. Because no

woman in her right mind would be offered the opportunity to gain insight into Nick Masters and *not* take it. Particularly if she were feeling a little unsteady. Like her feelings were too big to fit into her body, and like she was barreling toward something she'd never had before.

So, right or wrong, I read on. The next one had a big line through it, like he'd rejected the thoughts, either for falsehood or maybe he just didn't like the words.

Chances.
I have not been known to follow. Not after chances.
I have not been able to dream. Not of chances.
I have not been determined to fight. Not for chances.
I have not been deserving to know. Not of chances.
Now I know.
I will follow you.
I dream of you.
I will fight for you.
I will endeavor to deserve to know you.
I will take my chances with you.

I glanced over into the kitchen. Nick stood at the sink, but the water was off. Maybe drying something. He had a dishwasher, so I wasn't sure. But there was one more section on these open pages. I wouldn't turn the page—I wouldn't invade his privacy that way. Even my desperate, needy little heart had a line.

Miraculous things happen with your hands on me. My hearts stops, clearing all interference. Nothing will interrupt the pads of your fingers tracing my jaw. Silence will greet the press of your lips. Stillness answers the slide of your skin against mine. The ragged muscle in the cage at my chest, so weak from disuse, only starts again when you whisper my name. The whip of the word reminds me of breath and I take it. The stolen seconds between us have changed me—

My hands shook. That one extended onto the next page, and every atom of my existence wanted to keep reading. His words were sensual and full of so much meaning, I could hardly swallow. In fact, I couldn't. I shot up, desperate for a drink.

"You okay?"

"Uh... yeah..." I pushed past the couch and practically stumbled to the table. He hadn't cleared the glasses, thank goodness, and I gulped down most of the water remaining in mine.

"Summer?" He came close, a hand on my back. "What is it?"

I wiped my mouth, buying time. I couldn't very well say I'd read his book. Could I? And if I did? What would happen? Was it the kind of thing that disappeared off the page once read? Did it remove the sentiment, to be written down?

"I, uh..."

Get it together! I couldn't find words. Something about *his* words had shaken me, created a shuddering weakness at the pit of my stomach. In fact, on that note, I might retch. The muscles of my throat worked, and I took the last sip of water.

His hand rubbed gentle circles in the curve of my lower back as he watched me. His eyes, intense and concerned, made the suffocating sensation intensify. And I knew I wouldn't calm down, not here. I wouldn't be able to sit down over there and see that book and not be torn to shreds.

"I'm so sorry, I'm feeling kind of bad all of a sudden. I'm going to run home." I grabbed the jacket we hadn't moved from the back of the chair no one sat in and yanked it on. "I'll grab the dinner stuff on—another time."

"Okay. Do you need medicine? Do you want me to come—"

"I'm fine. I'll be fine. I'm sorry."

And with that, I was gone. Out of his front door, with him reaching it seconds after I'd tried to cram it shut behind me. I choked back the sob rising in me, but the tears had started. Every step I took pounded the thought into me— *what the hell is happening right now?*

By the time I reached my house, I flung the door open, then shut it behind me and sank down against it. I tucked my head into my knees and breathed slowly.

I'd flipped out. *Flipped. The. Eff. Out.*

His words... all those gorgeous words, and they were about me. I knew it. And what they said, all of them together, painted a picture of Nick wanting me. With an intensity I didn't think anyone ever had. *Ever.*

And what that did to me?

Need. It made writhing, aching need crawl up from the depths of my belly and grip my heart in a vise-like fist. And the minute I recognized that, I ran.

CHAPTER TWENTY-NINE

Nick

These are just words on a page. These are nothing like the blood in my veins, which grows hot with the thought of you. These are nothing like my lungs that struggle for breath at the sight of you. These are only words, not like my wandering mind and its dreams of you. These words are nothing like this heart and what it feels for you.

I found the journal on the couch a few minutes after Summer had shot out the front door like she might die unless she reached home.

I skimmed the pages that lay open. *Damn.* She couldn't read those and think I was anything but completely gone for her. And she wouldn't be wrong.

Funny how she'd mentioned not wanting to scare me

away, and here we were. I messaged her, asking if she was okay. I paced the living room, wiped down the table, and still didn't hear back. I debated going over and knocking, but that was so far from my natural impulse, I trashed the idea. I didn't want to push her. She'd panicked, clearly, and me shoving my face in her door wouldn't take that away.

A full hour later, she responded. *"Sorry about running out."*

Well, better than silence. I debated saying outright that I knew she'd seen the journal. But something told me pressing her now wouldn't do anything for me. *"We should talk. When you're ready."*

Another few agonizing minutes passed, and then her message came. *"We should. Check in tomorrow after your training sessions?"*

At least it wasn't an effort to put me off more than a few hours. I could live with tomorrow, of course. I couldn't blame her for needing time, and I wanted her to have it if she needed it. Granted, I also wanted to go barge into her living room and demand to know why my bad poetry had thrown her so hard, because I hadn't made a secret of my feelings. Perhaps I hadn't shared them quite so honestly, but still. These weren't even the worst of what she could've seen in that book.

I petted Butter, focusing on the purr, the feel of the wispy longer fur around his ears. I never would've imagined a fickle little beast like him would be able to calm and center me, but he did. Just touching his softness brought me down from the worry about Summer and how things would go tomorrow to here and now. It didn't erase the concern, just like it hadn't erased the grief of the last few months after Rob had dumped him on me in January. But having another living being in the house, something purely his own and willing to coddle me a bit by letting me pet him and fuss over him now and then... it eased a primal tightness death and solitude had wrought in me.

I messaged Summer back, confirming I'd check in after my last session. Nate Reynolds had upped his frequency and had the last slot of the day. It didn't exactly surprise me, because he worked hard whenever he showed up to group trainings on weekends, and his general level of fitness was very high. He'd asked for tips here and there, and I'd helped him map out a solo-training plan he could do at home and the on-post gym. But he'd wanted more, almost like he was pouring himself into the physical to avoid something else.

Not uncommon. Happened all the time and frequently resulted in some amount of injury or over-training. So I'd need to evaluate where he was mentally and physically tomorrow.

I slumped down on my bed, the infernal journal next to me. Not shockingly, I both needed to and didn't want to write. Pouring myself out into it, knowing the words there had thrown her so... it didn't sound like the release I wanted. I wished I could go for a run, but it was too dark now, and it'd be a bit cold. March was spring in Germany, but that didn't mean warm just yet.

Instead, I readied for bed and slipped under the covers, praying sleep would find me sooner than later.

"Good."

Reynolds pushed from a decently low squat and thrust the bar above his head. Good natural form. "Two more."

He didn't waver, moving through the thrusters with the same determination he'd shown every time I'd seen him train. For someone seemingly so happy-go-lucky, he had genuine grit. I'd always read him as kind of a pretty rich boy who was good at Army, though he'd never treated anyone like that. My own prejudice at work. I liked seeing him in this context, though—he took direction, listened well, didn't balk at being pushed or challenged.

He let the barbell and weights plunk down gently. He hadn't gotten used to the fact that he could drop them altogether if needed. It was a safety precaution, and in competition, also helped with speed. I appreciated the consideration for the equipment, but he didn't need to be gentle.

"Now give me a quarter mile, and you're done."

He nodded and took off out the door. He wanted bulk *and* speed, so we kept some sprinting in the mix. Quarter-miles were perfect for pushing guys used to training to the Army PT test requisite two miles.

I'd only have a little over a minute, depending on how much gas Reynolds had left. But I'd been itching to message her all day, so I grabbed my phone and sent the message to Summer.

Me: *"Wrapping up here. Should be free in thirty."*

That'd give me time to get Reynolds cooled down and stretched out. Rob had come for an extra-long session today, but he'd already moved to the mats to wrap up.

Summer: *"The girls arrive in 45."*

Well, crap. I'd hoped they'd be showing up later, like maybe six. Five was early for a girls' night, no? I didn't want to rush the conversation we needed to have. Especially if for her it wasn't simply *thanks but no thanks*, I wanted the time. I wasn't about to confess my love—not there yet. But I could easily get there, and if we kept at this, I would. And I wanted to know if she thought she could too—even if it was purely hypothetical. I needed to know we could move forward, and her knowing I didn't want to keep it at *casually dating* was part of that.

Reynolds burst back in the door and tapped his watch, then walked in a loose circle.

"Good work. Last round, best round—good."

He'd improved. Even since earlier in the day, he'd improved, but especially since the fall when he'd really started showing up to the group workouts on weekends. *That* was what drew me to this—seeing people improve in ways they wanted. Seeing that satisfaction that only came from knowing you'd left everything on the table.

He nodded, huffing out a large breath, and eyed me. "How's Summer?"

Routinely, he brought up Summer or retirement. Not anything deep and probing, just making conversation. Probably making sure I wasn't a danger to myself. I'd popped on a mental health tracker after the new year, likely both because of the death in my family and a conversation I'd had with Sergeant Major Allen. It was the first time I'd mentioned retirement to him personally, and he hadn't seen it coming. I suspected he thought of me as someone who'd be in for more like thirty rather than twenty.

The idea of ten more years of this, sank low in my gut. No. I couldn't do it much longer. It wasn't any one thing. I'd had a great career. But I was ready for the next chapter. And I wouldn't mind if that chapter starred one gorgeous, stubborn, perpetually busy and helpful blonde. If I could only get her alone for a few minutes sooner rather than later and see if she had interest in moving forward too.

"Busy. She's got friends coming over tonight." I didn't know why I said that. He didn't want to know those details.

He seemed interested, though. "Yeah? Is Ariel going? She and Summer are pretty close, right?"

Ah. "I think Ariel was invited, yes."

He nodded, affecting nonchalance I'd gathered he didn't actually possess when it came to the woman in question.

"Sorry you had to spend your day training us and not with your woman." Rob patted my back and waved, keys in hand. "See you tomorrow."

I returned the gestured. "Drive safe."

Reynolds moved to the stretching mats, and I stared at the phone. Did I push or try to act like the timing for when I got to see her and talk to her again wasn't driving me into madness?

Me: *"I could help you clean up after?"*

I sent that without fully thinking it through. I just wanted a reason to see her. But she often rejected help in the kitchen, so I added, *"Or, if you refuse to let me help, I could sit and watch you, and we could talk?"*

The little dots indicating she was typing popped up, then disappeared a half dozen times. My stomach clenched, anxious she'd put me off another day. I could live with that —I would. But damn, I didn't want to.

Finally, she replied. *"Okay. I'm not sure what time we'll be done. Could be pretty late."*

Me: *"Just let me know."*

CHAPTER THIRTY

Summer

I'd been off all day. So far off, I needed a new recipe.

But the food turned out well, thank goodness. Sometimes when my mood was too far gone, whatever I touched in the kitchen reflected it. I supposed that, since I wasn't exactly upset or angry or anything necessarily bad, just overwhelmed and a little fearful, if we're being honest, I didn't need to worry about ruining everything I touched.

Usually, cooking helped. I could work my way through whatever problem I faced as I worked through a recipe—chopping garlic, sautéing onions, browning meat, seasoning, combining, rolling, stuffing, baking, whatever. It served to break down the larger issue into bites, and of course I loved the process of cooking so that fired off some endorphins to help things. Tonight, I didn't feel that kick of clarity that usually set in.

I prepped the appetizers for the oven—they'd go in right

as everyone arrived. Just five minutes to crisp them up. Otherwise, everything else was ready and waiting. I shucked my apron, smoothed down my shirt, and glanced out at Mr. Meier's house. From the kitchen, I could see part of his front walk, his front door, and around to his back door. He'd had a grandchild staying with him the last few weeks, so I hadn't seen him much.

My phone buzzed, and my heart leapt into my throat. Nick and I would see each other later, no matter how much later. He seemed to know I needed space. Or maybe that was what life with him would be like—never being pushed to face my ridiculous feelings. I doubted that. He was incredibly intuitive, likely because he spent so much time observing and thinking rather than speaking or preparing to speak.

Instead of something else from Nick, it was Ariel. My stomach dropped at her message.

Ariel: *"I'm so sorry to do this, but I can't be there tonight. I'm so sad to miss. Livie won't make it either. Please forgive me. We'll get together soon!"*

Me: *"Are you okay?"*

Ariel: *"Yeah. Livie's still not feeling good, and my mom is worn out. Eric's at a planning conference or something this weekend. I need to stick around here."*

Me: *"Of course. Tell Livie we'll miss her too and to come see me at the clinic Monday if she's still feeling bad! I didn't realize she was still in such bad shape."*

Ariel: *"You're the best. Tell everyone hi, and eat some guacamole for me."*

The doorbell rang, pulling me from the conversation. I missed Ariel—and Livie, for that matter—but I also admired Ariel's loyalty to her family and her sense of duty to them. Maybe that wasn't quite the right way to put it, but she showed up for them. I'd text Livie later to check in on her—I didn't realize she hadn't kicked whatever she'd been dealing with last time we had a girls' night. For now, I'd focus on enjoying the friends who could come and would hope to see Ariel and Livie sooner than later.

"Come in!" I said, genuinely smiling at finding Bec, Emily, and Katie on my doorstep.

They bustled in, unzipping coats and chatting as they came.

"It's weirdly cold for end of March. Shouldn't it be spring?" Bec asked as she hung her jacket and purse.

Emily widened her eyes in exasperation at the weather. "It *is* spring—this is spring in Bavaria. It sort of feels like winter except you get freezing rain instead of snow most of the time. But I bet you we have another snow or two before it warms up all the way."

She wasn't wrong. Spring was cold and crisp but also lovely. It also meant the summers, compared to many places, were fairly mild.

"That's just rude," Bec mumbled, glancing around. "Ariel and Livie running late?"

I took Katie's jacket for her while responding. "Sadly, no. They can't come tonight."

After a few minutes of regretting that reality, I shooed them into the living room. "I'm going to put the taquitos in the oven and grab the drinks. Get cozy."

I popped the tray in, enjoying the warmth that filled me at having my girls here. I'd needed this. And strangely, admitting that didn't throw me for a loop. It made me grateful to have friends like this, people I wanted to be around and looked forward to seeing. I'd had friendships, but not a close group in far too long.

I emerged with a tray of margaritas in highball glasses.

Not official margarita barware, but as I tended to be on the clumsy side, I didn't favor stemmed drinkware.

"Those look so good. I've been looking forward to this for what feels like forever." Emily accepted a drink and took a sip, then let out a sigh. "So good. Is it spicy?"

"Yes. You all said you like heat, so it's a jalapeno margarita. It shouldn't be *hot*, just a little... tingly." I wiggled my brows.

They all chuckled. I set the tray down on the coffee table and slipped back into the kitchen to grab a few of the appetizers while Bec spoke.

"Sounds perfect," she said, taking her glass. "This week —other than spending time with the man I love—has made me anything but tingly."

We all laughed again, and they each toasted each other. I set several platters down, including the now piping hot and crisp taquitos which I'd been looking forward to all afternoon, on the small table.

Holding my drink, I raised it to the middle of the circle we'd made by sitting in the different spots in my living room. "To friendship and Saturdays."

Katie said, "And a generous hostess."

Bec chimed in, her eyes wide on the table in front of her. "And amazing food and drinks."

Emily gave us a grin. "And tingles."

We all burst out laughing at that, but we raised our glasses high, then drank. The tart, spicy liquid refreshed and cooled my mouth, then warmed my belly. I scooted to the edge of my seat and waved dramatically over the food. "Apps are chipotle chicken taquitos with cotija crema. Bacon, chicken, and pepper jack quesadillas. Chips, salsa, guacamole."

"I love you. I'll say it now, and I'm sure again later. But I love you."

Emily didn't glance at me as she piled food on her plate. Bec and Katie did the same, and I breathed in the moment. The soothing, peaceful satisfaction of feeding friends settled over me, and my heart glowed with that familiar feeling.

After a few minutes of eating and exclaiming how delicious everything was, we relaxed into easy conversation about work, updating on the latest. Since they all worked at the Ed Center, their update was short and sweet. Then they turned to me.

"The donation drive's going decently well, I think. It'll run through spring break, but I know most stuff will come in before people leave for their trips. So I'm within about ten days of having a solid sense of the final amounts, and then I can get it sorted."

An anxious little spike shot up in my belly. I hoped it'd turn out to be a success. In theory, any amount of donations would be a success because it was food and boots the people receiving them wouldn't otherwise have. But in reality, I wanted to be able to quantify the amount of donations and have it sound impressive. It needed to signal my ability to manage.

"That's amazing. There's nothing we can do to help, right?" Bec asked, setting aside her now-empty plate.

"No. Truly. It's sort of on autopilot at this point. Thank you."

They wanted to help, and instead of that grating, I felt touched. I knew they genuinely meant what they offered. But it was fairly low-maintenance.

A smoky curl of concern rose in the back of my mind, but I mentally waved it away.

"And what about Nicholas Masters?" Emily asked with a sly smile.

I gulped down the sip of margarita in my mouth, immediately nervous and excited by the sound of his name. "Uh. We're dating? I think?"

Bec cocked her head to the side like it might give her a better view of the situation while Katie's brow furrowed. Emily finished chewing and jumped in.

"You think?"

"Well, we went out in London. And I know he likes me." I swallowed, my belly contracting with an anxious little zip. He definitely liked me. A lot.

Emily pointed at me. "What's that face?"

Bec chuckled. "Nice, Emily."

Emily held up her hands in innocence. "What? I'm just trying to get a read on this situation. We've got two of the most beautiful people *ever* circling around each other for months, and I want the goods. Have you kissed? No good?"

The furious blush burned in my cheeks. "We have. And... uh, very good."

I laughed, and the smile exploded on my face. Why deny it? The chemistry between us was not an issue.

All three of them exclaimed something along the lines of "Yes!" and "Ooh!" like they were celebrating with me. The silliness of that, and yet the sweetness, struck me. How wonderful to have people rooting for me like this. To celebrate something good or fun in my life.

It threw into sharp relief how alone I'd been. I didn't think of myself that way because I hosted dinner parties and had a social job, but I had very few people who knew me. That these women were here, supporting me, wanting to know about the details of my life, made my chest feel like someone had inflated a balloon behind my ribs. I cleared my throat of the emotion creeping up and smile at them.

"He's just... different than I expected," I admitted.

"Different, bad?" Bec asked.

"No. Different like... I never imagined someone like him existed. Like I was expecting a cake from a box mix and instead got something baked from scratch, with top-notch ingredients. Like he's a little too good to be true, and I don't know what to do about it."

There. Got it out. I'd been circling the thought all day, but it seemed silly. He was, after all, a human man. He was kind of grumpy and a bit awkward in social situations. He could be stingy with his words.

Yeah, or extremely generous with them.

Too true. His letters, and though I shouldn't have seen or read it, his journal. Plus, we did have good conversation. We'd talked about all kinds of things at this point—childhoods, goals, travel, interests. I hadn't tallied it all up, but he probably knew more about me than anyone else ever had.

And that, more than the feelings scrawled across his pages, was what scared me most.

The three women sitting in my living room looked stunned by my last comment. Not surprisingly, Emily spoke first. "I'd say if you like him, you just... keep dating him."

Simple enough on the surface, sure. "Right."

Katie reached out and set a hand on my arm. "I can understand your thinking. I felt that way about Noah. Sometimes, it even made me feel bad, like what could I have to offer this guy? But Noah, like Nick, is not perfect. And once I let myself see that, it got easier."

I nodded.

Then Bec chimed in. "And if you want to know what's happening between the two of you, ask. No one can read minds. He's probably wondering the same thing. And if you care about him, being a little vulnerable to get some clarity on your relationship isn't a bad idea."

My smile was thin, but I spread it wide to cover the discomfort her comment stirred in me. *Vulnerable.* What a horrendous word. And exactly the reason I'd flipped and run away last night. Nick always had a way of making me feel exposed, and somehow, seeing *his* intimate thoughts in that book had made me feel raw and naked.

"Good idea. Thanks, ladies." I held up my glass and dramatically took a few chugs, at which they laughed.

"So, Katie, tell us when you guys pack out and what your PCS is going to look like," Emily said, mercifully shifting the attention from me.

I listened as Katie gave us the details on her move, and while Bec agonized over job prospects in Kansas, where she and Thatcher would move this summer, but only for a year. We migrated to the table after a while, gorged ourselves on fajitas, and eventually, they left. Like I promised, and only because I'd promised myself I would, I texted Nick to tell him they were gone, just shy of eleven. I half expected he'd be asleep, while at the same time knew I wouldn't be that lucky.

Five minutes after I sent my message, a quiet knock sounded at my door.

CHAPTER THIRTY-ONE

Nick

You'll have to pry it open. Wrench back the rounded, hollowed halves. Peek into the blackened middle. Ease the fruit from the shell, careful of its edges, its softness, its fragility. That's the only way you'll taste the sweetness.

The last six hours had been long. They'd moved so slowly, I'd ended up getting in a second workout after dinner. I normally hated to work out in the evenings if I didn't have to, but I'd needed some way to expend the anxious energy building inside me.

The tentative smile that greeted me made my stomach dip. She was so beautiful, and I didn't know how this conversation was going to go.

"Come in," she said, her voice a little rough.

"Did you have fun?"

A genuine smile now. "Yes. It was great."

"It still smells good. What'd you make?"

She listed the dishes, all of which were no doubt excellent, and took a seat on the couch in the living room. Adrenaline raced through me so hard my hands shook, but I took slow breaths to keep calm. I sat next to her—not too close, because I already felt like I might be suffocating her with all the *feelings* I had.

"So..." She squinted up at me.

Well. Let's get to it. "I'm guessing you saw my journal."

She swallowed and bobbed her head.

"And you thought it was about you?"

She blinked. Nodded.

I cracked a half-smile. "The ones I think you might've seen were inspired by you."

Maybe couching it in *inspiration* would help soften it. Based on the page that lay open when she left, it could've been worse, but the words were certainly... impassioned.

She didn't speak. Usually, she spoke constantly, filling the room and the space between us with words, but now, I couldn't have bribed her. I was groping around in the dark for some way to break through and get a conversation going, because me just blundering along here wouldn't do me any favors.

"I'm sorry if they made you uncomfortable. I didn't plan for you to see them. I've been journaling and writing poetry since my teens. It was a way to cope—to process things. And there's a creative element, so don't let it upset you."

If she weren't sitting half a foot from me, studying my face, I would've crushed my eyes together at the idiocy of those words.

To my immense relief, she set a warm hand on my wrist. "You don't need to apologize. *I* do. I invaded your privacy by reading it, and then I just... had no idea what to do with myself."

I nodded, understanding. The alternative might've been to pretend she hadn't read it, but she wasn't dishonest like that. Leaving had been the best option, if I looked at it like that.

"I don't feel invaded. But I am concerned."

"Understandable."

I waited. Ready for her to take over. I willed her to let me understand.

"So. I was overwhelmed," she started, then chuckled low.

I appreciated her ability to laugh at the situation. That bolstered me.

She inhaled slowly and turned her eyes to me.

"I've never met someone like you. I've never been with anyone so..." Her gaze flickered around the space, like she might find the right word hiding in the corner of her living room. "Thoughtful. Intense."

My shoulders stiffened. *Intense* was a word I often heard from women I dated. Granted, I hadn't bothered in quite a while, but it was never used as a positive term. They wanted a relationship, but with someone easy, sunny, fun. Occasionally, I stumbled into fun, but I was, by nature, intense. That'd ended more than one relationship before it really began. Summer must've seen my reaction, though I wasn't sure I'd moved visibly. She grabbed my hand with both of hers and held it. Relief and wanting sliced through me at the connection.

"Those things are good. I like that about you. But it's very different than what I'm used to." She swallowed, seeming to marshal her bravery. "I've never felt about someone the way I do about you. And paired with the writing, I just... I needed some space. I was embarrassed I'd snooped and read your obviously private thoughts, and I then didn't want to lie to you or pretend it hadn't affected me. So I ran home and acted like a totally immature—"

Those things are good. I like that about you. Having her say them, just like that... I raised my free hand to brush across her high, smooth cheekbone. "It's fine. We're here talking about it."

What I really wanted to say? *And how do you feel about me?* But I wouldn't press her on that point right this minute. What she'd admitted was enough.

"We are."

I couldn't help the smile that came. "So what do you want to do now?"

She huffed. "I don't—I mean, what do *you* want?"

Our gazes locked into one another, and my whole center of gravity shifted to her. The pull in my chest, my whole being, made me wonder if I'd be skewed toward her indefinitely.

"You."

Her lashes fluttered.

"I'd like to date you. Seriously. And move forward together like we might stay together."

Lightning bolts of nerves raced through my chest. *Well, it's out there now.*

"Okay."

Her answer came out a bit breathy but sure. No hesitation. Though I could've gone for something more than *okay*.

"Do you want that too? There's no pressure here. If that's not what you want, just say the word and we can figure out a different—"

"I do." She squeezed the hand she still held tight. "I want that. With you. With us."

That sure, clear confirmation was all it took to relieve the day's worth of tension that'd cycled through me since the minute she'd bolted last night. I let out a long breath. "Good."

She leaned up, and her warm lips met mine. She may have meant to start a soft kiss to seal our decision, but everything about the last few minutes, the last few days, had set me on edge. Having her close, touching her, loosed a hunger in me I stupidly hadn't seen coming.

She didn't seem overwhelmed at the touch, at the sure progress of my hands from her face down to her neck and then back. Her hands roamed over my chest and arms, like kissing was the only time she had permission to explore me. I made a mental note to make clear she could touch and take whatever she wanted, whenever she so chose.

"I missed you. Isn't that stupid? It's only been a little more than twenty-four hours, but I did," she whispered into my neck, sending fire into my veins.

"Not stupid," was all I could scratch out.

She ran a hand over my hair and down to my neck where she cradled my head. The feeling of that gentle palm made me pause. The growing need for her, the desperation to be as close as possible, slowed, quelled by the affection and sweetness of the gesture. My gaze found her face, and I searched it for meaning.

"I like you, Nick."

A sharp breath tumbled out like a laugh. "Good. I more than like you, Summer."

~

More than an hour later and so far past my bedtime it wasn't funny, I lingered at her door, wishing I didn't have to say goodbye. But I did.

My hands at her waist, I spoke quietly. "I hope feast night goes well tomorrow."

Her brow furrowed, and her hand traced along my right pec. She must not have realized how her touch affected me —couldn't possibly know, or she wouldn't do that.

"You're not coming?"

"I didn't know I was invited."

She tilted her head to the side. "Of course you are. You're my boyfriend."

The word sounded almost comical, and yet it shot a thrill straight through me. I liked being something of hers. "I guess I am."

Her brows raised. "You *guess?*"

I chuckled low, relishing her indignation. "I am. *I am.* I just hadn't thought of it in that term, but of course. And you're my girlfriend."

Some primal part of me raged at the word for her. I didn't want her to be my girlfriend. I wanted her to be *mine.* But girlfriend was a good first step. A necessary step, too.

Her answering smile lit up the room, and she pressed her hand flat in the center of my chest. "Yes, I am."

We smiled at each other like idiots for a minute, but my watch buzzed at the hour. One a.m.

"I hate to, but I have to go. Art and Alicia will be in by eight."

"Go. And I'll see you tomorrow night."

She leaned up on her toes to press a kiss to my lips. I caught her behind the back and held her there for a minute, storing up the touch until I'd see her again.

"Sleep well."

I jogged the half block home, anxious to get to bed. Eager to review the events of the night in my mind. Resolute that, at some point, this return trip wouldn't be necessary.

CHAPTER THIRTY-TWO

Summer

Nick didn't come to feast night.

I couldn't be upset. And I did understand. Disappointed? Yes. But I genuinely did understand—or, I could empathize. We'd talked in the late afternoon, and I'd mentioned a few people who were coming. He'd asked who else, and then we realized he didn't know any of them.

First, this boggled my mind. The Kugelfels community was so small, I didn't understand how he could live here and not know these people. They were from all different agencies and offices on post. Granted, none of them were military. But I could tell the minute he realized it, when the space between us, even the cellular, metaphysical space or whatever, filled with dread.

So I'd given him the out. And he'd taken it.

I tried *so* hard not to feel anything more than missing

him. But that disappointment crept in. I wanted him with me. If we were going to be together, I needed him to participate. And I knew he would show up if I pushed him or even asked him to.

I hadn't. I'd heard his tone and told him he didn't have to come, and though a small part of me had hoped he'd insist on it, I tried to accept that his staying home was right.

The evening went well. The new recipes I'd tried were a hit, though I'd made notes to tweak the goat cheese tartlet, and I didn't love the clove in the chicken dish. I never really liked clove, so that shouldn't have been a surprise.

Everyone had filtered out quickly, the threat of a thunderstorm fueling their exit. I insisted all the more they just get going and avoid driving on slick Bavarian roads in the pitch black since so few of the country roads had streetlights. But moments after the last person had gone, before I'd even emptied the table, someone knocked.

And who should it be but Nick, his T-shirt soaked through and plastered to that glorious chest. My toes curled in my shoes. He was generally stunning, but showing up on my doorstep, rain-soaked, his tattoos shadows under the sopping fabric? This might've topped the shirtless snowstorm moment.

"Hello," he said, his eyes sparkling.

"Hello. Would you like to come in?"

His lips twitched. "Only if you'll let me help you clean up."

A warm, sweet feeling bloomed in my chest.

"If you insist," I said, turning aside and gesturing for him to enter. I closed the door behind him, my breathing fast. Like, stupid fast. But the sight of him like this darn near knocked me out.

He didn't go far, once inside. In fact, he sort of crowded

me but didn't touch me. Rain drops tracked from his hair down his face.

"Would you like a towel?" I asked, tucking my hands behind my back so I couldn't maul him.

"Yes, please."

Ooh. Wow. He had a little grit in his voice tonight, something that told me he had come to clean up, and then some. I scuttled down the hall to the bathroom, grabbed a towel, and returned to him. He took it from me and wiped his face, ran it over his hair and neck, and then pressed it into his arms and chest.

"Shirt's pretty soaked," I said, my voice sounding weird. Like I'd eaten a raw

Scotch bonnet pepper and singed my throat.

"It is."

"Maybe you should take it off."

Eyes on me, he handed me the towel. My stomach dropped down, down, through the floor, straight through to the other side of the world. His fingers gripped the hem, and slowly, he peeled up the thin, sodden material to reveal what I now considered my favorite piece of art. Truly. Stick him in the Tate Modern, folks. Wow.

Every breath accentuated the curves of his muscles, all cinched together and stacked, the picture of discipline. Maybe that was why the sight affected me the way it did —a kind of total body experience. Because I knew the life he lived to maintain this. He would never pretend it came about easily or without effort. He'd spent years honing this body, both for his profession and his future plans.

That shook me from the all too real grip of his physical beauty. The future. One we'd said we'd walk toward together, and yet we hadn't actually talked about what it could look like. Last check, we had entirely different trajectories.

"We should probably wring that out."

He nodded and followed me into the kitchen. I focused on this small task—wring out his shirt. I walked to the sink and reached out a hand, palm up, without looking at him. If I kept allowing myself to, I'd end up touching him. And if I did that... well, the kitchen wouldn't be likely to get clean.

"I'll do it," he said, his voice gruff and surprisingly close.

I turned just as he stepped up to the sink, *right* next to me, and wrung out the shirt.

"Did it just downpour the whole time you walked over here?" I asked, amazed at the amount of water dribbling into the sink and working not to admire the strength of his hands or trace the tendons and veins in his forearms.

"It was barely a drizzle when I stepped out, so I decided I'd jog over, but as soon as I hit the sidewalk, it opened up. Felt more like a southern storm that way. Should've grabbed my jacket." He gave me a wry grin.

A pang hit me at that. I liked everything about him. Everything. Of course I liked his appearance—*duh*. But that little smile, and the fact that he'd come without me even calling or texting. Like he'd been watching for people to leave. Like he wanted to be here as much as I wanted him here. I could get over his reticence to socialize with people he didn't know. That wasn't the end of the world.

All kinds of winged things fluttered around in my belly.

"I doubt I have a shirt that would fit you... or even a sweatshirt. I've never been one of those people who keeps her ex's shirts or anything. But let me go see if I can find something." I squeezed the arm nearest me as I passed him, his skin pebbled and cool under my hand.

"Thanks."

I escaped into my closet, ransacking it for anything that might work. I had to have something he could wear. He had to be cold, if not freezing. My house was fairly warm, but he was well and truly soaked just moments ago.

I had not one T-shirt larger than a women's large, which I knew would look like a child's size on him. The only idea I did have, I delivered to him and did my best to keep a straight face.

"So. This is all I could find that might even begin to cover you."

A brow flared, and he smiled.

"Looks cozy." He took the item from me.

"It is."

My voice had dropped and sounded weirdly sensual. But as he slipped his long, muscled arms into the sleeves of my bubblegum pink fuzzy robe, some of those grippy, desirous feelings eased. I burst out laughing.

He scowled. "You give me the robe to wear, then laugh at me?"

He pulled the sides together. They'd overlap on me, but they didn't quite meet in the middle for him. He tied a quick knot in the belt, then held his arms out for me to take in the full picture.

I laughed harder. "How is it that small on you?"

The sleeves came nearly to his elbows. What was mid-thigh length on me hit him just below the hips. The belt cinched just above his belly button, and the pink color clashed with the olive green of his pants, which were also quite wet. The best part, though, was his face. He found the humor in it, once again proving my judgement of him from weeks ago to be false. I'd assumed a man this pretty couldn't have a sense of humor, especially not about himself. But there he stood, now striking subtle, ridiculous poses in the robe.

"It's super soft. I might want one of these." He brushed his hands down the front.

"I think we should find you one in your size."

And then, I just had to. I couldn't resist him anymore. If the sight of his skin and muscle had drawn me in, the image of him donning my bright pink robe with no hint of embarrassment, only good humor, finished me off.

I walked to him with arms out, and he immediately accepted me into a hug. My head rested at the base of his neck, and my hand stroked up along the center of his back, over the robe.

"Thanks for coming to help," I said, almost in a whisper.

"Of course."

We lingered in the embrace. Standing in the middle of my kitchen wrapped up in Nick Masters, being held close and smelling the rain and soap scent of him, had emotion clogging my throat. I should've been tearing the robe off him, mapping those muscles with my hands, but suddenly, I felt like weeping.

And we couldn't have any of that. No indeed. So I pecked a kiss to his neck, then pulled back—all the way back, out of his reach, and twirled around to set to work on dishes. If I let him see the tears shimmering in my eyes, he'd worry. And then I'd probably lose my grip on the tears and they'd fall.

I didn't want to think too hard on the reason simply hugging him had brought me such comfort and peace, so much so I couldn't stand there doing it without a crush of emotion flooding in. Allowing the full gravity of the moment to set in—the sense of rightness, or tenderness, or intimacy—couldn't happen. So I set to work, and seconds later, with no complaint or question, he joined me.

CHAPTER THIRTY-THREE

Nick

Forgive me while I look my fill. I need to etch that little scar on your chin very carefully into my mind. I have to get the whorl of blue and gray in your eye just right. I have to make the memory of the curve of your cheek last until next time.

I counted Art's reps, knowing he'd lose track and do too many. The flowing movement of kipping pull-ups, the kind that used momentum to assist the arms and torso to complete high reps, proved mesmerizing this evening.

Two days later and I still couldn't stop thinking about Sunday night with Summer. I hadn't planned to show up soaking wet, nor had I anticipated taking off my shirt. The way she'd looked at me then... my gut clenched at the memory.

I'd waited for her to touch me, willed her to, begged her to in my mind. But she didn't, even if her gaze felt like fingers tracing the grooves between muscles, every line of ink down my arms. Though we'd kissed plenty of times before, I still felt the hesitation of being a beast in her living room, so aware of my size and hers. I didn't ever want to seem the aggressor. And the fact that she hadn't touched me, not until she left to find something for me to wear, spoke volumes and reinforced my impulse not to pull her to me and devour her.

Then the fuzzy pink robe had taken the edge off. She'd laughed so hard, I could tell she'd needed the release, and I'd chuckled along with her, unafraid to look the fool to her in that moment. The hug, though... As so often happened with her, the hug sent my mind racing around the globe of dreams I carried in my mind. Then it was done, and we worked together, not talking, until we'd completed the cleanup.

I left with another hug and a short, sweet kiss, and a plan to talk this week before I left on spring break.

And so far, we'd texted. But we hadn't talked on the phone, and stupidly, we hadn't seen each other. I'd noted the words at the time—*"We'll talk this week"*—and immediately felt the sliver of worry. Why wouldn't we *see* each other this week? We'd managed that last week, and we could do it again.

I'd long since given up expecting to understand Summer based on her actions. I could easily admit I didn't have experience with women enough to make an educated guess, and even if I had a hundred women in my past, I suspected I'd still find deciphering Summer to be like reading an untranslated manuscript. I didn't know how much of it was me and my inability to guess what was on her mind when things shifted like they had during the hug, during the half hour after as we cleaned, and how much was her.

Whatever the case, I missed her. And her food drive was coming to a close soon—during spring break, in fact, so I couldn't help her since I'd be traveling. I'd offered assistance more than once over the last few weeks, but she'd brushed me off. Perhaps there really wasn't much I could do. But she'd mentioned a few times how she'd been expecting more donations and hoped people would remember to drop stuff off before the break.

And I decided I could help with that. So after a talk with CSM Allen and LTC Wolfe, I spread the word.

On Thursday that week, we finally found a few minutes late in the evening to connect. Whatever odd feeling I'd gotten when I left her house Sunday subsided when she asked me to come over for a few minutes tonight.

"The donations have practically doubled this week," Summer said with a giant smile, then wrapped her arms around me.

I ducked my head into the hug and inhaled the scent of her, placing a kiss on the smooth skin of her neck.

I liked that place. Such a soft, vulnerable part of a person's body. I relished being this close to her, being able to press my lips just behind her ear before pulling back.

"You don't have to stop doing that, you know." Her voice had dropped, and the look in her eye told me she meant it.

"I want to hear more about your week."

I wanted closeness, yes. Contact. It felt like a need more than ever before. But I also had no interest in purely physical exchanges. I'd had too many relationships that devolved into that. When knowing me got challenging, when understanding how I thought or processed things or simply *was* became effort, there was a shift to gratifying baser needs. That's all well and good if you don't want more, but I always had. And after a series of failed efforts at it in my twenties, the last one maybe just after thirty, I hadn't even attempted anything like this until Summer.

So no. I wouldn't continue the progress of my mouth and hands. Especially not when we'd had an unusual dynamic together last time I saw her. I set her away gently and squeezed her waist.

"Fine then." She scowled, but a small smile pulled at her lovely mouth. "What was I saying? You scrambled my brain, Sergeant."

I smiled and sat on her couch. "Donations."

"Ah, yes. So, as I'd hoped, they've taken off this week. I think people must be prepping for spring break and really making an effort. I'm so relieved!" She slumped down and rested a head on my shoulder.

I laced our fingers together. My stomach flipped at the small contact and the ease of it. "I'm glad."

And I happened to know that at least part of that was thanks to my soldiers, and the others in the OPFOR. Who knew getting out of a few PT days would be such a motivator?

Well, I did. Which was exactly why I got the incentive approved. LTC Wolfe was more than happy to support the effort, especially since the battalion's schedule had been non-stop. Even little things like this, he'd said, helped morale. Might not've worked in a typical unit, but the rules when stationed OCONUS tended to be more relaxed, especially here at Kugelfels with our odd schedule, so no doubt the soldiers took the opportunity and ran.

"Are you ready for your trip?"

A small pang of longing hit at the question. I wished with every bit of me she could go with me. Seven days with her, no distractions, just experiencing a new place and watching her savor the local fare. How I wanted that.

"I'll finish packing tomorrow. Roll out early Saturday and back next weekend depending a little on how things go."

I'd deliberately left the schedule flexible toward the end of the week. Since this was the first longer trip I'd taken anywhere other than back Stateside, I'd wanted to give myself flexibility. Part of me had feared hating the travel or being miserable and mired in grief the whole time. I didn't know what would happen, but now, maybe I'd come back a day or two early. Spend a little more time with Summer since I wouldn't have any training session that weekend.

"Good plan."

"Hope so." I exhaled, unable, or maybe just unwilling, to keep the words I felt coming in. "I've missed you this week."

Summer stiffened, then sat upright. "Busy week, as always."

A false cheeriness I didn't understand tinged her words. "Did I say something wrong?"

Her lashes fluttered. "No. No."

I inspected her. Red at her cheeks, a little flush up her neck, and not the good kind stemming from close contact.

"You sure? Seems like maybe my saying I missed you made you..." Uncomfortable? Upset?

Her brow furrowed, and she pressed her lips together, studying me. After a large breath, she spoke. "I've had a few exes who didn't appreciate my tendency to... overschedule myself."

My eyes narrowed. Admittedly, I hated the sound of those *few exes*, but also the latter words there. "Do you feel *overscheduled?*"

"No. I don't."

"Then you're not."

She blinked. "Just like that?"

I nodded. "Just like that."

"So, when you said you missed me, you meant..."

I grabbed her hand and held it in both of mine. "Something like you probably meant when you said it last weekend. I meant I like you, Summer. I like seeing you. I miss seeing you on the days I don't get to see you."

Her lips turned up ever so slightly, and she leaned close. "I missed you too."

CHAPTER THIRTY-FOUR

Summer

Sunday night, I'd sent him off with barely a peck to his cheek. I'd wanted to throw myself at him and lock him in my bedroom for hours, especially after the wet shirt incident. But I'd felt it so clearly as he helped clear the table, then wiped down the stove. I wanted him there. I liked his help—no, I *loved* it. I'd been looking forward to him showing up, and I hadn't balked at him helping.

And then it hit me. I didn't just *like* his help... I was starting to need it. That thought had sent my heart racing, and I'd needed him gone. I couldn't explain it, other than knowing I couldn't keep looking at him, enjoying his warm, large presence, appreciating his help and kindness. I'd needed him gone.

I'd kept away from him for four days before missing

him, and knowing I wouldn't see him next week during his break had driven me to invite him over.

Next stop, you're barefoot and pregnant in his kitchen, just like you should be.

I could hear my father and brothers snarling their BS, and that was how I knew I'd gotten way too rattled.

"Idiot. You're such an idiot."

The words rang false in the quiet of my car, now parked outside the clinic. I didn't actually think I was an idiot. Having feelings for Nick, enjoying him... I'd wanted a relationship like the one we were building. I always had. When he'd said he missed me and then clarified that he meant just that, that he missed me... honestly, it'd broken my brain for a minute. Could he possibly mean that? Nick wasn't someone who said anything he didn't mean. I'd meant it when I said it days ago, so why couldn't I believe he did? But I'd never had someone *not* guilt me for being busy.

I had been in relationships before, just not in a while. Two years since the last one, before I moved here. And honestly, it hadn't been hard to leave because I got that all the time—the guilt-tripping. That feeling that my own ambitions should take second place. I'd dated a soldier then, too, and he'd been busy. But when he said "I missed you," what he really meant was, "Why are you so busy? Why can't you do what I want to do all the time?"

Believing that Nick didn't think that... it was hard. I wanted to take him at his word, and he'd been nothing but honest. But the last guy was one of several who seemed so irritated I had my own life, even after I started dating them. I didn't get that—wasn't I a more interesting person? Didn't men want women who were independent, not clingy?

Actually, I knew better than that. I often tried to trick myself into believing that's what they wanted, but so far, my lack of *need* for a man had been the crux of every break up I'd had. Either I got tired of them being disappointed in me for not needing them or they did.

The fact that I felt I might end up needing Nick... I didn't know what that meant. I'd genuinely never felt that way, and I'd been trained to think that when I did, it'd be a bad thing. So far, things with Nick felt good. *So* good. I didn't want those old mindsets to sneak in and steal all that away.

Or worse, to find out he didn't mean what he said, and he was like everyone else.

I took a deep, cleansing breath and cleared my mind. I couldn't make changes or figure things out about any of that right now, but I could use this lunch hour well.

I had restless energy out my eyes, so instead of taking a normal lunch, I gobbled my salad in the car and drove around to the sites. I wouldn't have to off-load them all because people didn't tend to steal canned goods, plus that was what I had planned for tomorrow. But I wanted to see.

The community mail room's drop site was bursting. The table had additional cardboard boxes set up on top and underneath, all of which were brimming with cans. Excitement bolted through me. This would be such a good donation to the community.

Two younger soldiers wandered up, each holding commissary bags bulging with cans.

"Oh, thank you for these. That's great," I said, smiling wide at both of them.

"Anything to get out of Masters' PT for a few days, right?" The taller soldier elbowed his friend.

"What's that?" I asked, a little twinge of dread nipping at me.

"Colonel Wolfe and Sergeant Major said if we bring a

full bag of cans, we can skip PT Monday through Wednesday of the week after spring break. No question, that's why everyone I know dropped stuff."

If they said anything else, I couldn't hear them. A sick feeling welled up in my esophagus, and I bolted back to my car. *"Anything to get out of Masters' PT..."*

He'd done this. It had to be him. I'd dodged his requests to help, insisting there was nothing he could really do. Short of hauling the stuff to its destination next week, I didn't have anything he could help with. So he'd done this.

I drove back to work, a muddled mess of thoughts clogging my brain. He must've assumed I'd appreciate the help. Some small, quiet part of me could recognize I *should*. But all I could think about, all I could feel, was that sick, oily feeling I got when someone helped me. I'd owe him now. I'd worked so hard not to have to owe him, and he just kept piling it on.

Soon, it'd all go the same way. He'd be disappointed when I refused his help, then it'd grow into frustration and potentially anger. And then we'd be done, and I'd be left with far less than I'd started with.

I groaned in frustration. My thoughts were a mess. I pushed them all down, away, and shoved out of the car. I'd pour myself into work this afternoon and deal with this tangle of feelings and my hang-ups later.

Major Hall gave me a small smile that didn't quite reach her eyes.

"I'm glad the donations are going well—I noticed the one outside the PX is nice and full too. I'm a bit concerned that this project has taken your time and you haven't found something that demonstrates your managerial capabilities."

My heart sank. "This was the project I was hoping would help with that."

That smile turned down in a kind of regretful smile-frown. "I'm not sure it does that. And that's okay. But you'll want to think about highlighting managing and delegating to other people, not just resourcing and planning."

A wave of embarrassment crashed over me. "Of course. Yes. I have one other idea I've been considering, and I can bring that forward. I—I'll find a way to show I can manage people."

"It's not all or nothing, of course. And nothing outside of work is actually going to demonstrate you can do this job. So in some ways, you can't show you do the job until you do it, but we want you to show you *can* do it before you're hired. It's tricky, but you're a strong candidate. I can't speak to the other applicants, but it isn't a large pool. The job will close in a week, and then we'll begin scheduling interviews."

I swallowed and nodded. "Thank you for the information."

I slipped into the bathrooms, locked a stall, and covered my face with my hands.

Why had I thought this canned food drive would show them my managerial skills? I'd been so caught up in the logistics, thinking that'd show my ability to manage, I'd completely lost the thread of managing *people*. And what that translated to was not me strong-arming an event into place, but learning to delegate. Learning to be a part of a team, but as the person driving it. Accepting their efforts, counting on their help.

I breathed in slowly through my nose, staying the tears threatening.

You will not cry about this right now, at work, when you still have a half hour before the day ends.

~

I cried long and hard when I got home, all the pent-up emotion from everything, particularly my stupidity, crashing down at once. The memories of my family guaranteeing I'd fail if I left, promising I'd be back, pressed in close all the while.

Nick messaged to ask when he could come over, and that sent a new wave of frustration.

Me: "*I never asked you to incentivize the food drive.*"

Nick: "*I thought it'd be a good way to encourage the soldiers to donate. Wolfe and Allen were on board.*"

Me: "*I don't appreciate you doing that without talking to me.*"

It took him several minutes to respond.

Nick: "*Can I come over? Just for a minute.*"

I hesitated. I wanted to see him. So, so much. But I couldn't sort through this with him here. Before I responded, he called. I answered without a chance to think better of it.

"I'm sorry. I should've talked to you."

"It's okay," I grated out.

The apology gave me no satisfaction. What I wanted was him. Here. In front of me. Telling me I wasn't a prize dunce for getting so off-track with the whole thing. I wanted to see him and know I didn't need him, that I just wanted him.

But the aching, raging *need* rose in me and begged me

ask him to come over. And all of that, all the twisted-up feelings of the day, paired with that cold, stark need, had me clenching my jaw against any such confession.

"Can I come hug you goodbye?"

His voice came out low and sweet and stabbed me right in the heart. *Yes. Yes. Come hold me. Hug me. Stay.*

An ugly sob burst out of me, but I slapped a hand over my mouth. I cleared my throat, sucked in a breath. "I'm worn out. Today was tough."

"Are you okay?"

"I—" I loosed a sharp exhale and hardened my resolve. "I'm fine."

"Summer, you have to talk to me. How can we do this, if we don't talk to each other?"

"Do what?"

"Be in a relationship. Care for each other."

"I'm not good at that. I don't know how to do that." My stomach curled into a fist, drawing so tight, I could hardly breathe.

"I don't understand. We already said that's what we're doing—we're dating. Exclusively."

Frustration with myself, with him, with the whole damn day boiled over, an unwatched pot I couldn't even try to remove from the heat.

"I don't need a babysitter, Nick. I'm not someone who likes to be checked up on. I've lived my life being independent, doing my own thing. I don't need someone telling me they miss me when what they really mean is I should slow down, I should ease off whatever obligations I've chosen to engage in, to make time for what they want me to do."

A pause came from his end, then, "I don't want you to stop doing the things you enjoy. I said I missed you because I do. I like you, Summer. I think I might even—" He grunted, then continued. "I care about you. I want to be around you. I want to talk to you. I don't know how to help you understand I don't have an ulterior motive."

Bitterness like I'd only tasted one other time in my life rushed to my throat, and the words spat out. "Well, don't concern yourself with helping me understand for a while, okay? You take your trip, have a good time, and we'll see what happens."

"We'll see what happens?"

For the first time, heat entered his voice. Frustration, and maybe disappointment. Maybe hurt. Good grief, how many times had I heard those same things from other people. I'd never cared so much until him. That should've made me hang up all the faster, but instead I calmed, just a little.

I blew out a breath. "Listen, I'm sorry. I just need sleep. Space. Something. I'll talk to you next weekend, okay?"

"Okay. Night, Summer."

I waited an hour, hoping he'd knock on my door and bust past my mile-high defenses. That somehow, he'd know only part of me wanted to push him away while the rest of me wanted to hold him to me and never let him loose. I trembled at how cold I'd been, how opposite to what I actually felt. But that smaller part screamed louder today after the events with Major Hall and even the news of Nick's interference.

By Sunday of that same weekend, I felt hollowed out. My efforts to spin all this into something positive failed and failed again. All my mantras and smiling into the void meant nothing right now.

Ariel called, and I clutched at the phone, desperate for someone to connect to and tell me I hadn't done an insane, horrible thing by sending Nick away without seeing him.

"Hey, how have you been?"

"I'm good. Enjoying the last big hurrah with the family all together here. Your text earlier worried me."

I'd sent her a little SOS message. I'd never been good at leaning on friends, but I wanted to. I could admit that, and somehow, it seemed far less terrifying.

"Sorry. I'm fine. But I think I've broken everything good in my life, and I'm broken."

My voice caught on the last word. Until that moment, I hadn't ever said those words, even in therapy, even though they resounded clear and true through me.

"Why do you say that?"

I liked that about Ariel. She didn't immediately spring to my defense and tell me I hadn't done anything wrong. She just asked the question.

"The way I grew up, the culture in my family and all that—I've had therapy for this. I have. But lately, I've been finding the idea of needing anyone to be unbearable. I've always struggled to accept help, and I knew that was a hold-over from childhood. But with Nick..." I sucked in a breath. Saying his name hurt.

"With Nick?" Ariel asked gently.

"I think I need him. Like, *love him* need him. And I am... not mature enough for that."

She chuckled into the phone. "I'm not sure that's quite right, but maybe it is. Only you can tell for sure."

I exhaled, a small measure of relief coming from just saying these words out loud to someone. "I don't know how to do this."

"Be in a relationship?"

"Ask for help." I sighed. "Sorry, this is all messed up because I've bungled not only things with Nick but also my whole resumé builder project thing. I'm basically a mess. And I think I need to ask for help."

And something distant and timid said, *It's not just help you need. It's trust.* But help was the tangible, fixable problem I could present a friend with, and so I listened to her response.

"I know how hard that can be. But you should ask whoever you need to, and ask as many people as you need to. I didn't reach out when I needed it—before Jim and I married and definitely not after. It was pride and maybe the reluctance to bother anyone. But if I had, I would've saved myself so much grief. And I would've saved myself period, I think. Sooner than I did, anyway. I know that's totally different, and it may not actually apply, but I wholeheartedly support you asking for help."

"I'm sorry you went through any of that. And thank you. I will. I'm going to."

I could hear the smile in her voice. "Good."

I inhaled a full, slow breath, my lungs filling for the first time in what felt like days.

"And for what it's worth, I think you should consider that loving someone isn't quite the same as needing them, and that it could be a really wonderful, freeing thing, instead of something that ties you up."

We ended the call not long after, and her words filled my mind, along with a new determination. I couldn't change my gut reaction to some of these things, but I could work on that. I could get help with *that,* for sure, and then I could reach out and ask for help for the idea blooming in my mind.

And when Nick returned, I'd talk to him too. I'd apologize and see if he could forgive me for being so cowardly and awful. I'd see if we could find a way forward. I'd see if that disappointment could be replaced with... something better. Properly set expectations, maybe, and good communication. Things real couples did when they were trying to work through something.

Before we hung up, I'd asked for *her* help. My idea to rectify the whole food drive, resumé mess would require lots of hands. As I knew she would, she happily agreed.

And after? I didn't feel terrible. I felt... lighter. Like I had someone on my team who'd help me get through this. I'd grown to love the women I now called friends, and I could ask *them* to help me without fearing what they might say later.

Why couldn't I get there with Nick?

CHAPTER THIRTY-FIVE

Nick

I'm staring at this grass of a battlefield on which too many died. I'm thinking of Grass by Sandburg and Dulce et Decorum Est by Owen. I'm thinking of what a strange, storied brotherhood I joined when I shaved my head and laced my boots that first day nearly twenty years ago.

France was beautiful. The battlefields I visited were somber, yet already bustling with springtime life. Such a poignant contrast to the brutal death wrought in those places during World War One.

I did whatever I could to keep my mind off Summer, but what that ended up looking like was much of my notebook alternating between war memorials, reflections on battle and life as a soldier, and thoughts of her.

I didn't return early. Why would I? Butter was taken care of—his beloved Danielle, the pet sitter, was checking in twice daily because I spoiled him rotten. He'd probably be mildly offended if I showed up a day early and deprived him of any of her affections.

Plus, I'd only come back and have to avoid seeing Summer, wondering about her, aching for her. I'd never expected her to be upset by my incentivizing donations. It simply didn't make sense, and no matter how I sliced it, I couldn't make myself feel bad about it.

One conclusion repeated in my mind—something else had to be going on. She wouldn't be that upset about more donations. She wouldn't be that upset about me saying I missed seeing her. She'd admitted she was tired, needed space, and we'd now had eight days of space. No communication whatsoever.

I'd swung from hopeful to fatalistic during my travel, and by the time I got home, I just wanted to see her. If we could talk, maybe she'd help me understand what she needed. Maybe she'd show me she could accept help and rely on another person without losing her mind seconds later.

My heart thudded heavy in my chest as I walked to her house. This was it. She pulled open the door, revealing her in relaxed jeans, sneakers, and a white T-shirt with *Don't Worry, Be Happy* printed in scrawling script on the right side. She'd pulled her hair into a ponytail, her face looked fresh and clear of makeup, and taking her in, a shudder slipped through me.

Then, the other parts of this moment registered. Her red eyes. The Military Police officers, two of them, sidestepping where I stood in the doorway. Only after seeing them did I register the two MP vehicles parked on the circle.

They hadn't parked directly in front of her house, though, and I'd been so one-track-minded, I hadn't registered the oddity of their presence there. Until now.

"What happened? Are you okay?" I moved fully inside the house and inspected her, but other than the red eyes, I couldn't tell.

Summer spoke to the two MPs. "Thanks for coming. Let me know if you need other information or anything."

They departed, and she closed the door behind them, then locked it. My heart thundered in my ears.

"Summer."

She crossed her arms tight to her body. "Dennin was here. He didn't get in, but he really freaked me out. He started out calling me baby, saying he knew I'd been giving him looks. I didn't open the door, obviously, but told him I hadn't been. That made him mad, and he started yelling about how I shouldn't be calling him crazy while he was banging on the door. I called the MPs, and they actually got here really fast."

That schmarmy jerk that'd been here one of the first times we'd spoken. I'd hoped he'd fade into the abyss, but no dice. She'd mentioned he'd torn down her flyers, but this was a very problematic escalation.

Ire like I rarely felt rose in me, and I wanted to crush the kid—because he was little more than a kid. Probably mid-twenties, clearly immature, and apparently couldn't take no for an answer. Maybe more disconcerting was the thought that he might be truly unhinged, not just imma-ture and too persistent. To think of what could've happened if she'd been coming home, unlocking her door—

I pulled in a breath. "Why didn't you call me? I would've come right over."

She made a *huh* sound, and I heard it. The demand, the lack of care.

"I'm sorry. I don't—that's not—I'm glad you're okay. I'm sorry it happened. I hate that he was here again. I'm glad the MPs were nearby and could respond. Did they arrest him?"

She cradled herself, like she needed affection but wouldn't take it from me. We'd parted on fairly bad terms before the break, and the last week of silence certainly didn't point to the closeness I'd thought we had. I couldn't just gather her up in a hug like I wanted. I wouldn't be someone trying to take something from her she didn't want to give, especially after what'd just happened.

"I told him I was calling them. He ended up leaving a few minutes before they arrived. I got his license plate, and I actually did file a complaint with them the day after he showed up a few months ago. He spun it to say it was a misunderstanding, but I think having both incidents on record should help."

"I'm sorry."

"They were going to track him down right now. Said we'd see more patrol cars out here—they don't normally do a lot out this way since it's just you and me from post."

The military police from Kugelfels didn't technically have jurisdiction in Germany, but because of the large population of Americans in certain neighborhoods, they did patrol regularly. If there was a disturbance, typically the MPs stepped in first unless it was emergent.

"It's so stupid. I've never had to do that—I called 911 at first. I panicked and totally forgot that's a US thing. I've lived here almost three years." Her voice shook, and she swiped a hand over her head.

My chest tightened hearing her like this. Knowing what

caused it. "It's just one of those things that's automatic. You did a great job getting help."

At least she'd called and not refused to. I said a silent prayer of thanks she hadn't been so stubborn about it that she didn't reach out.

She moved into the living room and stood by a chair. I followed and stopped a foot away.

"Are you up for a hug?"

She tucked her arms tighter to her. "Better not. I'll probably just start crying again."

My spirits, already low, sank further. She was hurting and upset, and this was not the time to be selfish and wish she'd let me hug her. Yes, it might bring her comfort, but I wanted it to help *me* feel better too. I wanted to hold her, feel her whole and safe, and reassure myself she was okay.

She cleared her throat and sat, so I followed her lead and did the same, a cushion away on the couch.

"So, hi."

A surprised chuckle released a modicum of pressure in my chest. "Hi."

"How was your trip?"

"Uh... good." I shifted in the seat. "Are you sure you don't want to talk any more about—"

"I don't want to give that jerk another thought. I know I will, and I am going to have to deal with that at work, too, but right now, I want to talk about last week."

"Okay." She could drive this train, and I'd ride along.

Her lips flattened at the edges. "I've been thinking a lot about our last conversation."

I nodded—good. I would've been extremely disappointed if she hadn't.

"One of the things that happened that day was a bit of a

reality check. My boss basically said the food drive was useless in terms of my resumé."

I straightened. How could doing something good for the community be useless?

"The point was to demonstrate my ability to lead other people, to corral volunteers or something along those lines. And my default has always been to go at it alone. I got so focused on making sure I'd be able to claim it as *my* project, I even lashed out at you for being so thoughtful and helpful." She swallowed, like a swarm of nerves had hit her.

"I'll admit I didn't see that one coming."

She shook her head. "I'm sorry for that. I wish I hadn't gotten upset. I know a lot of my feelings regarding people helping, even on a project explicitly to help other people, is rooted in old issues that created bad habits. I've let that slip in a lot lately, and I'm going to work on that."

I nodded again in acknowledgement. Commenting on her admitting her *issues* didn't seem wise.

"I talked with Ariel, too. She thinks I need to work on asking for help. She has her own story about that, but it convinced me I need to. I've come up with another project, one that I think will be amazing and also *require* help. It'll require me to solicit it from friends and the community at large. So I'm going to be reaching out to Emily, Katie, Bec, Ariel, and of course, anyone else who wants to join to make it happen."

The small smile on her face should've warmed me. She felt good about this news—maybe even proud. Planning to ask for help was clearly a big step for her, and verbalizing that so clearly likely counted as another one.

But what I heard there was that she'd ask anyone but me for help. That she'd ask people for help for work but didn't see that translating to any problems between us. At some point, I needed her to need me. Wasn't that how relationships worked? Not in a simpering, sickly way that drains a person, but in the way that says *I trust you.* I want you, I need you, and those things are true because I trust you. Without the need, to some degree, wasn't it all still just physical?

I tamped down the jump of worry that we'd never get to that place and resolved to listen. To be here, right now, and hope that the next stop in this conversation would shift to *us.*

"That sounds good. Let me know if I can help."

Her eyes softened, and she reached out her hand. The fact that we hadn't touched yet certainly stood out.

Her soft, warm hand in mine calmed me. I'd missed her to a ridiculous degree while I was gone, particularly since we'd parted on such negative terms. The slip of her palm against mine renewed my hope we could find a way forward, even if not much about the conversation had to do with the primary issue between us.

"O-of course you can."

"Of course?"

I kept my gaze on our interlaced hands, willing her to continue. After another moment, she did.

"I'm sorry for how I spoke to you before your trip. I'm sorry I got upset with you for helping when all you were doing was making the food drive better for everyone." She scooted closer, not breaking eye contact. "It was messed up to make you feel like helping was wrong."

I nodded again, relieved. "Thank you."

She leaned in and pressed her lips to mine. Softly. So softly. Like the kiss might gentle my worry, the very real concern still coursing through me. Because of that, I pulled back.

"I appreciate your apology. I think we have more to talk about."

Her lashes fluttered. "Okay."

"I'm glad you're going to ask your friends for help with this project. I'm glad Ariel's insights helped you."

She watched me, wariness creeping into her expression like she could feel the *but* coming. Why was she still so wary of what we'd been building? Or, what I'd hoped we'd been building.

"I want you to think through how that could work between us. As I said last week, I care about you. I want to be with you. But we can't continue keeping score."

"Keeping score?"

"Yes."

Her head reared back. "I don't keep score."

"You do. By worrying about owing me whenever I do something for you. Can you honestly tell me that's not how things started between us?"

I'd suspected, and the events of the last week or so had clarified that. Her overreaction about my helping the project, and even my confession about missing her.

"I don't know what you mean," she said, though it sounded more defensive and less truly confused.

"Do you not?"

She just stared at me, face so full of upset, it nearly gutted me. We shouldn't have done this today. Now.

"I'm not trying to be cruel or accusatory." I held her by the shoulders. "I want us to figure this out."

She leaned back, so I immediately dropped my hands. She didn't seem inclined to speak, so I raced to clarify and dispel any possibility of her misunderstanding me.

"I want to be with someone who can trust me. I want to trust that person. Not in an unhealthy, codependent way, but in the way that people who truly care for each other rely on each other. And I don't want to keep score. I don't want you to either."

She didn't seem to move or breathe, so I pressed on. "I want us to be together. But if we do that, we need to be on the same page about how that might work."

She nodded then, and the strap of tension around my chest loosened just a bit.

"Think about it. Let me know if that's something you want too."

She stood, so I followed, wishing we could keep talking but knowing it made sense to part now. Continuing to force an emotional conversation after Dennin, and even after being apart so long, just didn't feel right.

"I'll think about it. I—" Her chest rose with a big inhale, then she smiled like nothing was wrong. "I've got people coming soon. Feast night."

"Why don't you cancel? You've had a crazy afternoon."

Something in her face hardened, and the look was pure determination before she forced a smile. "I don't *want* to cancel. I'm not letting this change anything."

I exhaled silently, pushing away the disappointment. I wished she'd give herself a break, but at least she'd be in a crowd. "Right. Hope it goes well."

She kept that bright grin on her face as I walked out.

"I wish—"

I cut myself off, swallowing the words. I wanted to say, *I wish you'd trust me. I wish you'd let yourself rest. I wish you'd give yourself room to feel whatever you need to feel.* But I couldn't say that without harming the tone between us. She would think about things. And I would hope she'd decide she could take a chance with me.

"What?"

"Nothing, really. I'll talk to you when you're ready."

And maybe it would be better for her to have the time to herself, cooking and entertaining in the way she loved, without my interference.

Or maybe her refusal to acknowledge an upsetting situation, to deal with the fact that trusting me terrified her, would lead us to what I should've known was coming all along.

CHAPTER THIRTY-SIX

Summer

I didn't need time. I'd already decided I wanted to try with Nick, and that meant facing my revulsion of needing someone else head-on. I didn't need more therapy to help me with asking friends for help, but I would need someone wiser than me to help wade through the relationship kind of trust. Because that was what it boiled down to—trust. He'd nailed it when he said that, and it struck me *hard*. I had to trust that Nick wouldn't use my need for him against me.

My love for him.

'Cause, yep, I loved him. Seeing him speak so clearly and gently yesterday, when he had every right to push me away, confirmed it, as though I hadn't already known.

As though that, underneath all of this, wasn't the real reason his help, care, and concern made me panicky. When love was synonymous with debt in your childhood, it was hard to shake that correlation, even decades later. Until Nick, I'd never cared enough to get past this point—the point when my boyfriend recognized how messed up I was.

And his response to seeing the MPs—as panicked as I could imagine him. He didn't get ruffled, but the man had been shaken, finding me there with two cops. I'd felt guilty for not letting him know. I sensed maybe he thought my not calling him was significant. But in truth, I'd been so upset and thrown by the idiot showing up on my doorstep again, then bungled the actual call itself, I hadn't had much space to think of anything but observing everything Dennin said and did so I could give a clear report. I hoped it'd be enough to make sure he wouldn't think he could do it again.

My insistence on not being in debt had hurt me in a real way this time. When I'd reported the first incident, I should've listed Nick and Rob as witnesses. I hadn't, and apparently, that meant it was Dennin's word against mine, so in the end, he was given a counseling and nothing more. Had I given the full picture of what happened and named Rob and Nick, who would've corroborated the events, they might've given him a no-contact order. It could have made a difference, though somehow, I doubted it.

And I didn't want to think about Dennin. Any thoughts about that were wasted—I'd done what I could, and I'd meet with Major Hall tomorrow. I didn't want to be stupid, but—

I shook my head at myself while scrubbing the last pot left from the dinner party. Calling myself names, putting myself down, that wasn't going to help. I knew that. The real issue here was Nick, not Dennin, in that going forward, I did have to do something about Nick. I hoped the case was closed with Dennin.

The men I'd dated in the past hadn't been ready to face this trust stuff down with me, but it seemed like Nick might be. I hoped so. And that didn't even touch the fact that he'd be retiring soon and might not even live in Germany long enough to matter.

Every second with him matters.

Ugh, the cheesy little echo in my mind was right. I wanted every possible second. It'd push me, *he'd* push me to go beyond the surface, beyond the knee-jerk reaction of shutting down and rejecting help, need, even real emotions like sadness and love. He'd want all of me, and I wanted all of him.

His brooding soul still mulling through grief and loss. That quiet part of him he'd already shown me. The demanding coach. The ridiculously tender cat dad. The awkward party guest and stubborn friend. I wanted all of him.

But I'd need to show him. I considered texting him tonight and asking him to come help me clean up—a small sign of the changes I'd been slowly working on for weeks. Or years, depending on how you looked at it.

I needed him to know I'd thought carefully about it, and I had to make him certain of me. But I didn't want to make him wait, nor could I stand to. The surety had hit right as the MPs drove up, as my adrenaline started crashing. And truly, the only reason I didn't let him hug me was exactly as I said—I would've broken down. And I wasn't ready to say what I needed to say. I'd only just registered the truth and how much I wanted it.

But this was my chance to truly show him. So I would get ahold of him and make a plan, so he'd know I wasn't keeping him hanging. The problem? He started a rotation today, and genius me didn't think through the realities of that. We hadn't really been in the full swing of dating during the last few rotations—I wouldn't have expected to text him and get a response. But the whole bad reception out in the training area thing *really* cramped my plans.

I sent a text anyway, hoping maybe it'd get through. I kept it simple, tried not to be cryptic.

Me: *"I am ready to talk when you are. I know the rotation lasts until next week. Let me know when you can talk. Stay safe."*

I had the strongest, craziest impulse to say *I love you* right there at the end. Of a text message. As mentioned, *like a crazy person.* But I didn't.

A twinge of worry picked at me all week, though. Spring rains had made driving out in the training area, known as the box, a bit treacherous. The dirt roads could slide out and cause real problems for the military vehicles. My first year here, a tank rolled over and very nearly killed several people during one of the spring training exercises.

The reality of this—feeling worry for Nick—struck deep. Though Kugelfels was a training base, that didn't mean safety. It didn't guarantee security. Sometimes, I fooled myself into believing that all these men and women were simply playing war games, practicing for days I hoped would never come. But small things like flood warnings could change the dynamics for them and could mean real-world injuries. Exhibit A—Nick's, Thatcher's, and the other soldiers' injuries from the accident in January.

Since there was nothing I could do for him by worrying, I threw myself into work, delivering meals to a few families with new babies and organizing the event I hoped would make an impact.

I'd shifted mindsets—finally. I didn't want to be so focused on the job that I couldn't see anything else around me. I'd let that happen already, and it couldn't continue. That drive to achieve, to gain more financial security and rub my parents' nose in my success though they'd never know about it... time to move on from that blinders-on, nothing-else-matters approach. So when I gathered my friends on the Friday, the first day of my event and the last of the most intense days of the rotation, they all beamed at me.

"This is going to be great." Katie grinned as she surveyed the tables piled with donations.

"I can't believe we don't do this more often," Emily said, folding a pile of baby onesies.

"I can't believe I forgot about it."

We called the event a swap for the community, but it was primarily geared toward lower enlisted soldiers who might be in need, and even more so, soldiers participating in the rotation who might be in need. Quite a few countries sent contingencies of soldiers who had families back home struggling. We'd rounded up donations of used clothing, toys, and other items, sorted them, arranged them, and now eagerly awaited people arriving.

The timing hit perfectly, if a bit suddenly. I cursed myself for not thinking of it sooner and giving people more time, but the prospect of having a place to give away all their too-small clothes and outgrown toys proved alluring for the women of Kugelfels. The entire multipurpose room in one of the community buildings was filled with tables brimming with used goods for anyone to come and take. Just take.

And the best part? Sharing the victory with my friends. Because it was a kind of victory—seeing what felt like miles of things lined up, waiting to find the right person who might need them. We'd spent hours and hours this week setting up, and I'd taken the day off so I could prep. I looked at my watch and saw the minute hand slide into place right then. Noon. The swap was officially open.

Bec shuffled in the door a minute later. "Sorry I'm late. Donna ran into car trouble coming back from her lunch."

"You're fine," I said, a thrill of delight running through me. "This is the easy part—walk around, answer questions, fold stuff that gets messy."

Bec didn't have any days off since she'd taken quite a few after Thatcher's accident, but she'd be here during her lunch hour and then after. Emily had taken the whole day, as had Katie. Livie would be here tomorrow. Ariel would arrive in a few hours. They'd shown up for me, no question, and had done it joyfully.

And Nick... hopefully, Nick had gotten my messages about today. He'd responded to the first one and said he looked forward to talking after the rotation. Then nothing. I'd watched for his car, the lights at his house, and I would swear he hadn't been home the entire time, but that seemed unlikely.

Still, I didn't ever see him or signs of him, so today would be the first opportunity. I didn't know what time he'd finish up his obligations. I hadn't received any sign that he'd seen the text telling him the swap started today, that it was the new project I'd thrown together in record time, and that I hoped he'd come see.

Several spouses wandered in, coffees in hand. The closest thing to a Starbucks was the small coffee shop that shared the building with this multipurpose room, *Brew*. They made decent coffee when the machines worked and provided an option on post. Since the post itself was situated ten minutes from the nearest town and twenty from any stores and restaurants, the shop had a corner on the market.

Excitement swirled in me as more people filtered in. No soldiers yet, but the military and contractor spouses would be the first, and some of the best, customers. My goal was to see as much of the stuff on tables and displayed throughout the room go to specific people, but whatever we had leftover would be donated to locations in the surrounding area.

The satisfaction of being here and seeing my friends and several other people I knew from work or feast nights, folding clothes, answering questions... nothing about this felt like failure. Sharing the burden had been a relief, and genuinely no part of me had clutched at the duties, reluctant to delegate or rely on others.

Honestly? After the joy of seeing how the community rallied to donate so much so quickly, and how amazing the volunteers had been, the primary feeling I had was relief. I'd wondered if my ability to work with others had been destroyed over the last few months of hoarding plans for the food drive and getting so addled about how to accomplish a goal.

And though at one point, I thought I'd worked through all those nasty reminders of my past, the last few weeks had shown me I hadn't. Maybe we never fully tuck away the hurts and have to be vigilant against them, or at least keep learning from them. This moment felt like a culmination of lessons learned from both my past and now this iteration of me. *This* lesson would carry me forward and remind me, yet again, that working with others and receiving help and being open with people wasn't weakness. It was an asset and a strength, and it made good things happen. I swallowed down a gush of emotion that wetted my eyes.

"You okay?"

Nick's voice startled me from my moment, and I whipped around.

"Yes," I said, taking him in.

Camo paint caked on his face and flaking off at his

temples. His hair was matted down from his patrol cap, and maybe his helmet before that. He looked rumpled, exhausted, and completely gorgeous. "Hi."

His blue eyes settled on mine. "Hi, Summer."

Oh, the warmth in the way he said my name sent a burst of pure joy through me. I balled my fists, like that would help me not first throw myself at him and kiss him, and second, make a fool of myself by confessing every big, scary feeling I had for the man right here next to the collection of costume jewelry.

"Hi, Nick. Thank you for coming."

"I wouldn't miss it," he said, his eyes sweeping over the room. "Looks like you've been busy."

"*We've* been busy. I had a total of ten volunteers helping me this week setting up and then on shifts throughout the weekend."

"That's great." His voice sounded a little gruff, probably from lack of sleep.

"You don't have to stay. I'll be here on and off all weekend. It's done on Sunday, and we'll load everything up in boxes that I have someone delivering to donation sites on Monday. But I am hoping you can come to feast night?"

His brows shot up, then settled again, like he hadn't meant to react that way. "Uh, sure."

"Great. Thank you for coming. Go get a shower and sleep. I'll see you later this weekend." I set a hand on his arm and squeezed.

Before I pulled away, one of his large, warm hands covered my own and held it there. Flutters filled my belly at the touch and the typically intense Nick look he gave me.

"See you Sunday."

He slipped out the door just as another big group arrived to browse. I got lost in the bustle, which provided a nice distraction from the longing pulsing a little stronger now that I'd gotten to see him for just a moment.

Soon.

Soon we'd talk, and I'd tell him everything, and hopefully, his feelings would be the same.

CHAPTER THIRTY-SEVEN

Nick

I never realized how much I could enjoy a room full of people as long as you're one of the people in the room.

After cleaning up and eating to my heart's content on Friday night, then paying penance with Butter since he didn't appreciate not seeing me at least every once in a while despite the pet sitter's faithfulness, I slept in Saturday.

Until seven.

After going to bed at eight the night before, I didn't need more than that. Fortunately, I had several training sessions planned for late morning, so after some quiet time reading and sipping hot, properly brewed coffee, I kicked into gear.

All the while, I avoided thinking about Summer. Just like I'd done during the rotation. I could've come home more than I did—I usually made it back every few days to shower and eat something substantial and hot. But I didn't have it in me to be near her and not wonder about her or glance toward her house and notice if her lights were on.

When I did get reception, having a message from her came as a huge relief. I hadn't realized how much of my unconscious had been wrapped around that. Not that it should have surprised me, but I'd deluded myself into thinking I'd left the ball in her court and I'd deal with whatever happened as though it wouldn't wreck me if she decided to walk away.

Her triumph at the swap yesterday had made me happy for her. Genuinely happy. I hoped it signaled something new for her—the ability to ask for help and the ability to trust those whom she had asked.

Did it bother me she hadn't asked me? I wished I were the kind of man who could say no, it didn't. But I couldn't avoid the feeling that she might trust her friends or colleagues, but trusting *me* was a different level. And beyond simply assisting with hauling stuff to a drop site or whatever it might be, trusting me in a romantic, intimate relationship *was* different.

The training sessions Saturday kept me from focusing too much on her. The evening proved to be fraught with all kinds of useless longing and curiosity and a fine edge of desperation that then turned into me sipping Scotch and reminiscing about the first time Gran poured me a drink, then laughed when I sputtered and coughed at the first sip.

Mercifully, the loss that'd been etched so deeply into my heart didn't burn like it often had. Time had passed, yes, but I couldn't ignore that hope for a future with someone pressed into me and muted some of that grief. I prayed it might work with Summer, but if all she'd given me was the hope of having *someone*, of not being entirely alone for the rest of my life? I'd be thankful for that until the end. Those resigned, morose thoughts accompanied me to bed.

By Sunday at just before six, I'd dressed in a navy-and-gray plaid shirt and jeans, ready to be social. Or as ready as I ever managed to be. Seeing Summer at her home when she was surrounded by strangers and having to sit at a table and watch her interact with them when all I wanted to do was be alone would be challenging to say the least. I'd done whatever I could to mentally prepare, but by four this afternoon, all I could do was pace and give my meal prep for the week half effort.

The cool April air was scented with early spring blooms, but the heady tag of garlic and sesame wafted out of the open door. My stomach clenched with hunger and anticipation.

Thatcher Wild shook my hand as we entered Summer's house.

"Good to see you, man. Rob said you put him through the wringer yesterday and today."

His girlfriend, Bec Jones, preceded him through the door, and I followed behind both of them.

"He did well."

Thatcher and I chatted back and forth as he took Bec's coat and hung it, then ushered her in. They'd both been here before, so they knew the drill. I prepared myself to peruse her cookbooks again, when Summer peeked out the kitchen and said, "Nick, can you come help me?"

My heart jumped into my throat at the sound of her

voice, at those words. I looked around, wondering if there might be another Nick somewhere I hadn't met. She'd disappeared back into the kitchen before I could do much more than gape, so I hustled to reach her.

Inside the kitchen, steam rose from a pan, but everything else sat on platters. How she managed to time everything so it came out so perfectly at once amazed me.

"You wanted help?" I asked, though my voice came out more like a croak.

Her bright eyes sparkled at me. She nudged something around the sauté pan with a wooden spoon without looking and said, "Yes. Please."

My throat tightened. Maybe I hadn't slept as well as I thought. Maybe I was more of a lost cause for this woman than I realized. Either way, I stepped forward, willing and ready for whatever she might need.

"Say the word."

"Can you just keep these moving for one more minute? My phone will chime when it's done. Just don't stop stirring, pull the pan, and scrape them into this." She pointed to a small glass bowl to the left of the stove's eye.

I nodded and took over, savoring the fleeting brush of our fingers when taking the spoon's handle from her. She bustled around, somehow everywhere in the kitchen. When the alarm went off, I lifted the pan and scraped what looked like breadcrumbs, garlic, and maybe chili flakes into the designated bowl.

"Can you help me take everything in?"

I whipped around to find her holding a tray of soup bowls with steam rising between us.

"My pleasure," I said, like this wasn't completely new. Like her asking for my help in the kitchen wasn't historically unheard of for a feast night, and certainly for our relationship.

Seated around the table were all familiar faces. Just like the last time I'd attended. Then of course there was that one time I *didn't* attend, but maybe that was why the crowd tonight was composed of friendly faces. I delivered the tray to the sideboard, then distributed the bowls of what looked like a golden-brown broth with coin-thin slices of mushroom and scallions. Behind me, Summer walked with another tray, adding garlicky sesame chicken wontons to each person's bowl, then sprinkling the breadcrumb mixture on top if they wanted.

"This smells so good. I'm not sure anything has ever smelled so good in my life," Rob said, then wiggled his eyebrows in acknowledgement of being there. He hadn't said a thing yesterday, little sneak.

"I'm glad. I've done the broth recipe before, but this is a new wonton mix, so let me know what you think."

She continued around the table, and I slipped back into the kitchen to retrieve the next dish, marveling at the ease of the moment.

My usual dread of sitting and talking to people would've been diminished by recognizing that I knew every person around the table. But assisting in serving gave me something to do with my hands, an excuse to move around and not have the attention turn to me. Doing it with Summer, in tandem, felt natural. *Right.*

Everyone filtered out quickly, like they had the first time I'd attended, and left only Summer and me. Wordlessly, we cleared the table, rinsed dishes, and loaded the dishwasher. I washed a pot while she put away any leftovers—I didn't even have to talk her into letting me do it.

I should've felt calm slipping over me as I swished the suds around, but instead, everything felt heightened. The light tap of her shoes against the floor kept my mind pinned to where she moved in the room. The hiss of the water in the tap as I rinsed the pot sounded sharp against the *thud, thud, thud* of my heart.

Something was coming. I'd worked all evening not to let my hopes gather themselves and storm the village, but here they were, pitchforks in hand, ready. But for what? Summer had pointedly asked me for help at least four times tonight. She'd actually said the words, "*Nick, can you help me?*" so there could be no confusion.

That she'd filled the list of people here tonight with those I knew also hinted at all of her actions being very purposeful. And at this point, as I dried the pot, smoothing away droplets of water, the thump of my heart sounded more like thunder. We'd almost finished cleaning up. Whatever her answer, whatever future lay head, would be made clear any minute.

Her voice interrupted my scattered train of thought.

"Can you stay a while, or do you need to—"

"I can stay."

A pleased smile flashed at me, and she bit her lip.

"Good." She held out a hand. "Come sit with me in the living room."

I set down the now-dry pot, tossed the rag over the edge of the sink, and took her hand. They always felt soft compared to mine—no callouses. But her hands weren't all that soft. They were strong. They were hands that healed, helped, and nourished.

I love these hands.

I swallowed the thought as we sat side by side on the small couch.

"You seem very serious. What's going on in that head?" She squeezed my hand, then placed her other one on top.

"I was thinking about how generous you are. How much I like that about you."

She frowned and looked down at our hands for a moment before pinning me with her gaze. "There is one person I haven't been very generous with."

My brows rose slightly, but I didn't speak. My heart felt like it might beat out of my chest, but I didn't speak—I needed *her* to.

"It's been a long couple weeks, and I've missed you." She smiled at me, almost shy, and inched closer on the couch, her hands still wrapped in mine.

"I've missed you too."

"Really?"

I exhaled a laugh. "Yes. That can't be a surprise."

She looked happy, and a little pained. "I didn't know if I could hope for that much—that you'd still care for me. But I wanted to be able to *show* you that I get it. Trusting doesn't come naturally to me. It's scary. And I've never been with someone who has been as scary in that regard as you."

"I'm *scary?*"

A breath whooshed out of her. "I'm not explaining this right. What I mean is, I've never been with someone I *wanted* to trust. Who made me feel safe and cared for and like they really might want to be with me because they... cared about me."

My chest tightened at the thought, at how thin and frail a relationship would be built on exchanges and record-keeping. "I do care about you, Summer. So much."

I love you. Damn, the words were right there, but this was her moment. I'd take my turn in a minute.

"I know. I know you do. You've shown me that, you've told me in a dozen ways by now, and I've been so scared to trust it. To trust *you.* But the last few weeks, as I've practiced asking friends for help and trusting them to do what they said they'd do, I've realized how I've failed you. I haven't been willing to ask you for anything because I was too scared you wouldn't deliver. And I don't mean that to sound like I expect to be given a bunch or—"

"I know that's not what you mean." I couldn't keep the smile from my face.

Her gaze jumped to my mouth, then back to meet my eyes. My stomach dropped, and in seconds, we were wrapped in a kiss so molten, I almost melted into the couch. Her lips claimed mine, demanding and eager and hot. Her body pressed against me, one hand on my back, the other in the short hair at my nape.

She pulled back, breathless. "What I'm building up to is that I love you, Nick. And until I realized how I'd kept myself from trusting you, I didn't see that—that so much of my weirdness about having you help or saying you missed me, was rooted in the fear that you had power over me. Because of how I felt. How I feel."

Warmth and joy burst through me, racing through my body to the tips of my toes and fingers. "I love you. I've wanted to say it."

No eloquence to be had here, not with the sheer overwhelm of elation, relief, and pleasure.

She laughed—a pure, beautiful sound. "I'm so glad. Though I'll admit I would've liked it in writing so I can refer back to it."

I chuckled along with her. "I will put many things in writing. Very soon."

She grinned, kissed me again, then sobered. "I've got a lot to learn about what this looks like."

"Me too. I've never done this either. But we're doing it together. We'll figure it out, one day, one challenge at a time."

CHAPTER THIRTY-EIGHT

Summer

All the tied-up places in me seemed to have loosened. Stress I hadn't realized I'd been carrying for weeks and weeks melted away. And joy—so much joy swarmed me, I hardly knew what to do with it.

Five days after what could inarguably be identified as the best night of my life to date, I exited the interview with the hiring committee feeling good. Feeling like I'd done everything I could, been honest and open and frankly a bit vulnerable. I'd explained the failure of my first project—the problem with running a drive by myself, and how I'd gotten off track. Then the success of the second effort and how rewarding it was for not only me, but the volunteers and community. More than that, I delineated my perspective on the clinic, on patient care, and a host of other questions they lobbed at me.

I wanted this job. I wanted the raise and the increased responsibility, and I wanted the challenge of something new. And I'd just admit it—a sliver of me still wanted that just so I could mentally thumb my nose at my family. They wouldn't know, and if they did, they likely wouldn't care, but in the same way my silly car gave me satisfaction, advancing in a job that helped people, that meant something *to me,* was a small victory. If I was allowed to fall back into old thinking patterns and learn new lessons, I'd decided I was also allowed to take a little selfish pleasure in still proving them wrong.

That said, I'd settled into accepting that it might not happen. And if the last few weeks had taught me anything, it was that I needed to open myself to possibilities beyond my narrow focus. Nick had busted into my life completely unexpectedly, and I couldn't imagine anything better than being with him. My friends had elbowed their way into my heart, and I couldn't have been more thankful.

If the job didn't work out, I'd find something different. Or, maybe I'd just stay in the same job and enjoy that role. It didn't have to be so dire that it drove me to lose sight of what mattered, of my feelings and relationships and the possibility for happiness outside of what I'd marked out for myself.

Nick hadn't solved all my problems. In fact, he'd solved none of them. But he'd given me a gift—a chance to see my fears, confront them, and begin working on them... *with* him. We talked long into the night and had talked every day since. To be fair, often I did most of the talking. He still wasn't going to become an avid socialite or even verbose in conversation, but he spoke honestly, and he listened better than anyone I'd ever met.

On top of all that, the harassment from Kent Dennin

had officially ended. Apparently, he'd been harassing at least two other women, one of whom he grabbed in the commissary in full view of a whole crowd. He'd been given a no-contact order for her, but paired with the episode at my house and another woman's account of his harassment, the guy was getting officially chaptered out of the Army. While I'd hoped I wouldn't have to deal with him again, the specter of that had been an insidious little stressor. Knowing the case was closed, and that he'd been removed from his duties at the clinic so I wouldn't ever see him again, had brought those concerns to rest. That relief and the hopeful feeling I had for moving forward had made the last little while shaded with a giddy kind of joy.

I reached my house, energy and excitement buzzing in me. Nick and I had a date planned for tonight. At some point, we'd go out somewhere, but I suspected he was as exhausted as I was. After nearly a month apart, aside from quick conversations and our one longer talk Sunday, we hadn't seen each other. We needed time, space, and no rushing.

I changed out of my interview clothes, thankful it'd come at the end of the day so I didn't have to change back to scrubs while at work. My hair was down and straight, makeup on point, and the ice-blue silk dress I wore looked good. *Really* good. I wanted Nick speechless, and not from his introverted tendency to observe, think, and then speak.

I felt incapable of words whenever I saw him after any amount of time. I wondered when that'd wear off—of course it would, if we stayed together. And for once in my life, I hoped, prayed, and planned for us to.

I'd bought fresh strawberries for our dessert. Nick claimed he had everything else ready from the list I'd sent him. Tonight, we'd cook together, eat together, clean up together. And hopefully, a few other fun things together. After slipping on a light jacket, I practically skipped down the sidewalk to his house.

His door swung open before I reached it to knock.

"How'd it go?" he asked, taking every bit of me in like my hair or legs or heels might give him the answer.

My huge smile gave me away as I shucked my jacket and the bag containing the strawberries and jumped at him. He caught me around the hips, then stood so my head was higher than his. Looking down into his handsome face, I said, "Very well." Then I kissed him for all I was worth.

After a moment, I broke free, and his beaming smile made my stomach flip. "It wasn't perfect, and I'm honestly not sure if I'll get the job. I think I'm competitive, and from what Major Hall could tell me, which was basically nothing, I am in the top three. But I don't know."

He set me down in a graceful move so full of raw strength, I had to press my lips closed to keep from making an audible, unladylike sound. There were advantages to dating someone who lifted heavy things for his job.

"When do you..." He swallowed, blinked. "Uh..."

I didn't try to hide the pleasure that blazed through me at the way his eyes slipped down my body, then slowwwly back up. When he met my gaze, he tried again. "I mean, when..."

I chuckled, then pulled him to me by the placket of his shirt and kissed him again. Just one quick, firm press to his perfect lips. "When do I what, Nick?"

His eyes narrowed, and his lips twitched. "When do you find out about the job?"

Ah, darn. He recovered so quickly. Still, points for the lost train of thought. Many thanks to this silky, sexy dress and my general feeling of badassery wearing it. I felt good already, but I would never deny that his blatant apprecia-tion made me feel downright fabulous.

"Next week sometime."

Butter had descended from his throne on the back of the couch and swirled around my legs. I bent to pet him a few times. When I straightened, Nick held out a hand, then raised mine to his mouth and kissed the back. "What happens if you don't get the job?"

I saw the question there—the thing we hadn't talked about. "I'll be upset. Definitely disappointed, and not gonna lie, I'll probably cry at some point. I've had my eyes on this position for just under a year now, ever since I heard Cindy was thinking about retirement. But I've also realized there's more to life than making more money and being obsessed with having that tangible sense of security. I didn't realize I'd gotten so focused on that, and I don't need to be. Plus, I do genuinely like my current job."

"Will you move?"

I set my hands on either side of his waist and gazed up into his eyes. "It's early days for us, so I don't know what answer you're looking for here. But I can tell you I want to stay in Germany, very much. That said, I know you have plans to move back to the US, and I don't like the idea of putting an expiration date on us."

"I can train anywhere."

We watched each other as the words sank in.

"What about going back home?"

He shook his head. "There's no one there I'm going back to. I planned on it because I had no other way to deter-mine where to go when I finished. But..."

My blood thrummed, and my head felt light. This was a big deal. A huge deal. But we'd confessed our love. We'd planned to be together. And I'd enjoyed every moment of being with him the last few months.

"But..." I urged.

"I can change that plan. Based on... whatever factors I decide."

And though he wouldn't say it directly, he'd stay here with me. If it made sense when the time came. He wouldn't pressure me now, but we could decide together.

My arms slipped around his back, and I hugged him to me, my cheek resting against his firm, delicious shoulder. When I pulled back, he had that peaceful, sweet look I loved seeing on him. "I look forward to seeing where we land."

"Me too."

EPILOGUE

Nate Reynolds

Eric and I both shook Nick Masters' hand. The Army was losing a great soldier, but at least he still had about a year left. He'd brought in his paperwork indicating his intent to retire and had just finished up his meeting with the CSM.

"You've got a lot to be proud of, Sergeant Masters. You let me know if there's anything we can do for you as you make the transition."

"Will do, sir. Thank you."

"You're going to keep kicking my ass, right? Dropping your packet doesn't mean you've suddenly started coveting a life of leisure?" I asked, knowing full well the man's plans were just the opposite.

"No, sir. I'll make sure your workouts are extra challenging."

"Glad to hear it. And tell Summer congratulations. I

hear she got that promotion." I'd heard Ariel talking about it with Livie. Summer would be the nurse supervisor over at the clinic—good for her.

"Thanks. I'll tell her." He nodded, and with a wave, left silently.

The congenial air to the room shifted immediately. Eric eyed me, more criticism in those ridiculous eyes of his than I'd seen in a long time. Maybe ever. The fact that he'd tucked it away when Masters came in, right as we'd started this conversation, told me he had himself fully under control and was letting me see that look for a purpose.

"Just tell me."

I heaved a sigh. "I don't know what you want me to say."

His lips pressed together and he blinked. "Are you really going to avoid this?"

"I'm not avoiding anything."

He crossed his arms and leaned back in his desk chair. Oh okay, so we're going for the stare-down, are we?

Two can play at that game, my friend. I'd stopped being intimidated by him about the sixth month of my time as a platoon leader when he was a captain—and my company commander. Right around the time I'd met Ariel, in fact. More than fifteen years ago, for sure, so if he thought this little commander act was going to be a thing now, then he could shove it.

"Seriously? You're giving me the look?"

That stone-faced stare had caused many a young soldier to cower in the wake of errors. In the end, though, people knew Eric Wolfe was for them—he rooted for his soldiers, worked for them, and when you knew a guy had your best at heart, it was hard to be too terrified.

Worried about disappointing him?

Now that could make me shudder, if I thought about it. But I wouldn't, and so the glaring needed to stop.

His turn to loose a sigh. "We haven't talked about this before, but—"

"Then why start now?"

His frown deepened. "Seems to me that inviting my sister to move in with you is a pretty good reason."

My pulse sped up. *Okay, here we go.* I'd been waiting for this talk. He was right—we'd never really talked about my feelings for Ariel or her lack of them for me, but he'd known. For a long time, if I had to guess. Small things like him telling me how she was doing, or giving me the heads-up she was here. Since she'd moved to Germany, he'd seemed pleased with our friendship—encouraged it at every turn, even.

The fact that he was just now bringing up Ariel's moving in, more than a full month after she'd done it, showed true restraint. Granted, he'd asked if there was going to be a problem when it first happened, but that was far different from actually addressing my feelings for her in the same context. I wasn't fool enough to think he hadn't wanted to before now—likely the only reason he hadn't that day was because Ariel could've overheard us.

"She needed a place. I had room. Simple as that."

He raised one brow. "Really."

"Yes."

He waited another beat, then spoke. "So your being in love with her for the last... what has it been?"

Then he waited again, like I would actually answer the question. Like his saying that out loud wasn't a punch to the gut.

"Decade at least, right?"

My jaw clenched. No need to respond.

"That has nothing to do with any of this?"

I shot to my feet, the insinuation a low blow. "You must think I'm a real jackass if you think I offered her a room in my house to get close to her."

He stood. "The only reason I haven't already talked to you about this is because first, Ariel forbade me from saying anything while she decided, and I wasn't about to take that choice from her. She's had enough choices made for her these last few years. And two, once she moved in, Livie made me promise not to get involved and 'make things weird.'"

I almost smiled. God bless Livie, though my chest twisted at the mention of what Ariel had lived with for too long. "Well, mission failed."

He grunted in frustration. "Listen to me. I care about you both. I'm concerned about this situation. Just tell me I don't need to be—that you've tucked away your feelings, that everything's speeding along like you guys are brother and sister, and I'll relax about it. Won't bring it up again."

I swallowed and inhaled. Brother and sister, we were not. What we *were*, I didn't know. I couldn't tell him because I hadn't figured it out myself.

"Tell me I don't need to worry about this, Nate. Tell me it's all friendly, low-key, smooth sailing."

I grabbed my patrol cap, planner, and keys from his desk. "I don't know what to tell you, but I can't tell you that."

Thank you for reading Nick and Summer's story! I hope you loved them! You can grab the finally book in the series, Nate and Ariel's story, today!

ALSO BY CLAIRE CAIN

Veterans of Silver Ridge Series

Small Town Veteran Romance

Love Undercover

Romantic Suspense Light

Back to Silver Ridge Series

Small Town Romance

Exceptional Mission Unit: The Cardinals

Military Romantic Suspense

The Silver Ridge Resort Series

Small Town Romance

Soldiers Overseas Romances

Sweet Military Romance

The Rambler Battalion Series

Sweet Military Romance

Married to the Military Series

Military Marriage of Convenience Romcoms

ACKNOWLEDGMENTS

If you're one of the odd ducks who reads acknowledgements and you've read more than one of mine, then you likely see the same people popping up repeatedly. This is because they are most excellent people, and they seem to be bound and determined to help and encourage. Thanking them here is such a small thing, but I hope they all (you all!) know it is heartfelt.

First to my husband, for being my first quiet hero (though he is not at all broody). Thank you for loving the Pride & Prejudice (2005) movie even a fraction as much as I do.

Thank you to my kids, who are crazy and awesome and hilarious. Big kids, your tenacity through a strange year of learning and change has reminded me that resilience and strength can look all kinds of ways. And tiniest tot, thank you for the pure sunbeam you are.

Thank you Emma, Caroline, and Amanda for your thoughtful feedback in the beta reads. This book is stronger thanks to your insights!

Thank you, Zee Monodee, for bringing Summer into 3D. I'm so glad she didn't stay a little paper doll, and that's thanks to you!

Thanks you Amanda Cuff, for polishing this baby and for the words of encouragement!

Thank you Rainbeau Decker for the gorgeous photo on

the original cover and all the work that came before and after snapping this image!

Thank you Emma for designing the original cover and adding so much lovely detail, along with providing an eagle eye. Also thanks for the hours of phone calls and all of the friendship and encouragement you've gift me.

Thank you, Jamie, for being an understanding ear, a bright mind, and a dear friend.

Thank you, Julie, for your unwavering support and friendship.

Thanks to the Claire's Sweet Readers group, and all the readers who've chosen to dive into this series! I hope you've enjoyed these books, and I especially hope you enjoyed Nick and Summer.

ABOUT THE AUTHOR

Claire Cain lives to eat and drink her way around the globe with her traveling soldier and three kids, but is perhaps even happier hunkered down at home in a pair of sweatpants and slippers using any free moment she has to read and cook. Or talk—she really likes to talk. She has become an expert at packing too many dishes in too few cabinets and making houses into homes from Utah to Germany and many places in between. She's a proud Army wife and is frankly just really happy to be here.

You can also join Claire's facebook reader group for exclusive content and fun: https://www.facebook.com/groups/clairecain/

Website: http://www.clairecainwriter.com

E-mail: Claire@ClaireCainWriter.com

Newsletter sign-up for new releases, exclusives, and freebies: http://www.clairecainwriter.com/newsletter

www.ingramcontent.com/pod-product-compliance
Lightning Source LLC
Chambersburg PA
CBHW051217190726
48288CB00006B/2002